The Medium M

The Medium Murders

Jack Murray

The Medium Murders

THE FIFTH KIT ASTON MYSTERY

Jack Murray

Jack Murray

Books by Jack Murray

Kit Aston Series
The Affair of the Christmas Card Killer
The Chess Board Murders
The Phantom
The Frisco Falcon
The Medium Murders
The Bluebeard Club
The Tangier Tajine
The Empire Theatre Murders
The Newmarket Murders
The French Diplomat Affair (novella)
Haymaker's Last Fight (novelette)

Agatha Aston Series
Black-Eyed Nick
The Witchfinder General Murders
The Christmas Murder Mystery

DI Jellicoe Series
A Time to Kill
The Bus Stop
Trio
Dolce Vita Murders

Danny Shaw / Manfred Brehme WW2 Series
The Shadow of War

The Medium Murders

Crusader
El Alamein

Jack Murray

Copyright © 2020 by Jack Murray

All rights reserved. No part of this publication may be reproduced, distributed, or transmitted in any form or by any means, including photocopying, recording, or other electronic or mechanical methods, without the prior written permission of the publisher, except in the case of brief quotations embodied in critical reviews and certain other non-commercial uses permitted by copyright law. For permission requests, write to the publisher, addressed 'Attention: Permissions Coordinator,' at the address below.

Jackmurray99@hotmail.com

This is a work of fiction. Names, characters, businesses, places, events, locales, and incidents are either the products of the author's imagination or used in a fictitious manner. Any resemblance to actual persons, living or dead, or actual events is either purely coincidental or used in a fictitious manner, except when they really were alive.

ISBN: 9798510439670
Imprint: Independently published

The Medium Murders

A NOTE FROM THE AUTHOR

This is the fifth book in the Kit Aston series. If you've been on this journey since the first, thanks! I recognise that, despite best efforts, errors have crept into the previous books. These have been corrected over time. Thankfully most of you have chosen to forgive rather than condemn. In return, I hope you've been rewarded by, what one sympathetic reviewer described as, 'a great yarn'.

The latest addition to the series, as with the other books, explores new territory while remaining true to the idea of historical mystery. Enjoy!

I hope you'll consider leaving a review on Amazon. It really makes a difference…

Prologue

Blenheim Palace, Oxfordshire, August 1908

Winston Churchill knelt before the white-robed druid. If he didn't look like a bloody fool, then he certainly felt like one. What could he do though? Everyone else had been through the initiation. They'd all supplicated themselves before the Grand Master or whatever he called himself. Was it High Priest? Yes, that was it. High Priest. Must remember, he thought. And promptly forgot.

Ridiculous really. He swayed slightly and fought to control himself. The thought that he should have waited until after the initiation before taking the third brandy crossed his mind. His head was swimming a little. The alcohol, the hint of a chill coming into the air, and the fact he was kneeling before a fake druid at a mock temple dedicated to a Greek goddess all felt like he was in a dream.

Tomorrow he was seeing Clementine Hozier. He would bring her here and ask her to marry him. The druid cleared his throat. He wondered what her answer would be. He wondered what she would think if she ever got wind of this little spectacle. Perhaps the Grand Master druid could stay around to conduct the service. Did they do weddings?

Or just cause funerals?

Human sacrifices. Yes, this was their forte. They did this in Greece, too, didn't they? Maybe hosting the ceremony at the Temple of Diana wasn't such a daft idea after all. Behind the druid, he could see the pale Ionic columns of the temple rising to the sloping roof. Churchill focused his gaze on the sky. Not even the hint of a cloud. It all felt very Mediterranean. All except for this distinctly un-Mediterranean priest.

At that moment, Churchill was unsure whether to laugh or squirm. The next words of the High Priest damn near pushed him over the edge.

'*Nequaquam ut oblitus esse pristina sua consuetudine, Et non duxitadanimum?*'

Latin?

Since when did the druids speak a language that did not arrive to the country until a few thousand years later? Then the words of the High Priest took shape in Churchill's mind. He almost added to them himself.

The Medium Murders

'For auld lang syne, my jo. For auld lang syne.'

Churchill's friends, sitting facing the High Priest, could see his shoulders shaking. A tell-tale sign that their friend was no longer taking the business seriously. Of the priest, it was impossible to know what he was feeling. He was wearing a false grey beard. *De rigeur* for druids, apparently. The long flowing white robes completed the rather theatrical appearance. There were a few other priests standing either side of him looking solemn, at least as far as it was possible to detect through the bushy beards. They, too, were clad in robes. Damn shame they were not all wearing those. Winston should have insisted, really.

With the initiation finished, a grinning Churchill went to join his friends. They were with a dozen other dark-suited men all sat in a semi-circle witnessing the events. A distinctly undruid-like round of applause broke out amongst the assembled congregation. Churchill, by the merest of whiskers, refrained from giving a cheery wave as he would have done instinctively on the campaign trail. It took an even greater effort of will to stop himself lighting up a cigar. He would have done anything for another drink right now.

This was all just a bit of fun. With any luck the initiations would be over soon. They could all return to the house and get on with the real business of the evening. Drink, chat, and more drink.

And then there was Clemmie. Dearest Clemmie will you marry me? Perhaps it was just as well they were doing this nonsense tonight. It had taken his mind off the morrow. A big day in his life. A big day in anyone's life.

He was bored now. Another initiate was going through his admission to the Ancient Order of Druids. A slight breeze caressed his face. A light brush. Like a reminder. For the first time that evening he felt a real chill.

The Medium Murders

1

London, September 1920

A short, squat, bull-necked man walked along the street with a sense of purpose in his stride. The pinched look on his face was a defence against the cold night air. And it was getting colder. Accompanying him was a taller, leaner man with a ruddy complexion. His sharp face did not so much suggest shrewdness as scream it from a hilltop. Following the two men was a woman whose age could have been anywhere between forty and sixty. She was tall, slender, and walked with a bearing that was almost noble.

Ahead they could see a group of policemen shining torches. As they neared these lights, three uniformed policemen emerged from the house. At the opposite end of the street, a man wearing a thick overcoat, an even thicker scarf and a homburg crossed the road to join the policemen. Peeking out from the homburg, spreading like a contagion along his cheek, were grey whiskers. They all arrived at the scene a few moments later.

'Dr French,' said the shorter man. The man with the impressive whiskers nodded.

'Bulstrode,' replied the good doctor without much enthusiasm. He gave every impression that he wished to be somewhere else. This could just have easily meant with someone else. He disliked Detective Inspector Bulstrode and his partner-in-crime, Sergeant Wellbeloved. If ever a man had been misnamed it was this sergeant, thought French. As nasty a piece of work as had ever clutched a pair of handcuffs. Both of them.

Two peas.

'Shall we?' said Bulstrode and he walked into the room without waiting for a reply. Wellbeloved, Dr French and the woman followed Bulstrode into the room.

The new arrivals looked at the body of the dead woman. The wound in the neck made asking the cause of death somewhat redundant. This left Bulstrode temporarily at a loss. Then he remembered the woman who had accompanied them here. She was standing back from the group covering her mouth either from horror or because she was feeling ill.

Bulstrode rolled his eyes and returned his attention to the young woman. He knelt beside the body and looked at her stomach. He sensed the doctor kneeling down beside him. He lifted the arm and tested its flexibility. Bulstrode's eyes had not left the woman's stomach.

'Looks like a star.'

The Medium Murders

'Of course, it's a bloody star,' said French. 'Look, why don't you do your job and ask me for an estimate on time of death.'

'Go on then.'

'I'd say twelve hours. No more than twenty-four.'

Bulstrode looked at his pocket watch. Twenty past one in the morning. He looked at Wellbeloved. With some irritation, he noticed the sergeant was still standing well back from the corpse.

'Squeamish?'

'Funny.'

Wellbeloved stepped forward and examined the body. He moved over to the other side and looked at her face.

'Do you know her?'

Wellbeloved shook his head but remained silent.

'Sure?' persisted Bulstrode.

The sergeant stood up, narrowed his eyes, and nodded to his boss. Bulstrode looked at him closely. He seemed unconvinced. Then he turned around to the woman. He motioned for her to come over and look at the body.

'What do you think you're doing, Bulstrode?' said French angrily. The whiskers were not the only Victorian aspect to the good doctor. Bulstrode ignored his Victorian sensibility.

Reluctantly, the woman stepped forward; her eyes were fixed on the corpse. She stopped for a moment in front of the doctor. French looked into her dark eyes.

Neither said anything. There seemed to be something diabolic in those eyes. Or something else.

The woman broke away from the gaze of the doctor. She felt a slight breeze from the open window. The trees rustled outside, and a few leaves blew into the room falling like teardrops near the body.

'Is this the woman you saw?' asked Bulstrode.

'The woman nodded and turned away. She walked out of the room, out of the house and away from the crime scene. Then Bulstrode realised what he'd seen in her eyes: anger.

As she walked away the tears stung her eyes. This was exactly what she'd seen. The woman. Those markings. It was overwhelming. Her chest felt tight; her breathing laboured. She felt faint. It was always this way when she sensed spirits in the air. Evil spirits. The intense awareness of something malevolent.

She heard footsteps behind her. Running. She ignored them. He knew where to find her.

The sergeant finally appeared alongside her. She looked at him for a moment then continued walking. His face betrayed fear. Anguish.

'You knew her, didn't you?' said the woman.

Wellbeloved glared at her. Now anger replaced the anguish.

'Couldn't you have done something to stop them?'

The Medium Murders

The woman stopped. Then she did something that caused the group of policemen outside to spin around in shock.

She laughed.

'Stop them? How?' She waved her arms in the air like she was conducting an orchestra. Then she stopped and glared at Wellbeloved before laughing again.

'Do you think this a magic trick? Like pulling a rabbit from a hat?'

Wellbeloved tore off his hat and threw it angrily to the ground. He turned away from the woman, unsure of what he would do. He caught the eye of Bulstrode who had come outside to see what was going on. His boss was looking at him strangely. It was time to regain control. He spun around to the woman and pointed at her.

'You should show more respect for the dead.'

The woman looked at him perceptively.

'Perhaps you should show more respect for the living.'

She turned away and continued walking. After a few yards she stopped. Wellbeloved looked at her and shrugged his shoulders.

'Take me home. You have people to see now, don't you?'

-

As it happened Sergeant Wellbeloved did have people to see, but how this woman was aware of this, God only knew. Then again, if she wasn't a charlatan, why wouldn't she. This was worrying on several counts. He cursed himself for his reaction to the crime scene. He'd acted like a fresh-faced constable. He turned and jogged back to Bulstrode.

'Can you tell me what on earth is happening?' asked Bulstrode. Had there not been other police present, his language would have been a good deal sharper.

'Sorry, sir, she wants to go.'

Wellbeloved shrugged in the way that men do when confronted by that very rare specimen: the unreasonable woman. As a lifelong bachelor, Wellbeloved's experience of this subdivision of humanity was somewhat limited. In fact, his exposure to women came principally from frequent, recreational trips to brothels. There, he found a more compliant class of female. Except Fenella, of course, but she was strictly for those occasions when he'd behaved badly.

Bulstrode rolled his eyes. It was late. He wanted to go home. Dr French, standing on the doorstep, was lost in thought. He seemed to be fixated on the woman whose graceful figure was receding into the distance. Slowly, French became aware that Bulstrode's eyes were on him. Without averting his gaze, he asked a question.

'Was that Eva Kerr?'

'Yes.'

French did not react to the news. He looked at the detective and remembered there was work to do. But not by him. He put his gloves on and indicated the body with a slight tilt of his head.

The Medium Murders

'You can take her away now. I'll examine her tomorrow morning.' He paused for a moment then said, 'Actually, I think we'll make that the afternoon. I can get nine holes in, maybe.'

'Yes, sir,' replied Bulstrode before wondering why he had called the doctor, sir. He realised he did not know what rank the doctor held. He sounded like a toff though. Rank was relative. The doctor lived in a different world.

They both turned and looked at Wellbeloved trotting towards Eva Kerr. His heart sank as he saw a taxi pull up. A gaggle of reporters tumbled out. A bad night was about to get worse. He felt like howling to the moon but swore instead. He felt a touch on his arm. Doctor French nodded to the reporters and smiled grimly. There was little trace of sympathy as he echoed Bulstrode's thoughts.

'Looks like you have another Medium Murder on your hands.'

2

London, Belgrave Square, September 1920

The front door swung open to Kit Aston's apartment in Belgravia. After a month away in the United States, Kit entered the luxurious flat to the sound of his dog, Sam, barking happily and jumping up to greet him.

'Hello, boy,' said Kit bending down to pick up his excited, and excitable, Jack Russell. He was rewarded for his endeavour by having his spotless face licked clean by the little terrier. This prompted loud laughter from both Kit and his manservant, Harry Miller.

'It looks like you're forgiven, sir.'

'It certainly does. I'm sorry, old chap, it was a bit long, wasn't it?'

Sam stopped licking and regarded his master for a long moment. If he didn't quite nod in agreement, then his eyes certainly had the look of 'don't-do-it-again-buster'. Kit looked at his little dog affectionately. He'd missed him greatly and a wave of guilt coursed through him. He stroked Sam behind the ear. This was something that had the little terrier virtually purring.

In fact, Kit could distinctly hear purring.

The Medium Murders

'Good Lord, Harry. He's never done that before.'

'Ah, yes, sir,' replied Miller. 'There's a few things I've been meaning to tell you.'

One of the more astonishing aspects of Sam, at least as far as Kit and Harry were concerned, was his seeming ability to understand human conversation. One moment, Sam was a chap of the canine variety, earning a well-deserved cuddle from a returning master, the next he was a ferocious wolf on the hunt for his prey. In a flash, he jumped from Kit's arms onto the leather Chesterfield sofa, barking for all he was worth.

Kit looked at the object of Sam's wrath. He found it sitting curled up on his favourite armchair. He turned to Harry with a quizzical look on his face.

'Isn't that…?'

'Simpkins, sir.'

'Yes, Simpkins.'

He turned back and looked past Sam, who had worked himself up into a fine state of fury at the dark form residing on his master's chair.

It was a cat.

A black cat, in fact. The feline in question continued to ignore Sam. Such a wilful lack of fear in the presence of a fearsome beast like Sam was never going to sit well with this canine. The intensity of his verbal attack reached a new level of vehemence. Simpkins turned and looked at Sam for a moment. This caused the little dog to stop barking. Then Simpkins returned his attention to the examination of his paw.

Sam turned around and looked up at his master. If he could have shrugged his shoulders at that moment he certainly would have done so. Kit, meanwhile, turned to Miller, one eyebrow raised.

'You were saying, Harry?'

'Countess Laskov, downstairs, died the day before yesterday.'

'Really? I'm sorry to hear that. She must have been in her seventies at least.'

'Seventy-three, sir.'

'Good innings these days. How, may I ask, did she pass away?'

'Natural causes, sir.'

Harry Miller detected relief on his master's face. It was a little too early in the morning for murder. Anyway, it had been a long journey by sea and then by train back to London. Sleuthing was the last thing on Kit's mind.

'Well, I suppose we should go to the funeral. It'll be tomorrow, I suspect. Aunt Agatha will want to go, too. They were acquaintances. I'll be sorry to break the news to her.'

The two men looked back at Simpkins. The cat stared back. Even Sam was looking up at the two men. The room was silent for a moment.

'And Simpkins?' asked Kit.

The Medium Murders

'Well, sir, after the ambulance took the countess away, he came upstairs and started to scratch on the door. I heard the scratching and opened it. I saw him come in and sit down on your chair. He hasn't moved much since.'

'Really? But what about Countess Laskov's maid? Tunney, wasn't it?'

'Tunstall, sir. She moved out of the apartment. I haven't been able to find out why, but I did hear a slamming of a door one evening, so it clearly wasn't on good terms.'

Simpkins listened intently to the conversation without raising any objection to its veracity. His ears were upright and trained on the two humans who were, by now, discussing his future. Sam was all ears, too.

'How does he get on with Sam?' asked Kit.

'How does Sam get on with anyone?' This was more of a point than a question.

The two men looked at the terrier and the black cat. Once more, silence reigned until Sam offered a growl. The prospects did not look good from his perspective. The dark intruder had not been summarily dismissed. Every passing second was one too long in Sam's humble opinion. Then he heard Simpkins purring. Sam turned around to Simpkins and then back to Kit as if to say, 'You're not going to fall for this?'

'Well, we'll hold onto the little fella for the moment and see tomorrow, or whenever the funeral is, if there are any takers.'

Conscious that he'd been standing rather longer than expected, Kit moved forward toward his chair. He smiled down at Simpkins and motioned him off.

'There's a chap. You're on my seat. Any chance you could move along?'

Simpkins remained on Kit's chair. By now he'd gone back to cleaning his paw. Kit turned to Miller. The look on Miller's face was by no means sympathetic to his master's predicament. It was clear that Kit was on his own.

'I say, old boy, you're sitting on my seat.'

Kit suspected he was not alone in thinking this pleading was somewhat unbecoming of a war hero, spy, chess grandmaster and, well, a member of the nobility. Simpkins appeared unimpressed by this. He was not for moving.

Moral support from Miller did not appear to be forthcoming for Kit. In fact, his manservant was now laughing uncontrollably. At the very least, Kit decided, Miller should be complicit in, what was becoming, a shattering defeat.

'Fine help you are.'

Miller held his hands up in acknowledgment. The extent of this mea culpa was undermined when he had to use his hands to support himself against the wall, such was his amusement.

'Well,' said Kit, 'I suppose I could sit here for the time being.' He walked over to one of the two Chesterfields facing one another and sat down.

Strategic withdrawal complete, he asked Miller for some tea. In such situations, crises even, an Englishman can have no better comfort indeed, no finer inspiration for ideas, than a pot of tea. With milk.

As Miller went into the kitchen to make the tea, a thought struck Kit.

'I say, Harry,' shouted Kit.

'Yes, sir.'

'I remember Countess Laskov had a manservant, too? Bentham or something like that?'

'Yes sir,' called back Miller. 'He left just before Tunstall.'

This was odd. To lose one member of staff was unfortunate. To lose two, mused Kit, was bordering on empirical proof of Wilde's dictum. However, dying a matter of days afterwards was, frankly, stretching credibility too far. It all seemed like something from one of the *penny bloods* so beloved of his aunt and uncle.

A few minutes later Miller entered the room pushing a trolley. On it was a silver pot containing the magic elixir and some biscuits. Another thought struck Kit.

'You said there were a few things, Harry.'

'Yes, sir,' said Miller who lifted the pot and began to pour tea through a tea strainer. As he did so, there was a knock on the door.

The two men looked at one another. Nothing on Miller's countenance suggested he was expecting a visitor. The knocking became persistent. Miller set down the pot and tea strainer and went to answer the door. Kit heard the door open and the sound of a man's voice. It was a voice he knew very well.

This didn't make it any less incredible that he was here. In the normal way of things, he didn't pay house calls. Something told him such a visit was unlikely to be social. Nor did it bode well. He was barely through the door after solving a case in the United States and it looked like another one was heading in his direction.

Kit looked longingly at the tea and then towards the lounge door. It all seemed a bit early in the plot. After all, it was barely mid-morning.

The door opened and his visitor walked in. Miller had no idea who the man was, but he guessed, correctly, that Kit would know him. Kit rose from his seat and extended his hand. He glanced at Miller. The look on Miller's face suggested this was the other thing.

Kit looked at the man in front of him. He was slightly shorter than Kit. He wore a navy overcoat and supported himself on a stick. Kit knew for a fact that there was a sword inside the stick. The man was not quite elderly but nor was he middle-aged. Silver hair peeked out from under his Homburg. The final touch was a monocle that may or may not have been plain glass.

'Kit, I'm so sorry to call on you like this. You may guess I wouldn't have done so if this wasn't a matter of the utmost urgency and, frankly, delicacy.'

'Yes, sir. Please sit down. Tea?' asked Kit hopefully.

'I'm sorry Kit but I don't have the time. Would you be able to accompany me to Whitehall now?'

The face of Sir Mansfield Smith-Cumming, "C" to those who operated under him at the British Secret Service, suggested refusal was not an option. Kit smiled and accepted his second defeat in as many minutes.

'Yes, sir. Would you like Harry to take us?'

'No, I have a driver outside.'

Sam began to bark, clearly unhappy at seeing his master leave so soon after arriving. This prompted a smile from Smith-Cumming. A moment later it turned to a frown. Kit noticed this and looked down in the direction of Sam and Simpkins.

'Something wrong, sir?'

Smith-Cumming shook his head.

'Let's hurry, Kit.'

3

London, Grosvenor Square, September 1920

The reunion of the Cavendish sisters, after a month spent apart, highlighted wonderfully well the difference between chaps and the fairer sex. When Kit had met Harry at Kings Cross, Mary had sly enjoyment from the curt nod and handshake between the two men. In addition, there was a quick aside from Kit on his manservant's lack of activity having made him gain a pound or three.

Mary, meanwhile, gave Miller a gentle peck on the cheek, declared herself delighted at his complete recovery from the injury incurred while chasing 'the Phantom'. After Miller received his reward, Mary looked archly at her future husband. Kit, meanwhile, was oblivious to the source of his fiancée's amusement. He could see something had entertained her. That he didn't know what bothered him not in the least. It was part of the endless fascination she held for him.

Thankfully any shilly-shallying on the platform was brought to a swift conclusion by Aunt Agatha. Business-like as ever, she got things moving by suggesting Harry

The Medium Murders

arrange for their valises to be delivered to the two addresses. Twenty minutes later he had deposited the two ladies back at Aunt Agatha's sumptuous abode in Grosvenor Square.

The door had been answered by the ever-reliable Fish. Aunt Agatha's elderly butler responded to his ladyship's call with all the speed and enthusiasm of a pale-throated South American sloth.

The reunion of Agatha and Fish was as brief as it was, well, brief. Within seconds of her arrival, Aunt Agatha was dispensing orders to her aged servant. This was something of a shock to his system. He had found the peace and quiet over the last month very much to his liking.

Mary looked at her sister, Esther, for a moment, then they embraced. There was no mistaking the warmth and affection between them. The embrace lasted a few minutes and a tear or two was shed. Finally, they stepped back from one another. A smile broke out on both their faces. A moment later, Esther Cavendish's eyebrows rose hopefully.

A shake of the head from Mary.

Then Mary tilted her head slightly and her eyebrows rose slightly. This was met with a shake of the head and a mock-sad face. With the information duly communicated, they realised Aunt Agatha had entered the room a little more silently than usual. They turned towards her. She had observed their reunion with what can only be described as a face on her.

'Do you think I'm completely senescent?'

Mary shook her head and Esther, not knowing the meaning of senescent, followed her sister's cue.

'Good. Please remember your Aunt Emily is only a phone call away.'

A phone call and a few hundred miles was not far enough, thought Mary. Agatha turned the full intensity of her gaze on Esther.

'You, young lady, are to be married in a few weeks. Let us not speak of this again. You have both been warned.'

They certainly had. If they were going to talk about such matters, and clearly both were very keen to do so, it was best done well out of earshot of their septuagenarian bodyguard. Emphasis on 'body'.

Both smiled by way of apology, but Agatha's mind had already moved on to other matters. Natalie, Agatha's French maid appeared in the doorway.

'Madame, the valises have arrived.'

'Excellent. Tell Fish to bring them in.'

In fact, the estimable Fish was standing outside the room. He had heard the order with a heart that did not so much sink as crash to his feet. He walked outside and saw around ten rather sizeable bags that would require transporting into the house and up three flights of stairs.

The Medium Murders

He turned around and was just about to give silent vent to a stream of words that he'd first learned sixty-one years ago when he saw the young French woman looking at him.

Fish smiled valiantly but suspected his attempt at a smile was more like that of a chap facing his ever-understanding wife following a convivial evening at the pub with other, like-minded, chaps. Natalie saw the poor butler's face and immediately recognised the cause of his dismay.

'I will help you, Monsieur Fish,' she whispered with a wink.

The combination of what she said, and how she said it, the low Gallic purr, and the slow wink, almost Fish finished off. He nodded in gratitude and turned, with something approaching youthful vigour, to the task in hand.

As Agatha took on the project of reintegrating their belongings into the Grosvenor Square household, the Cavendish sisters took the opportunity to escape into the city. Whilst it would be nice to report that their early conversation covered the health and happiness of the family members visited as well as the impressions of the exciting places seen, alas one topic dominated their thoughts.

'Perhaps I'm becoming paranoid, but at one point I was convinced even the seagulls were spying on us.'

'She's incredible. Do you know, she was telephoning Mrs Bright every evening to check on what I had been doing that day right up until she stepped onto the Aquitania? Richard's mother was rolling her eyes every time the phone rang.'

'Essie, do you ever get the feeling that the Cavendish sisters' devotion to their virtue is not trusted?'

Both girls burst out laughing as they walked along Brook Street towards the city centre. They concluded that Aunt Agatha understood them all too well. Esther stopped momentarily and looked up at the sky. It was midday. The sun was attempting, and failing, to peek through a thick blanket of clouds.

'Not very far away now, I suppose.'

Mary giggled and said, 'Six weeks to your wedding night.'

Esther smiled but then her face grew more serious. In a moment Mary's face changed and became more reflective.

'It's not even a year since we lost Grandpapa. You don't think it's all too soon?' said Esther.

Mary hugged her sister.

'If you remember, he was trying to marry us off. You to Kit and me to…' she stopped for a moment, unable to utter the name of the man who had killed her grandfather.

The Medium Murders

'They're due to hang him the day after the wedding,' said Esther.

Mary nodded then said, 'Let's not talk of him, Essie. Let's think of the future. I know it sounds banal, but I really think Grandpapa would have wanted this. He'd have been delighted to see us so happy with men like Richard and Kit.'

'I know.'

The two sisters walked on in silence for a few minutes, lost in their memories. Just ahead they saw Claridge's. They looked at one another and grinned. Lunch in one of their favourite restaurants was the order of the day and the perfect place to catch up on their month apart. They ducked into the hotel just as the first droplets of rain began to fall.

'We didn't bring an umbrella,' pointed out Esther, sadly.

'Excellent, we'll just have to stay here until it stops.'

Esther grinned, 'Good point. I'm sure Aunt Agatha will understand.'

At this moment, Agatha was concerned with weightier matters. The luggage, most of which was still sitting on the street, was in danger of being soaked. While there was no questioning the doggedness with which Fish was performing his duty, Agatha could not help but note that the pace was paralyzingly slow. Even with Natalie's help, it was clear that the poor man was struggling. She felt a stab of sympathy for her aging butler.

He was getting on a bit.

Perhaps the time was soon coming when she would have to decide about Fish. As this thought crossed her mind, the rain began to fall more heavily. She looked at the poor man struggling with the baggage. An image came into her mind of two young men. Her husband, Eustace 'Useless' Frost and his manservant Judson Fish.

So long ago.

The view the from library became obscured by the rain running like tear drops down the window but Agatha's mind was in another century. She could still hear the laughter of the two men. She could still see the first time that 'Useless' had looked at her. The whispered aside to Fish and then his leaving them alone on the platform to perform some duty or other. Of course, he'd been sent away to allow 'Useless' an excuse to engage her in conversation.

So long ago.

Was it really forty years? Where does the time go? It could have been yesterday as far as Agatha was concerned. The sights, the sounds, the heat, and the smells were still with her. All she had to do was close her eyes. Such a wonderful time. And sad. Fortune distributes its gifts unequally. We find that out in the end, don't we?

The Medium Murders

Poor Fish.

Agatha woke up an hour later. The rain was battering against the window like small stones thrown by a rough boy. Someone had placed a tartan blanket over her to protect against any drafts. She looked around her. The room was empty. The girls had probably gone out to lunch. No doubt they had much to talk about. Adventure. Romance. Aging aunts denying them the rich tapestry of experience they desired so much. This made her smile. She was performing her role to the hilt; for role it was. She remembered another. An aunt who had performed a similar duty in her life.

The door opened quietly, and a head peaked in. It was Natalie.

'Madame, *je m'excuse.*'

'It's quite all right, Natalie, I was awake. Thank you for putting the blanket on me.'

'It was Fish, madame.'

'I must thank him then.'

'I have unpacked everything, madame,' said Natalie.

'Very good. Actually, can you join me for a moment?'

Natalie looked a little nervously at Agatha before walking over to the library window where Agatha was sitting. Agatha gestured for her to sit down. This was unusual and set Natalie on edge for a moment.

'I want to talk about the future. Specifically, your role, Natalie.'

Now Natalie Doutreligne was very worried indeed. Agatha read the look on her maid's face and put her hand up to reassure her.

'I know that when I first engaged your services, Natalie, it was on a short-term basis.' Agatha paused for a moment. How she was going to phrase the next part of this conversation was something she wished she'd given more thought to.

'Clearly, the circumstances were unusual.'

Acting as a seductress to Aunt Agatha's nephew who was on the cusp of a potentially damaging marriage certainly qualified as being unusual, thought Natalie.

'Oui, madame.'

'Quite. However, Natalie, I must confess that your performance of the, shall we say, more traditional requirements of a maid have impressed me. In fact, I was rather hoping that we could extend your contract indefinitely.'

This was unexpected. Natalie's mouth dropped open. Agatha's eyes widened slightly which hastened Natalie's mouth to resume its normal aspect.

'Madame, this is very kind of you.'

'Quite,' said Agatha, unsure if this was a yes or a no. She raised her eyebrows a degree or three to suggest that an answer would be welcome to her job offer.

Natalie did not have to think too hard about her answer.

'I would love to stay, madame.'

The Medium Murders

'Capital,' said Agatha, tapping the table in a spontaneous gesture of happiness. This was good news, and she was sure it would be seen as such by the girls and Kit. The only question remaining was the status of Fish.

'Would you be a dear and ask Fish to join me for a moment. That will be all.'

Natalie rose from her chair and went to find Fish. Her happiness at the job offer, she realised, was tempered by a worry for what it would mean for Fish. One did not have to be a Cambridge academic to see that his vigour was not what it once was. She hoped that madame did not intend dispensing with the venerable butler's services. This would throw a new light on her own intentions.

Several minutes later, Fish appeared in the library. The long wait was something Agatha was used to by now. She watched him slowly make his way over to her. Judging by the tick of the clock, the journey of a matter of yards took almost thirty seconds. She gestured for him to take a seat.

For Fish, being asked to sit down was a rare event. He remembered an occasion at the outbreak of the War. The second Boer War. While he did not necessarily feel on edge, his senses were on heightened alert.

'Fish. How long have you been in service now?'

'Many years, milady,' answered the butler truthfully.

'Well, I'm sure neither of us needs to dwell on how long you have been of service to me. Suffice to say it has been a considerable amount of time.'

Fish nodded. A sadness fell upon him. He could see in Agatha's eyes that she knew what he was thinking. Even more reason to get to the point, thought Agatha, no point in shilly-shallying.

'I have just asked Natalie if she would like to stay on as my maid.'

This was a surprise to Fish. He had anticipated the young Frenchwoman would leave their service upon their return. At this point he began to wonder what this meant for him.

'You're no longer a young man, Fish.'

This was not looking good, thought Fish, even if it was true.

'Perhaps the time has come to think of life after service.'

Did such a thing exist, wondered Fish? Service was all he'd ever known. He was the son of a butler. His grandfather, too, had been a butler. The world outside was an abstraction. His world was *here*.

'Of course, it's up to you,' continued Agatha.

Better, thought Fish.

'But I wonder if you would not be happier with a reduction in your duties. Let the younger ones pick up the strain.'

Much better.

The Medium Murders

'What do you think, Fish?'

The question was thrown at him so unexpectedly, Fish was lost for words. Lady Frost wanted his opinion. An opinion on a subject related directly to his future. A few seconds passed and Fish struggled to arrange his thoughts into something that would sound comprehensible.

'I know this is a bit of a shock,' prompted Agatha.

Fish finally felt it was time to gain some sort of control on the direction of travel.

'I have no complaints, milady.'

In fact, he rather enjoyed his life. Lady Frost could be a harridan when she wanted but her demands were minimal. Having Natalie continue would certainly be pleasing to the eye, although he was certain he'd been caught by her, on a few occasions, enjoying her rear aspect. However, she was French and, if anything, it was an additional, if not particularly onerous, duty for him to fulfil.

Agatha was unsure if her thoughts had penetrated her butler's consciousness sufficiently, so she came to the point.

'What I am driving at, Fish, is that you should consider semi-retirement. I would add that I have no wish to see you leave this house. You can continue to oversee the staff, but we should think to a future where the younger ones do the work, and you enjoy a richly deserved rest.'

The interview finished on this highly satisfactory note. He understood that Natalie was to assume the role of housekeeper and that the two of them would recruit a new maid to take over many of Natalie's duties.

Yes, thought Fish on his way to the kitchen, a satisfactory outcome. He decided it should be recognised with a small, celebratory tipple. Perhaps he could persuade the young Frenchwoman to join him. If he remembered correctly, there was a bottle of wine high up in one of the cupboards. He could help Natalie reach it. This would, of course, require that he hold her waist while she stood on the chair. Not to do so would be unsafe and, certainly, ungentlemanly.

4

Kit and Smith-Cumming sat in silence for most of the journey. Smith-Cumming's only comment was to observe that the weather was about to turn. Rather than converse on a subject that held no interest for either man, Kit waited to see where they were heading. He didn't have to wait long. They pulled up outside a building Kit knew very well. His friend Charles 'Chubby' Chatterton worked there.

The War Office building on Whitehall was relatively new, despite its rather Baroque appearance. It had been completed just over a dozen years previously. The Whitehall-facing front from the second floor upwards had a row of Ionic columns. Along the roof were placed a series of sculptured figures symbolising Peace and War, Truth and Justice, Fame, and Victory. At the corner of the trapezium-shaped building was a decorative dome. Kit thought it somewhat overdone.

The two men hobbled up the steps. Each instinctively helped the other. Both had lost part of their legs. Smith-Cumming had lost his in a car accident and performed the amputation himself using a penknife to escape the wreckage; Kit had lost his during the War.

They took care going up the steps into the War Office as the rain had made them a little slippery. Once inside the main doors they were confronted with yet more steps. As much as he liked his friend 'Chubby', he rarely visited the offices as the steps were such a torture. Kit hoped that their meeting was on the ground floor.

'Up a flight,' said Smith-Cumming, dashing Kit's hopes. The spymaster noted the rueful grin and nodded.

'Yes, a bit of a pain really.'

They arrived outside an office with a large oak door. The sign on the plate beside the door read: The Secretary of State for War and Air. Kit raised his eyebrows and followed Smith-Cumming through the large doors. They were met by a man Smith-Cumming introduced as the Parliamentary Under-Secretary of State, Arthur Peel. Kit smiled at the dark-haired man before him. His moustache seemed to cover not only his face but half of London also.

'Hello, Arthur,' said Kit, shaking the hand of 1st Viscount Peel, the youngest son of Robert Peel.

'Oh, so you two know each other then,' said Smith-Cumming rolling his eyes in a manner suggesting he should have known that this class all knew one another. To be fair, they mostly did.

Beside Peel was another man in a dark suit. His greying hair was receding at the temples. A deep groove ran vertically between his eyes which were hidden behind round spectacles. A clipped moustache decorated his lip like a medal. The tightness of his lips matched well with the rigidity of his personality.

'This is Vernon Kell.'

Smith-Cumming added nothing to this. Kit sensed an atmosphere between them, like two prize-fighters meeting in the middle of the ring before a fight. Kell had once tried to recruit Kit and they had worked briefly together before the end of the War. He headed up the sister branch of the secret service, MI5 (g). This branch of the Intelligence service dealt with investigating espionage, sabotage, and subversion within Britain.

The look on Peel's face was quite grave so small talk was kept to a minimum. He led Kit, Kell and Smith-Cumming through to the main office. A man was standing behind an impressively large, and surprisingly high, oak desk. He was not large but his eyes compelled attention. He rose as they entered and walked around the table to greet them.

'Gentlemen, I'm happy you could come at such short notice,' said a voice that would one day become not just the most famous in Britain, but, perhaps, in the world. It was deep, textured, and warm. The voice of someone used to giving commands.

The Secretary of State for War and Air, Winston Churchill, shook hands with Kit and Smith-Cumming. Kit had met Churchill on a few occasions. Mostly social. Churchill was a Marlborough. The Marlborough family had been at the side of every King since William.

They went to an office with very high ceilings and portraits by Joshua Reynolds adorning the walls. It was a serious room where serious decisions were taken. The atmosphere was grave. Kit refrained from making any comments and waited for the men in the room to explain why they wished to see him. He didn't have to wait long. Interestingly he was not asked to sit. The five men remained standing as Churchill spoke.

'You are no doubt wondering why I have asked you here.'

Kit nodded but remained silent. His memory of Churchill was that he enjoyed speaking. At length. Well, thought Kit if he enjoys being centre stage, lead on Macduff. Churchill handed Kit an envelope. Kit glanced at Churchill then down at the envelope.

'Go on, open it.'

Kit did so. He removed three photographs. He studied the first photograph but said nothing. In the centre of the photograph was Churchill. It looked like it had been taken at least a decade ago as Churchill seemed much younger. Flanking Churchill were several men, some in suits and others in, more intriguingly, white robes. If Kit didn't know better, he would have said they were…

'Druids. Yes, Aston, they're druids,' said Churchill.

The second photograph seemed to have been taken at the same occasion, but it was difficult to be certain. Churchill was standing in the centre and some men were dressed in druid robes. This time there was, in addition, a woman in the picture dressed like a goddess. There was an olive wreath around her head, and she wore a long, flowing white robe. She was standing to the side of Churchill. Kit could see that she was young, perhaps in her twenties, and attractive. Her eyes stared stonily ahead into the distance.

'It looks like you weren't aware this photograph was being taken, Secretary of State.'

'I wasn't,' confirmed Churchill grimly.

The third photograph caused Kit to gasp. He looked at Churchill and then the three other men. Churchill's face had turned red with anger, his voice strained by fear and rage.

'I certainly wasn't aware of this photograph either. I have never seen this girl in my life before.'

Kit, reluctantly, looked down at the picture again. It showed the same young woman from the previous photograph. She was naked and clearly dead. Beside her were three robed and masked men. One of them holding the knife that had been used in the murder.

Kit looked closely at her stomach. There seemed to be something on it, but the photograph lacked enough detail to be sure if this was really the case or not.

'Yes,' said Churchill, noticing that Kit was looking at the young woman's stomach, 'I saw that too but it's impossible to see exactly what it is.'

'Have you any clue as to what to might be? Could it be some symbol related to the ceremony you attended?'

Churchill looked Kit in the eye. For a few moments there was silence as he sized up the man before him. He knew Kit, but not well. He knew of Kit, too. Everything. Smith-Cumming had briefed him the previous week. What he had just shared was an enormous leap of faith. If this became public knowledge, his career and, likely, his marriage would be destroyed. Kit Aston represented a last, desperate gamble. As he looked deep into the eyes of the man before him, Churchill saw his last chance. He wasn't certain if he felt reassured or just lightheaded with fear. He rolled the dice.

'Perhaps we should sit down,' said Churchill. 'I'll tell you everything.'

It was late afternoon before Kit returned to his flat. He walked through into the living room and noted that Simpkins was still residing on his seat. Beside him, on the Chesterfield sofa, sat Sam. There was a surprisingly accommodating silence between them rather like two old gentlemen at their club.

'No movement, I see,' said Kit.

'No sir, not much. Sam seems to have accepted the new arrival since your return.'

Kit went over and picked Sam up, much to the little terrier's delight. Simpkins glanced up but said nothing.

The Medium Murders

As there was clearly no chance that the cat was going to give up Kit's seat any time soon, Kit sat down where Sam had been sitting and placed the little dog on his knee. He risked stroking Simpkins behind the ear. Simpkins let him do this.

As Kit was stroking the cat, he noticed the collar for the first time. It was silver and looked like a star. As Simpkins was now pressing his head into Kit's fingers it was difficult to see it clearly. Kit assumed it was the Star of David. The thought of it reminded him of Countess Laskov's funeral.

'Harry, were you able to find out about the funeral?'

'You were right, sir, it's tomorrow morning.'

'Any word of the two servants?'

'No, sir, I asked my usual network, but they seem to have disappeared. By the way, the police are downstairs now. I observed their arrival around ten minutes before you came.'

'Now?'

'Yes sir, the Chief Inspector is downstairs.'

Kit lifted Sam from his lap with an apology. He looked at Miller and shrugged in the manner of a man who cannot help himself. This was greeted with a smile from Miller. A minute or two later, Kit was knocking on the door of the late Countess Laskov's flat. The door was opened a few moments later by a uniformed police officer. He looked at Kit suspiciously.

'Can I help you?'

Kit was rather hoping that this could be his line, but he smiled as he saw the Chief Inspector appear in the corridor behind.

'Your lordship,' said Chief Inspector Jellicoe, 'I wondered when you'd be down.'

Kit laughed guiltily. Was he so predictable? Probably. Jellicoe beckoned him to enter, and they shook hands. He led Kit into the main living room. It had been several months since Kit had last been in the countess's flat. Longer even. With a stab of remorse, he remembered it had been a pre-Christmas drinks party for residents in the building. Another life. A time before Mary.

'Well, Chief Inspector, as you already have me down for being a shameless meddler and curtain twitcher I may as well confess to my crime. Can I ask what brings you down here?' Kit emphasised the 'you' to indicate his surprise that it should be Jellicoe.

Jellicoe was a man not given to natural displays of warmth never mind outward appearance of happiness. He had a naturally melancholic mien, amplified by a rather exuberant moustache. This did not mean he was depressed. Kit had long since detected a sly sense of humour which he wove subtly into his conversation and interrogatory approach. His appearance was less a reflection of his personality than a consequence of the serious and often sad nature of his job. A job in which he had demonstrated no little accomplishment. Kit liked the

Chief Inspector as much as he respected him and that was a great deal.

'Good question, sir,' agreed Jellicoe. 'In the normal course of events such a death would be dealt with by other people. However, given the rank, and religion, of Countess Laskov as well as the apparent disappearance of her staff....'

Jellicoe left the rest unsaid and glanced at Kit, who nodded.

'Her death was of natural causes, though?'

Did the Chief Inspector hesitate just a second before answering yes? It was certainly Kit's impression. The failure to meet his eye had Kit's senses tingling.

'It was a heart attack, I understand,' replied Jellicoe.

Kit looked around the living room. It had changed much since his last visit. The walls had been given a fresh lick of paint and were now dark; much darker than he had remembered. The velvet curtains were black, long, and oppressive. Previously they had been a cream colour although Kit had remembered they had seen better days. Black candles rested on the mantelpiece. It was difficult to tell, but there seemed to be a star shape on them.

Jellicoe looked at Kit surveying the room. He said nothing until Kit's observations were complete. The two men looked at one another. No question needed to be asked.

'Very different from when I was last here.'

Kit explained, in detail, what he remembered from his previous visit. After a few minutes the two men parted. Kit expected that the Chief Inspector had his own work to do and did not want to take up too much of his time. He went back upstairs to the flat.

Miller was waiting for him in the living room. It was clear he was eager to hear what had transpired downstairs. Kit smiled at his manservant. Once again, he reflected on the good fortune that had brought the two men together. He owed him his life. Afterwards, Miller had taken well to the life of service as well as the more unusual aspects of his role which had included, over the last year and a half, burglary, spying and leading an armed assault on an Indian bandit stronghold.

'Quite a day, Harry.'

Kit proceeded to give the key highlights from his two meetings. When he had finished Miller suggested that a cup of tea might be in order.

'Something stronger, I think. Now, Harry, a question.'

Miller looked up from the drinks tray where he was preparing a brandy.

'How long do you think it takes for a young lady to make herself ready for the evening?'

'Hard to say, sir. An hour?'

'And if she were more like a chap?'

'Ten minutes, give or take.'

The Medium Murders

'I think that's close enough. Another question, how long would it take to drive from Grosvenor Square to Belgravia?'

'At this time, sir, no more than five minutes.'

Kit smiled and nodded in agreement. He went to his telephone and asked the operator to put him through to a Grosvenor Square number. Much to his surprise, the phone was answered quite quickly. This was a rare occurrence where Fish was concerned.

'Ahh, Natalie. Hello.'

'Your lordship. How can I help?' asked Natalie at the other end of the line.

'Is my aunt or Mary available?'

'Lady Frost is resting in her room and Mademoiselle Mary is in the bath, I believe.'

There was a pause on the line just long enough for Natalie to roll her eyes and wonder at how ridiculously alike, and simple, were men. Neither rank nor age made a difference in the matter of the unclothed female form. They worshipped as one.

Kit recognised after a few moments he should probably draw a halt to the delightful images coursing through his mind and convey a message instead.

'Would you tell the ladies that I have returned from my meeting with the Secretary of State for War and Air. Soon after arriving home, I bumped into Chief Inspector Jellicoe downstairs. He is investigating a death in the building. Thank you, Natalie.'

Message communicated, Kit sat down and looked at the clock. It was just after six thirty. Miller looked at the clock, too, and then their eyes met.

'Twenty minutes?'

'Less, sir.'

Sixteen minutes later, Kit's front door was virtually battered off its hinges by what sounded like a combination of fists.

'Looks like you were right, Harry.'

5

Mary and Esther arrived at Claridge's and went through the Davies Street entrance. A uniformed doorman greeted them as they entered. Inside, enormous chandeliers lit up the foyer. The black and white tiled floor gave the interior the feel of a painting by Pieter de Hooch. All around were young people, male and female, well-heeled and unlikely to be troubled by the need to work. It was as if every young officer from the War had come to Claridge's to celebrate their survival.

Esther grinned at Mary and gave voice to both their thoughts.

'Almost a pity we're taken.'

'Essie,' exclaimed Mary but she laughed all the same. Mary knew that she would never be able to persuade Kit to come here. To be honest, she liked him even more for this. Occasionally was more than enough for her. She didn't begrudge these bright young people their fun. She'd seen what War could do a young man. Why wouldn't you celebrate life? The censure many of these Bright Young Things received from older generations for living a life dedicated to frivolity was undeserved. Her generation had been tested to the limit in the fields of Flanders. It had not been found wanting.

She heard a particularly loud braying laugh from one young man clutching a bottle of champagne. The Cavendish sisters rolled their eyes in unison. Yes, their generation had proved resolute and courageous, but perhaps this did not apply to everyone.

They headed towards the restaurant and spoke to the maitre d' who told them that they would have to wait half an hour for a table. He suggested they wait in the bar.

'Why not?' said Mary.

The bar was crowded but quick thinking by Mary helped them nab a couple of free seats near the window. It was abundantly clear that their arrival had been noticed by many young men. Within a few minutes, an embarrassed waitress arrived and handed Esther a note. The waitress stayed by the table as she waited for their reply.

'Didn't take long for your admirers to make themselves known,' said Mary with a grin.

'Not just me, darling sister. Apparently these two young men would like us to join them for some champagne. They say they want to celebrate.'

'I can imagine.'

Esther looked at Mary quizzically then said, 'You can be, how can I put it, cynical sometimes.' This was said without malice and taken by Mary as a badge of honour.

The Medium Murders

However, she couldn't resist testing her sister's own set of standards.

'Shall we join them then?'

'You must be joking,' said Esther laughing at her own duplicity. She put the note down onto the table and scribbled a reply.

Mary read the reply upside down and nodded her approval. Then they ordered two cocktails. For the next twenty minutes Mary shared every detail of the recent trip to the United States. Esther was in shock at the level of risk to which Mary had exposed herself.

'Yes, I was pretty exposed at times,' acknowledged Mary, who had neglected to mention the dress requirements, or lack thereof, for her singing engagement at Lehane's in San Francisco.

They soon were invited into the restaurant by the maitre d'. The table was at the far end of the room. Mary's heart sank at the thought of having to parade through the restaurant with dozens of eyes on them. She suspected a few more notes would be zinging towards their table soon.

In fact, she was wrong. A more direct approach was employed by a couple of young men around the same age as Kit and Richard. Neither man could be said to be deficient in confidence, wealth or, to be fair, looks. It transpired she had met one of them before.

'I say, it is you, Esther,' said the first man. He was not especially tall, but his voice, dress, and manner bespoke rank.

Esther looked up and smiled.

'Hello, Xander.' She turned to Mary and introduced the new arrival. 'This is Alexander Lewis. Lord…'

'Never mind all that, Esther. Is this the famous Mary Cavendish?'

Mary smiled up at Lewis and nodded. She had, for a brief period, become famous amongst the titled class for volunteering as a nurse during the War under an assumed name. She was, by now, used to her notoriety.

'Can I introduce Bobby Andrews?' said Lewis. The man behind him seemed to step out from the pages of a romantic novel. Tall, dark, and handsome barely captured the dangerously easy grace of the man before the Cavendish sisters.

'I'm sorry if we are imposing. I did tell Xander to leave you in peace.'

'Nonsense, Bobby, Esther is an old friend,' replied Lewis. 'Can we join you?'

Esther looked at Mary and smiled apologetically. She desperately wanted to spend time with her sister, uninterrupted by the male of the species in full courtship mode. Mary accepted the situation was beyond their control.

'We'd be delighted if you joined us.'

The Medium Murders

What possible harm could come from it? They would know, surely, that she and Esther were affianced. If not, it would become apparent as they chatted. There was nothing unusual, never mind untoward, in four young people enjoying a lunch together.

The two men pulled two chairs over to join the girls. Soon they ordered lunch and a bottle of champagne.

There's nothing like the presence of an attractive member of the *gentler* sex to hasten the growth of antlers in the *weaker* sex. Within seconds of their arrival, and notwithstanding the immediate presence of two young adult bucks in the prime of condition, Esther and Mary's table soon became a focal point for young breeding males pawing the ground as they competed for attention.

Sadly, or fortunately, predatory chaps lack the devilishly subtle mind of their quarry. This is doubly prevalent when the hunting male is known by such soubriquets as Bunty, Tuppy or, most damagingly of all, Stinky. Their intentions are as clear as a full moon in a cloudless sky. Their courtship modus operandi rarely stretches beyond a 'what ho' before delivering the life changing question about making them the happiest of men.

The English gentleman's approach to romance is, famously, in marked contrast to the French or Italian men. For them, words and romantic gestures are necessary to cover for an absence of ruddy complexion and tweeds.

Paradoxically, the Englishman's more rudimentary methods are both a saving grace as well as his downfall. He is a participant in an ill-matched battle. Women are brought up knowing how their future must proceed along prescribed lines. Thoughts of love only intrude on the mind of a chap by accident. This is prompted, invariably, by the sight of an uncommonly beautiful face. Thus, a life spent in harmless pursuit of sport, joshing with friends, and recovering from hangovers is poor preparation for the one great game of life.

This innate incompetence is his salvation as it stops him from falling too much into the depths of despondency when the inevitable rejection comes. Furthermore, the rapidity with which he fires off these romantic rounds means he can try many times and, sooner or later, will manage to hit the target.

Several young men, mostly titled if their outlandish tweeds were anything to go by, visited the table under the guise of knowing either Andrews or Lewis. Whilst the latter seemed delighted by the company, it was abundantly clear that Andrews was livid. However, both sisters, as they admitted later, enjoyed the attention of these prime examples of the chap of the species. The afternoon passed pleasantly enough before Esther caused a wave of dismay to pass through the company when she announced it was time for them to return.

Offers to walk them home came pouring forth from these gallants. Polite refusals followed. No offence was felt as the sisters made manifest their gratitude by dispensing pecks on the cheek to each of their courtiers. This was as delightful to the recipients as it was palpably not enough for the tall, dark, and handsome prime male in the pack.

As they made their exit, Mary stopped for a moment at a publicity poster on the wall. Esther was already out the door and thus did not hear her sister say, 'That's interesting'.

The rain had eased off sufficiently for the girls to return on foot to Grosvenor Square. Their arms entwined and they walked happily along the street laughing at the remarkable mating rituals of the men whose company they had enjoyed these last few hours.

'I must say, though, Bobby Andrews was the absolute berries,' said Esther, laughing.

'Yes, he's certainly a dish. Bit too cocksure for my liking.'

'Really? More serious than Xander and some of the other boys. I think he liked you, Mary.'

Mary looked at her sister but, oddly, did not disagree. Normally, young men tended to fall for Esther. She was probably more beautiful and certainly more serene company. Mary was 'hard work'. In fact, she knew that Bobby Andrews was taken with her if the note he'd passed to her underneath the table was anything to go by. He'd invited her to lunch the next day. Mary had left the note on the table.

'Still, it was a nice way to pass the afternoon. I was relieved when the other boys arrived, though,' said Esther.

'I know what you mean,' said Mary, before adding, brightly, 'Maybe we can go back sometime.'

Esther collapsed into a heap of giggles. She had been thinking the same thing. The short walk back Grosvenor Square was barely sufficient to catch up on the more detailed aspects of their time apart. Perceptive as ever, Mary did hit on one topic that was troubling the future Mrs Bright.

'Has Richard decided about moving to Harley Street or not?'

Esther frowned and shook her head.

'He's not exactly a socialist but he really detests the way the system works presently. I think he wants to help people who desperately need it. That, unsurprisingly, excludes people like us. So, for the moment, he's doing locum. But that can't go on forever.'

'Good for him,' replied Mary.

'I agree but how that resolves itself remains to be seen. He'll need money to set himself up in London. Unfortunately, as you know, we're both a bit strapped.'

Mary raised an eyebrow at this.

'You know what I mean,' laughed Esther. 'Having a house with staff as well as setting up a surgery costs more money than my allowance will cover.'

The Medium Murders

Mary grinned and was about to say something when Esther's eyes widened in mock horror.

'Don't say live with Aunt Agatha.'

Natalie opened the door upon the sisters' return.

'Where's Fish?' asked Mary, surprised at seeing Natalie answering the door. Natalie explained the new arrangements which met the approval of the girls. Both felt guilty at having to ask the elderly butler for anything and ended up doing things for themselves.

'And Aunt Agatha?'

'She went to bed for a rest. It was a busy day. She went to an agency to recruit a new maid. Then Mrs Simpson was over.'

'Did they have brandy?' asked Mary.

Natalie nodded.

'How many?'

'More than one, mademoiselle.'

The three young women grinned at one another. It would be fair to say that after a rocky start, the Cavendish sisters adored Kit's aunt. They certainly didn't begrudge her a snifter or three in the late afternoon. As they were not due to see Kit until eight and Richard was still locuming in Kent, the girls decided to take a bath before getting ready for the evening.

Mary sank into her bath with a feeling approaching delirium. She sometimes read a book when so ensconced. Alas, in her haste she'd forgotten to pick one up. No matter, the feeling of the hot water and soap suds lapping around her body was compensation enough.

And in any other circumstances, she would certainly have stayed another hour. However, sometimes life has a cruel sense of humour. It distributes bounty and misfortune at random, often in bunches, sometimes mixed. So, it proved when she heard a knock on her door.

'Yes?'

'Mademoiselle, it's Natalie. Lord Aston has just phoned.'

Mary sat up immediately.

'He said that the lady in the flat below him died yesterday in suspicious circumstances and he went to see Winston Churchill in Whitehall.'

Mary's eyes widened.

'Natalie, can you relay this message immediately to Aunt Agatha and my sister, please.'

'But Madam is sleeping.'

'Wake her, Natalie. She won't mind, believe me.'

'Very well,' replied Natalie.

'Anyway, if I know my fiancé, he probably has a wager with Harry on how soon we'll arrive.'

6

Miller opened the door. This caused the three women on the other side to fall into Kit's flat. Thankfully, when such near accidents occur, women usually recover their dignity much more quickly than men. This is done through a variety of ingenious devices, the most popular of which is rapid, if hardly impartial, apportionment of blame elsewhere.

Suitably chastened for not giving sufficient warning of his intention to open the door, Miller beat a hasty retreat. Agatha ordered three brandies from him as he disappeared in the direction of the kitchen. Then Agatha followed Kit's eye to the table where, laid out on a silver platter, were three glasses of Napoleon.

'Ah well…at least you've done something right.'

Following this faint praise, eyes fixed on the prize, Agatha marched straight ahead, followed by a smiling Esther.

Mary glanced at Kit. Her eyes narrowed.

'Who won?'

'I had you down for twenty minutes,' said Kit.

'I did,' said Miller, reappearing at that moment carrying Sam.

'Well, I can see that my Lord and master no longer trusts me,' said Mary, before sweeping majestically towards the Chesterfields. The three ladies were now all seated and looking expectantly at Kit like children at a Punch and Judy show.

'Well, as you ask, yes I have recovered well from my long journey,' said Kit sardonically.

'Get on with it,' said Agatha. 'Save your common room humour for those fatheads at your club.'

The sisters Cavendish nearly clapped in delight but opted instead for smiles that would have had half the Church of England clergy engaged in a mass brawl for their attention.

'I can see I'm outnumbered,' said Kit.

'But not outvoted. Unfathomably, Essie and I are not entitled to vote.'

'Quite right, Mary. Now give us the skinny on what happened today,' said Agatha, her eyes glistening like a hunter in sight of the prey.

Just as this exchange took place, Simpkins rose from Kit's seat, stretched, and looked around the room. His eyes rested on Esther. He made his way over to her and settled on her knee.

'This is Simpkins,' said Kit by way of explanation.

'The Countess Laskov's cat?' exclaimed Agatha. 'What on earth is he doing here?'

'He wanted a place to stay,' replied Kit.

The Medium Murders

Esther smiled and began to stroke the cat on the head. Moments later, Sam jumped down from Miller's arms and darted around the sofas barking excitedly. Simpkins ignored him. A quick scan revealed that one lap was free. He looked up expectantly at Mary. Seconds later a pair of slender hand reached down and lifted him up before setting him down on an equally slender pair of thighs.

'I'm just the landlord apparently,' said Kit sardonically. He then broached the subject of Countess Laskov's passing first.

'Perhaps it's for the best,' said Agatha when Kit had finished. 'I gather she missed David horribly. But why were the police interested?'

'Alas, Chief Inspector Jellicoe was not very forthcoming. I sensed there was more to it than a heart attack. I think that we'll have to wait and see. Did you know, though, that she'd lost both her staff recently? They walked out on her.'

Agatha admitted that she was unaware.

'I suppose it's been a while since I've visited her.'

'Do you want to go to the service tomorrow?' asked Kit.

'I think, yes.' Agatha looked at Mary and Esther. It was clear that Esther had absolutely no interest in attending but Mary indicated she would join them.

'Well, it's very sad but life goes on. We'll all meet our maker someday. Now, Christopher, why were you with our esteemed Secretary of State for War and Air?' asked Agatha in a tone of voice that managed to combine disapproval for the office holder as well as a rebuke for her nephew for having a channel of access that would, unquestionably, have been denied to her.

Kit knew that this was an important moment. What he was about to reveal could probably have been classed as a state secret. However, he had no qualms about the integrity of his guests. The heat of curiosity was burning hot within his audience. Not to provide a detailed report on his meeting with Churchill might have resulted in serious injury and possible hospitalisation. Best to start with the headline, thought Kit.

'He might be about to be blackmailed. Photographs have surfaced of him standing with a bunch of modern-day druids and a young woman who was subsequently murdered.'

This was greeted with stunned silence. After a few moments Kit realised the stunned silence had become its own question and, by the look on the face of Agatha in particular, an answer was needed sooner rather than later.

It wasn't my idea, of course. I can't remember who first suggested it. Perhaps Sonny Masterson but I can't be sure. It had started a while back. I had some friends who were members of the Albion Lodge of the Ancient Order of Druids. They led me to believe the activities of the Lodge were less spiritual and more of a fraternal character. Certainly, it seemed harmless.

I knew several of the members, as I say, but there were many who were either not familiar to me or robed. I did not know the robed men, and truth be told, was rather bored by the initiation ceremony. Sonny and I decided quickly that it would be warmer back at the house.

The ceremony itself was neither here nor there. A lot of mumbo jumbo, a drink of some liquid that almost certainly contained alcohol and lo and behold, I was a member of the Lodge. As to the young woman, I have no recollection. In fact, I'd thought it was a boys' club. I remember we'd all imbibed a glass or two of jollity. I don't remember being so far gone that I wouldn't recall a young woman in our midst. Of course, I didn't think anything of it, and we left almost as soon as the initiation had finished.

Back at the palace, the bunch of us who had been initiated had a jolly good laugh about the whole thing. It would be fair to say that I was comfortably squiffy by the end of the night. We all were. I went to bed and the next thing I remember was Sonny shaking me awake, telling me that my then lady friend, Clemmie, was about to go home. This was a catastrophe as I had fully intended proposing to her that day.

Thankfully I was able to rescue the situation, although I felt uncommonly off colour. Clemmie and I married a month later. I made no mention of the Lodge and, to be honest, had little to do with them over the years. I must say, aside from when I am with a few of my pals, it had barely entered my thoughts since.

'When did he receive the photographs?'

'Last week. I know I thought this a trifle odd,' said Kit, seeing Mary's reaction.

'Where did all this take place?' asked Agatha.

'At Blenheim Palace. In the Temple of Diana.'

Agatha leaned forward. Her eyes fixed on Kit like a teacher interrogating a naughty schoolchild.

'Surely, he must have known most of the people at the ceremony. After all, why would they be invited to the family seat.'

'I gather there's a certain Masonic character to the thing,' replied Kit. 'They're not Masons as such, but I suspect Churchill and a few of his friends certainly are. I think secrecy regarding some of the druid priests would have been accepted. Churchill claims he barely knew more than half a dozen of the members and I've no reason to disbelieve him.'

'We'll need a list if we're to investigate them,' said Agatha.

'We?' replied Kit.

This comment went down like swear word at a baptism. Kit realised he'd, perhaps, made a tactical mistake. The look on Mary's face, never mind Agatha's, suggested a retreat was required, and rather quickly, too.

'Naturally, I will happily call upon your collective wisdom.' Kit felt his heart sinking like a French ship after meeting Nelson, 'However, the nature of this inquiry precludes anyone other than me being seen to investigate.'

As much as Mary was disappointed that she could not work alongside Kit, she recognised that to make an issue of this would be unfair.

'Humbug,' said Agatha.

Mary turned to Agatha and smiled in support. She looked back at Kit, raised her eyebrows and grinned.

'Perhaps you can tell us the names of the people Mr Churchill gave you.'

Kit sighed, which surprised Mary. It was clear he was reluctant, but he felt he owed them some sort of olive branch.

'Well come on,' prompted Agatha, impatiently. She motioned to Miller to refill her glass.

Kit reached into his pocket and extracted a piece of notepaper. He handed it to Agatha who was nearest. Agatha, in turn, reached for her pince-nez and read the names on the paper. When she read the final one, she looked at Kit in astonishment.

'Good Lord.'

Kit smiled and replied with more than a hint of scorn, 'Not so good, but certainly a lord.'

Mary and Esther, meanwhile, glanced at one another.

'Is anyone going to share the big secret?' asked Mary.

Kit took the paper from Agatha and handed it to Mary who immediately leaned over towards Esther so that they both could read it.

'Interesting,' said Mary and then she followed this with an exclamation before looking at Kit.

'Your father?'

'Apparently.'

'Does this mean I finally meet Viscount Aston?'

Mary made no effort to hide the edge in her voice. Kit looked at her sharply and then, remembering they were not alone, nodded. His face was neutral but the tension in his body was evident.

'It seems that way.'

Both Kit and Mary turned to Agatha. For once, her face was unreadable. They could not see the slight slump in her shoulders, the sudden shortness in her breath and the sadness that crept over her like a virus. She sensed that no good could come from this but now she was powerless to stop a chain of events that had been set in motion.

Perhaps it was time.

7

Bevis Mark's synagogue, the oldest in Britain, hosted the funeral service for Countess Laskov. Kit, Mary, and Agatha sat opposite the enormous Renaissance-style ark containing the Torah scrolls. They were on benches which ran parallel to the side walls, facing into the centre.

'Beautiful carving,' whispered Mary.

'Wood apparently,' said Kit, speaking of the marble-coloured shrine.

Mary looked around the synagogue in fascination. It was the first time she had visited such a place of worship. Overhead were seven brass candelabras symbolising the days of the week. The service began as Mary made a mental note to visit again.

Throughout the service, Kit's mind drifted. He had been to more funerals than any young man had a right to attend. The thought of some of the people he had lost caused a wave of grief to pass through him. Around him he could hear the stifled anguish of others. He wasn't grieving for the countess, although they had been on friendly terms. He wondered how much of the grief we feel at the funerals of those we are not especially close to is for one's own losses rather than for the person being laid to rest.

The service ended and they followed the procession out of the synagogue. Kit was surprised at how many seemed to know Agatha. They were of a similar vintage, he supposed.

One elderly man, tall and elegantly clad, with a woman who was of a similar age interested Kit, but they looked away when he spotted them. Something about the woman seemed familiar to him but he could not quite place her. After a few minutes Agatha put her hand to her mouth and whispered conspiratorially, 'Have you seen who's over there?'

A sea of black coats and black hats hiding grey hair confronted them. Kit was, clearly, none the wiser. Agatha nodded her head towards an elderly man accompanied by a woman perhaps twenty years his junior. They were standing ten feet away chatting to some younger mourners.

'You know Conan Doyle?'

Kit looked at his aunt affectionately albeit in a manner that younger people have done for eons to convey the fact that they are not complete fatheads.

Doyle glanced over in their direction and smiled. Moments later he was walking in their direction.

'Good Lord,' said Kit glancing at Mary and Agatha. 'Do you think he recognises me?'

The Medium Murders

Doyle joined them and said, 'Agatha, how good to see you again. Involved in any more cases?'

Agatha's eyes widened and there was an imperceptible shake of the head picked up by both Kit and Mary who looked at one another, eyebrows raised. For another time, thought Kit.

'Arthur,' said Agatha accepting his embrace. 'Lady Doyle,' she added, embracing the wife of the famous author.

'This, Arthur, is my nephew, Christopher. And his fiancée, Miss Mary Cavendish.'

Kit looked at the world-famous author. He was slightly shorter than Kit but broader. There was an undeniable charisma about the man. He radiated intelligence and geniality. His face was dominated by an impressive grey moustache that spread across his cheeks but could not hide the warmth of his smile.

'I can think of no more handsome couple and admirable, too,' said Doyle, shaking Kit's hand and bowing to Mary. 'I read of both of your efforts during the War.'

At the mention of the War, a shadow passed over the features of Doyle. The smile on Kit's faded and the two men looked at one another for a moment.

'I never met your son, Sir Arthur. I know many who did, and they spoke very highly of him.'

Doyle nodded but at that moment seemed too emotional to say anything further about his late son.

Instead, the group turned and followed the procession out onto the street.

'How did you know the countess?' asked Doyle.

'She was my neighbour, so to speak,' replied Kit. 'I have rooms above hers.'

Doyle stopped and looked at Kit.

'Really? I was in her apartment a few times. I wish I'd known.'

Kit laughed and said the same adding, 'I grew up reading your stories, Sir Arthur.'

'And I,' said Mary, brightly. Happy memories of her youth, which was not so long ago, passed through her mind. Reading Sherlock Holmes in bed after lights out. It was one of her first acts of rebellion. The look on Governess Curtis's face as Mary claimed to have read one book after another. Looking back on it now, Mary knew she knew.

Doyle waved the subject of his great detective away. He reddened slightly. He never got used to this celebrity.

'And you, Sir Arthur?'

'We had a mutual interest in psychic phenomena. Spiritualism, if you like.'

Doyle looked at Kit to see his reaction to this. Kit was only a little surprised. Although, it was well known that Doyle was a leading advocate of Spiritualism, he hadn't connected the countess to such an interest. The black candles in her lounge made more sense. Most obviously, she was a widow.

The Medium Murders

'Did you hold séances in her apartment?' asked an astonished Aunt Agatha.

'On one occasion we did. It was unsuccessful in reaching her husband,' replied Doyle.

That might be because it's a sham, thought Kit. Out of respect for Doyle and the late Countess, he remained silent. He hoped ardently that Doyle would not use the moment to evangelize the movement. In fact, he wanted off this subject. But…

'Have you ever participated in a séance?' asked Doyle.

'I met a number of people in France who were convinced about this new revelation, but I never joined them in any of their meetings,' replied Kit.

The procession had stopped as the coffin was put into a hearse. The family of Countess Laskov had requested a private burial, so Kit and his party along with Doyle parted at this point.

'You were circumspect, I noticed,' said Mary as they walked away. 'Do I detect scepticism lurking underneath that beautiful exterior of yours?'

Kit smiled at his fiancée and raised his eyebrows.

'You do. I wouldn't go as far as to say it's all nonsense, but most of these mediums are fakes. Worse than that, they prey on the grief of many people who are still suffering after the War and the flu pandemic. Sadly, Sir Arthur has given succour to this movement by his advocacy. I find it extraordinary that the man who created the embodiment of rationalism in Sherlock Holmes could have any interest in this area. Almost as fantastic as saying I'm beautiful. Thank you by the way.'

'You're welcome, milord,' replied Mary and grinned. Kit's heart skipped. Just over four months until they were married. Mary could read Kit's mind and she made a sad face. As ever, they were interrupted by Agatha who was blissfully unaware of the exchange that had taken place.

'We must make plans for going to Cleves.'

Kit stifled another groan at the thought of visiting his family seat. He wasn't sure if it was because he wanted to avoid his family home, his family or if he regretted that he had shared the details of the meeting. He realised the latter was as unavoidable as the idea that they would want to assist. However, the nature of the problem made it difficult to see what help they could provide. Then there was the nature of the possible murder.

It was clear there had been a ritualistic element to her death. What other explanation could there be? If the murderers were just wanting to hide their identity why choose robes? Misdirection seemed fanciful given they had taken part in a druid ceremony with a public figure on the grounds of one of the most famous palaces in the country. If blackmail was the end game, why now? The photographs were twelve years old. Rational thought was in short supply from whatever angle he considered the problem.

The Medium Murders

The next thing Kit had to say, he knew, would go down like support for prohibition at a cocktail bar.

Mary spied the faraway look on Kit's face. Increasingly attuned to his mood, she recognised his disquiet. She thought for a few moments and wondered if it had been prompted by Agatha's comment. If it had been, this would be disappointing.

'Come on,' said Mary. 'What are you thinking about?'

Kit looked at Mary but this time there was no smile.

'I have to see Spunky.'

Mary did not need to be a clairvoyant to know this would exclude both her and Agatha. Oddly, she did not mind. She had plans for the afternoon anyway which did not include him for a change.

She was going back to Claridge's to keep the appointment with Bobby Andrews.

8

Miller dropped Mary and Agatha off at the Grosvenor Square residence first before setting off, on Kit's instructions, towards 1, Melbury Road in West Kensington. The journey through London went quickly but Miller noted how more and more cars were appearing on the roads. The Rolls pulled up ten minutes later outside a tall red brick villa which overlooked Holland Park.

'I shan't be long, Harry,' said Kit getting out of the car.

Kit made his way past the security at the front door and up the stairs to the second floor where Spunky's office was located. Dawn, Smith-Cumming's secretary, met him on the landing, and she led him up to his friend.

Aldric 'Spunky' Stevens greeted Kit warmly.

'Kit, so good to have you back. Tell me more about your case in America. You can't keep a bloodhound down, what?'

Despite his fatheaded blether, Spunky possessed one of the sharpest minds in the Secret Intelligence Service, MI6. Spunky had been a part of the service since the middle of the War when he had been badly injured and unable to continue front line duty.

Kit gave a summary of the case he had stumbled into in San Francisco before moving on to the reason for his appointment. Before he began to speak, Spunky held his hand up.

'I think I know why you're here, old boy. As ever, I'm on the case.'

Moments later, Spunky extracted several thin folders from his drawer.

'I think you'll find the answer to your questions in there.'

Kit looked at the top two files. They were two of the names on the list given to him by Churchill. He leafed through them briefly and then glanced at the bottom file. On the cover was a name: Viscount Lancelot Aston.

'You keep a file on my father?' said Kit wryly. 'I would hardly have him down as a subversive or an anarchist unless you think being a dissolute adulterer sufficient qualification.'

The depth of Kit's contempt took Spunky by surprise. He knew that Kit and his father were far from close, but this was perilously close to outright animosity.

'Steady on, old boy. I'm sure he's no saint but then again, which amongst us are? These files are not ours. They belong to Kell's boys in MI5(g).'

Kit looked grimly at Spunky but said nothing in reply. The amount of information on his father was limited to known facts, mostly culled from Who's Who. On his relationship with Churchill, there was nothing.

'Has anyone else spoken to these men?' asked Kit.

'No. We were waiting for your return. We felt that it should be kept within…' Spunky paused as he searched for the right word.

'Our class,' replied Kit, eyebrows raised.

'That would be the size of it, Bloodhound. "C" rates your abilities as highly as I do. They thought it best to have your two brains on the case.'

'I'm not that smart.'

'Yes, you are but, as it happened, I was referring to Mary.'

Kit laughed at this. There was no use denying that he would have told her everything.

'She's desperate to be involved.'

'I suspect Agatha, too. Of course, that'll mean Aunt Betty.'

'I haven't done a great job keeping it secret, have I?'

Spunky shook his head and smoked languorously from his thin cigar.

'As you say, it's kept within our class.'

'Is there anything else I should know?' Kit looked at the disappointingly slender nature of the files on the table. It was clear he would have to go around to each of the men and speak to them about their recollection of what had happened that night. Hopefully some or all of them would be able to add new names to the list. It wasn't much to go on. A moment later, Spunky as good as confirmed this.

'That's all we have, I'm told. It's up to you now,' he said in his usual cheery manner that brooked no thought of his friend failing.

'Where to, sir?' asked Miller as Kit climbed back into the car following his meeting.

'The river, then keep driving.'

Miller glanced at Kit. His lordship seemed a bit down in the dumps. It wasn't too difficult to guess the principal reason; however, it was possible there were other things preying on his mind.

'The revolver might be quicker, sir. That way I won't get wet.'

'Good point, Harry. I'm being selfish.'

There was silence in the car for the next minute or two. The rain had returned in the guise of an annoyingly persistent drizzle. Kit toyed with the idea of looking inside the folders before throwing them down on the seat beside him.

'I think we'll have to make arrangements to go up to Cleves. There's no way of avoiding it.'

'Very good, sir. I'll look at the train timetables. This weekend?'

'No, maybe the weekend after unless we can crack the case before then. I'll start with the other names in these files first.'

'I should include the ladies?'

Kit let out a loud laugh at this and even Miller joined in. This helped lift the mood in the car. Perhaps it wouldn't be so bad. Perhaps his father would be on his best behaviour. Perhaps Marge would be less resentful. Then there was Edmund.

Brother Edmund. Was there a chance he'd grown up a little? Matured? Kit felt a stab of guilt as he thought of his half-brother. He'd sent some letters earlier in the year. They went unanswered so he'd given up. He knew it wasn't enough. What kind of a brother was he?

What kind of a son?

The longer you leave contact with the people you were once closest to, the more difficult it is to resume. It's like a wound that's left un-dressed, or a heart starved of love. Corruption sets in and the tissue dies. It wasn't just the cancer that had killed his mother.

So obvious, wasn't it? Yet here he sat, conscience-clouded, doubt invading his mind. There was another story out there, probably. It was in the eyes of his father, of Marge and of Aunt Agatha. It was told through the silences and the looks they gave one another. And who was he to condemn? If not a disloyal son, then, at the very least, he was an unloving and inadequate excuse for one. He'd never forgiven his father for betraying his mother. Nor, for that matter, had he forgiven Marge, ever the stage actress, for her role in this tragedy. She had played her part as the lover while his mother lay dying.

The result of this betrayal, Edmund, could hardly be blamed for his existence. Yet Kit knew he had tried to forgive his father and Marge. He'd tried to be a big brother. For a long time, he was Edmund's hero. Somehow, somewhere or someone had poisoned their relationship. It wasn't hard to guess who.

He thought of Marge.

As they drove along the street, Kit spied a newspaper boy selling an early afternoon edition of the newspaper. The headline on the pavement billboard read, "New Medium Murder".

'Harry, can you pull over a moment and buy me the newspaper. Look at the headline?'

'Good lord,' replied Miller, which implied he hadn't. Miller hopped out of the car and rewarded the young boy handsomely for his sales efforts.

A couple of minutes later they were on their way again. It was a short hop to Belgrave Square. Kit read out the key points in the article.

'Police are baffled - I hope it isn't poor Jellicoe - This is the second murder. Interesting that there is such a gap between the two.'

'The first was just before you left for America, wasn't it? Things went quiet on the case. Not sure what happened to the medium. She seemed to disappear.'

'The first was in Yorkshire. A middle-aged man. This one's a young woman. They haven't released any details.'

'Was it the same medium?' asked Miller.

'Yes,' said Kit, leafing through the paper.

'Eva Kerr?'

'Yes, that was the name.'

Kit continued to read through the articles, for there were more than one. As usual, the police were coming in for some criticism. Kit guessed this was for their refusal to feed the insatiable appetite of the press. As he reached the end of the article, he did something he'd never done before given the gruesome context of their discussion. He laughed.

'Something up, sir?' asked Miller, clearly as surprised as he was curious.

'You'll never guess who Scotland Yard have sent to investigate.'

They arrived at their destination a few minutes later. Kit stepped out of the car and walked up the steps towards his apartment building. He didn't see the big car parked across the road. Inside were two men. They watched Kit open his front door and enter.

'That's him?'

'That's him.'

'What about his man?'

They watched Miller disappear into the distance in the Rolls. The man in the passenger seat looked at the other man.

'I wouldn't worry about him. Come on.'

The two men stepped out of the car and moved towards the front of the apartment block.

-

Kit stopped outside Countess Laskov's apartment. He tried the door. It was locked. This was a disappointment, but he guessed Jellicoe would soon have bigger fish to fry if the news regarding the latest murder proved to be as significant as Kit thought it was.

He made his way up the stairs gingerly and into his apartment. Sam came running to greet him. He picked the little terrier up for a cuddle. Simpkins looked up from Kit's chair but did not seem inclined to give up his place or, indeed, offer much by way of greeting.

'Hello, Simpkins,' said Kit. 'I hope you're comfortable. Can I get you anything? A fish supper perhaps? Some wine?'

Simpkins appeared to understand he was being jested with and did not dignify the sarcasm with a reply. Kit sat down near him and began to stroke the cat behind the ear. This was better. Simpkins began to purr.

Meanwhile, Sam settled on Kit's lap, effectively pinning Kit to the seat.

It was while thus occupied that Kit heard a knock at the door. He waited a moment before realising that Miller had gone to park the car. After gently placing an unhappy Sam on the place beside him, he rose and went to the door. The knocking was persistent but not aggressive.

Kit opened the door and saw two men in overcoats standing before him. Neither looked like former public schoolboys or members of the clergy. One of the men had a nose that had been broken one too many times.

They seemed familiar, however. And not unfriendly.

'Your lordship, sorry to inconvenience you like this, but we'd like you to come with us.'

Kit glanced down at the man's pocket. He had his hand in there and seemed to be pointing a gun.

Kit looked back at the man and then recognition dawned.

'Good lord, isn't it…?'

Harry Miller was strolling back from the car park, just around the corner from the apartment. Not for the first time did he marvel at the good fortune that had brought him here. An early life spent as a burglar, a life nearly ended more than once in the fields of France and now, living with nobility in the centre of London. He was the luckiest chap alive. Just as he thought this, he felt the first spot of rain. He didn't care though.

Fifty yards from the front door he saw several men emerge from the apartment block. His senses heightened as the scene looked strange. Seconds later he recognised Kit climbing into the back of a car. He was just about to shout when he realised the men might be armed. Instead, he broke into a sprint. Just as he did so, he saw a taxi coming towards him. He hailed it.

Kit's car pulled out just ahead of the taxi. Miller saw Kit looking out the window at him. He did not seem particularly imperilled but, then again, he remembered his master was a cool customer in these situations.

The taxi stopped and Miller climbed into the back, slightly breathless. He was just about to speak when the taxi driver held his hand up.

'Let me guess. Follow that car?'

9

'We're just going out for lunch Aunt Agatha,' said Mary, taking Esther's arm and leading her into the entrance hall of the Grosvenor Square House.

'We are?' asked Esther, somewhat taken aback by this news.

'Yes, don't you remember, Essie?' said Mary, widening her eyes just enough to let Esther know how she should react.

'Oh yes, I'd quite forgotten.'

Agatha was not paying much attention to matters as it happened. In fact, she'd plans of her own which may or may not have involved the sisters. She waved distractedly to them as they disappeared to the coat rack. They were out of the house before Agatha realised that they'd left. She stood for a moment looking at the door nonplussed. Then she shrugged and went to the telephone.

'Betty Simpson, Fitzrovia 6263, thank you. I'll wait.'

A few moments later a voice came on the line.

'Betty, it's me. We have a new case. Good, I'll see you in a few minutes.'

The Medium Murders

She put the phone down and went into the drawing room to ring for Fish. Natalie appeared a few moments later.

'Yes, madame?'

'Ah, Natalie, any chance you could send up a pot of tea. Lady Simpson is visiting.'

'Very good, madame.'

'Why all the secrecy?'

'I'm going to meet Bobby Andrews,' announced Mary as they hurried along the street. Esther stopped. This forced Mary, who was holding her arm, to stop.

'Have you gone out of your mind, Mary?' She was genuinely shocked. Mary was, and had always been, a rebel, but this seemed to be pushing things to the limit.

'Nonsense,' replied Mary, 'Anyway, it's not just Bobby I want to see. I need you along as my cover.'

'Cover?' responded Esther, mystified.

'Of course, Essie. It wouldn't do for me to meet Bobby on my own.'

'I'm not sure it would do for you to be meeting him full stop, Mary.'

Mary burst into a fit of giggles and gave her sister a hug.

'Come on, we'll be late, I'll explain on the way.'

The sisters arrived at Claridge's around ten minutes later. Nothing seemed to have changed from the previous day. The noise was at a level bordering on intolerable. Hassled hotel staff glanced at the clock before realising they had another several hours to spend in the company of the idle rich spending their unearned income in their relentless rush to become spectacularly sozzled.

'Isn't it wonderful,' said Mary, narrowly avoiding a young man who had fallen at her feet.

Esther's face suggested that she didn't think it quite as wonderful as Mary. But she knew her sister well and she smiled.

'You should be an anthropologist.'

Mary grinned and looked at one amiably stupid young man standing on a table. He was demonstrating the correct way to rumba. The lack of music or, indeed, any sense of tempo, in no way inhibited his display. Each thrust of his hips was greeted with mild hysteria. From the men. The more polite members of the species responded with embarrassed giggling. It was a moot point about which the young man was more deficient in, intelligence or rhythm.

'I could write a paper on the topic of chronically stupid people. I'm sure it would be published in one scientific journal or another.'

Esther looked around and then spotted someone heading in their direction.

The Medium Murders

'Brace yourself, Mary.'

Bobby Andrews arrived carrying a dangerously seductive smile and a hint of triumph glinting in his eyes. Mary noted the look and glanced at Esther. Her sister successfully managed to remain impassive.

'Glad you decided to come back. Are you meeting anyone?' asked Andrews.

Mary looked him dead in the eye and said, 'You.' Out of the corner of her eye she saw Esther turn away.

'Perhaps we should go somewhere less crowded.'

'Excellent idea.'

They left the bar and walked into the foyer of the hotel and found some free seats near the door. The benefits of being away from the noise and moderate depravity were challenged slightly by the draught coming from the door. They ordered a pot of tea. This provided the dual benefit of giving them a reason to be there as well as warming their hands.

Andrews glanced uncertainly at Esther and asked how the wedding plans were progressing. Esther dwelt at length on these. She enjoyed every second of the young man's evident boredom. As Esther layered gratuitous detail upon superfluous tangents, Mary's smile grew wider. Finally, Esther put the young man out of his misery with an abrupt end to her novel-length summary.

'Well, I certainly wish you and Dr Bright well.'

Interestingly he neglected to ask Mary about her wedding plans even though he would obviously have been aware of them. The presence of Esther was having its intended effect. Reduced to making polite conversation, his charm diminished at a rate matched by the increase in his ennui. It wasn't helped by the fact that Mary seemed more interested in a procession of women entering the hotel and making their way past them.

Andrews finally noticed the source of Mary's interest and turned around to look at the procession.

'What's going on?'

'There's a speech taking place in the conference room,' replied Mary.

'Really? Anyone of interest?'

'Millicent Fawcett.'

It took a few moments for the name to register with Andrews; then he remembered that she was something to do with the Suffragettes. This presented a quandary. Whilst he had no gripe against the Suffrage movement, he could hardly be considered a supporter never mind an expert on their aims.

'Good lord, I didn't have you down for a Suffragette, Mary.'

'Suffragist, Bobby. Do you want to come?'

It would be fair to say, nothing on the face of Bobby Andrews, by this stage, suggested that he had the least bit of interest in listening to an old woman talk at length about why women should be allowed to vote. He saw Mary smile. Then she leaned forward, looking at him directly in the eye, with her hand on his knee.

The Medium Murders

'Maybe you can take me dancing afterwards.'

Esther nearly choked on her tea when she heard her sister make more than an indecently respectable stab at being a seductress. Mary was playing a dangerous game, here. Pretty well, to be fair.

They rose from the table and began to follow the crowd of women towards the back of the hotel. As they did so, a familiar voice called out to them.

'I say, Bobby. Hello Esther. Mary.'

It was Xander Lewis. Bobby Andrews turned and smiled grimly at his school chum. Meanwhile the girls received friendly pecks on the cheek from the ever ebullient, which is to say, squiffy young lord.

'Where are you all off to?'

'As it happens, old chap, I'm accompanying the ladies into the conference room to listen to Millicent Fawcett speak.'

Lewis was quiet for a moment then grinned.

'Name's familiar. Can't quite place her.'

'Suffragette,' replied Bobby Andrews.

'Gist,' corrected Mary. 'Suffragist.'

Lewis glanced archly at his friend and said, 'Well, if you three ladies don't mind being accompanied by a gentleman, I'd love to hear what Miss Foster has to say.'

Andrews looked down at Mary. Thankfully she was grinning. He rolled his eyes to indicate that he was not a buffoon like his friend. Mary's eyes narrowed slightly in a manner that almost had the young man forgetting his newly adopted beliefs and regressing to a more primitive resolution to his ardour.

The group found seats near the front. A low stage had been erected with two tables and four chairs arranged on it. There was a podium to the right of the tables. Behind the platform was a banner. It read 'Votes for Women'.

Mary looked at it and felt a surge of anger. The battle for the right to vote had still not been won. Only women over the age of 30 who were married had the right to vote. How could any just society permit this? How was it fair that half the population, until only a few years ago, had been denied a say in the running of the country. She shook her head at such inequity. She looked up at Bobby Andrews. He turned to her and smiled hopefully. His mind was on other things: principally, how best to turn this unexpected opportunity into a memorable evening.

It took a few minutes for the room to fill up and settle down. Mary glanced around with evident curiosity. The audience comprised around fifty women and a handful of men of all ages. The chatter silenced almost immediately as a few women walked onto the stage from a doorway just behind.

Mary gasped as one of them walked onto the stage. Esther turned to Mary and frowned a question. But Mary could not reply. Her eyes were on a woman who was staring none too happily, it must be reported, at her.

The Medium Murders

'Who is it?'

'Do you remember when you were in Brighton with Richard?' whispered Mary.

'Yes, you were on that Phantom case.'

'Yes. The woman I was acting as a maid for is on the stage, second from the right. We didn't exactly part on good terms.'

Esther grimaced then smiled.

Mrs Isabelle Rosling's eyes flicked back down at Mary and her group just as a youngish woman was introducing, at length, the keynote speaker. Finally, Millicent Fawcett stood up and walked to the lectern. The sound of loud applause filled the hall.

There was a genuine warmth as well as awe at being in the presence of this great champion of women's rights. She'd recently announced her retirement from the frontline of the battle, but she had not given up the fight. Beside the girls, Bobby Andrew and Xander Lewis clapped and cheered. A little too loudly, thought Mary.

Millicent Fawcett stood behind the lectern with her head barely visible over the top. A life spent campaigning for voting rights for women was etched in the thin lines of her intelligent face. It took a few moments for the noise of the clapping to subside. Then she stepped forward and began to speak, without notes, to her audience.

And they were her audience. Listening, rapt to their hero. Everyone, bar the two male companions of the

Cavendish sisters, was here for one reason only: the chance to see this legendary figure and, ultimately, to contribute to the ongoing struggle for universal suffrage. It was a privilege to be in her company. And the women and men in the audience were nothing if not privileged.

'We are on the eve of fulfilment of our hope. The goal towards which many of us have been striving for nearly half a century is in sight. I appeal to each and all of my fellow suffragists not to be overconfident, but to act as though the success of our cause depended on herself alone.'

Mary sat through the speech, transfixed. Even Esther, for whom the cause had been a more abstract idea found herself carried along by the words of a woman whose life had been dedicated to giving women a voice. Bobby Andrews, meanwhile, used the time to ponder the next steps in the conquest of Mary Cavendish.

When the speech ended around twenty minutes later, the audience rose as one to give the speaker their acclaim. None were more enthusiastic in their reaction, or less likely to have listened to a single word, than the two men sitting either side of the sisters. The two men had to endure several other speeches after Millicent Fawcett. The other speakers were, thankfully, greater in passion than duration. The meeting came to an end after an hour.

'Are you going to stay to try and meet Mrs Fawcett?' asked Bobby Andrews, keen to give the impression he was now a passionate advocate of women's suffrage. Mary smiled up at her suitor and noted, once again, that his dark eyes had a genuine flash in them. However, as dark and dashing as his eyes may have been, the intention sitting behind them was utterly transparent. Mary couldn't decide if this was intended or not.

'Nonsense. Let's go somewhere we can dance,' slurred Xander Lewis.

The sight of Mrs Rosling, apparently making her way over in their direction, made the idea of leaving for a nightclub more appealing than it might otherwise have been.

'Yes, let's,' replied Mary, taking Bobby Andrews by the arm and all at once giving rise to more than just hopes in the young man.

'Where to Bobby?' asked Lewis.

'Dalton's?' suggested Andrews.

'That's the ticket,' said Lewis.

Mary glanced at Esther and grinned. It was clear that her sister was caught between a desire to put an end to this adventure and a genuine curiosity to see the infamous nightclub in Leicester Square where bright young things mixed with the worlds of entertainment and crime. It was a lethal cocktail. Depraved, too, if the rumours were true.

'Wonderful,' said Esther, eyes widening in Mary's direction. She followed Mary's cue and took the arm of Xander Lewis, and they made for the exit thereby denying Mrs Rosling a chance to catch up with her former maid. Mary risked a glance back in the direction of the stage. She saw Mrs Rosling looking at them in a way that was less angry than genuinely curious. On the way out, all four made a sizeable donation to the cause which had occupied their attention for the previous hour.

Outside, it was beginning to darken. The nights were drawing in now. There was a chill in the air.

'So, tell me, how is the Earl of Gresham?' asked Mary.

'Father?' replied the Honourable Robert Andrews, 'Oh, he's a horse. Just some old people's problems.'

'Did I see a picture of him recently with our esteemed Secretary of War?' continued Mary.

'Shouldn't be surprised. They were at school together. Thick as thieves, they are.'

'Really?' said Mary, pressing her face against the arm of the gallant escorting her, 'tell me more. I find Mr Churchill a most interesting man.'

10

The shopkeeper looked at the woman in front of her. Without question, she was one of the tallest women he'd ever seen. One of the most formidable, too. Dark hair peeked out from underneath her hat. Her face was broad with high cheekbones and a strong jaw. It was difficult to reconcile this woman with the rather fine dress she was wearing. The smile was friendly if a tad demonic. It seemed at odds with the hard grey eyes and, if young Ernest Dalrymple didn't know better, the fact that she seemed to be chewing gum.

Accompanying her was another woman who was Lilliputian by comparison. The two ladies discussed the pearl necklace in front of them. It was clear they were politely disagreeing with one another about its merits. This was frustrating for young Ernest Dalrymple. He was desperate to make his first sale. Sadly, Mr Potter would not be around to see it. He'd just gone out to lunch when the ladies arrived. Ernest Dalrymple was left with strict instructions not to show any gems to customers. You couldn't be too careful, he said. But Ernest's enthusiasm was greater than his intelligence.

The discussion between the two ladies went on interminably. It covered tangential subjects such as dresses, hair colour and, in one particularly surreal moment, poodles. Ernest shrugged off such digressions as an immutable characteristic of the fairer sex. Thankfully, no other customers had arrived in the meantime. At one point, aware that Ernest was something of a bystander in the debate, the ladies invited his opinion on the necklace's suitability for the larger woman.

Ernest's earnest praise of the necklace and its ability to compliment the complexion of the lady in question failed to carry the day. This was evident when the smaller woman suggested they try a brooch instead and, oh, those two pendants over there.

Ernest was now convinced he was onto a big sale. These two well-spoken women were going to buy something. It was just a question of what. However, the difference of opinion was now becoming rather heated. Initially, young Ernest tried to smother a smile as the smaller lady made a rather insulting remark about the other lady's sweetheart. This subject struck Ernest as altogether unpromising territory for selling jewellery. By now, the argument had reached the topic of the height differential between the young woman and her intended. Ernest tried to bring the ladies back to the sale.

Alas, it was too late. The larger of the two women was now in tears. She stormed out of the shop. The smaller

The Medium Murders

of the two women looked at Ernest, shrugged her shoulders and apologised.

'We'll be back in a few moments,' she promised, and quickly followed her former friend outside. On her way down the steps, she removed a 'Closed for lunch sign', folded it up and threw it away. Waiting outside was another woman.

'Quickly,' said the woman. 'I can see Potter coming.'

The other woman raced into the shop. Inside, Ernest was all a flutter. He could have sworn he'd taken out a brooch for the women to look at. For the life of him, and it was a life-or-death situation on his first day, he could not see it. Just as he began to panic, the door opened. A lady of indeterminate age walks in. She smiled and asked to see the proprietor.

Ernest was now caught between looking for the missing brooch and dealing with the lady. In a moment, and with an understanding of the art of retailing that would stand him in good stead for decades to come, he decided the customer should come first.

'He's just popped out for lunch. Can I be of service?'

The lady spied various pendants and the pearl necklace that Ernest had been in the process of putting away.

Pointing to these items, the lady asked, 'Can I look, please?'

'Of course.'

Thankfully, as far as Ernest was concerned, she lifted the items. Instead, she used her right hand to move them about the counter. Unseen by Ernest was that her left hand. It was searching for the brooch left by her confederate under the counter using the gum she'd been chewing. The brooch was found in a matter of seconds. She made a face that did not bode well for the prospect of a sale.

'No, not quite what I was looking for.'

Ernest looked glum but was rather relieved when she said goodbye. He was now desperate to find the brooch before Mr Potter returned. Sadly, for Ernest, the pearl brooch was making its way out of the shop hidden in the woman's mitten.

Mr Potter, after a hurriedly eaten lunch at a nearby café, passed the woman on the steps. He'd been away less than fifteen minutes. What possible harm could have come in such a short period of time?

The woman, meanwhile, darted around the corner and jumped into a large eight-cylinder car which sped off just as the passenger door closed. The woman removed her hands from the mitten held up the brooch. All three ladies smiled and sat back to enjoy the ride.

The journey through London towards the Elephant and Castle passed quickly. A hint of celebration lay in the air courtesy of the shared sense of pride in a productive afternoon's work.

The Medium Murders

As they approached their destination, a pub named the Duke of Wellington, the three ladies saw a taxi stop rather suddenly at the entrance. A man did not so much exit the vehicle as explode from it onto the street. He sprinted through the entrance of the pub.

The larger of the three ladies looked at her two fellow 'hoisters'.

'This looks interesting.'

'What's going on?' asked the taxi driver to Miller.

'No idea, mate,' replied Miller, honestly. 'I saw my boss bundled into the car up ahead. Didn't like the look of that. Any idea where we're heading?'

'South of the river is my guess.'

They drove along in silence for the next few minutes before crossing over the river at Waterloo Bridge. The car containing Kit drew to a halt on Waterloo Street outside a pub. He handed the cabbie some change and leapt out of the car, running towards the entrance Kit and the three men had used.

Once through the doors of the pub, Miller entered the saloon section. It wasn't very crowded and there was no sign of Kit. He turned and made his way up the stairs. There was a smaller bar located on the second floor, but it was empty. Miller spied a corridor at the far end of the bar. He walked towards it. As he did so a man stepped out from behind the bar. A largish frame was squashed into someone of middling height. His nose had seen better days. Ears, too.

'The Gents is downstairs, sir.'

Miller was taken aback by the use of the word 'sir' and then he remembered that he was dressed in a suit. An expensive looking suit. The man was looking at him with some uncertainty. It looked like he was trying to decide whether to throw him out or frog march him to the back.

Miller gave him a third choice.

'I say,' said Miller, affecting an accent that would have held its own at Kit's club, 'I've come to see your boss. A few anomalies in his accounts.'

It was the word 'anomalies' that probably won the day. Dan 'Haymaker' Harris, a former middleweight boxer whose ranking had never reached the dizzy heights of the top ten, was not the brainiest of men. Eloquence impressed him. The man before him looked polished and seemed something of a toff. 'Haymaker' was under no illusions about his station in life. His job was not to think but to obey. This was particularly pertinent if the instruction was something along the lines of, 'Dan go hurt that person.' He tended to be deferential to his many betters.

'Come with me, said 'Haymaker'. As this was what Miller wanted, he followed the former pugilist to an office at the end of the corridor. A gentle rap on the door and then 'Haymaker' entered followed by Miller.

The Medium Murders

Kit was sitting facing a small, well-dressed man who looked like he'd been in the ring, too. Standing to one side was another man who was clearly the brother of the seated man.

The man behind the desk poured forth a volley of words towards the new entrants. Most of them profane. Dotted amongst them was a question around who the new entrant was and what he was doing here? You had to listen hard to catch it though.

Kit held his hand up which immediately silenced the abusive language and, simultaneously, reassured Miller that his master's life was not in imminent danger.

'This is Harry Miller,' explained. 'He's, my man.'

The final two words were repeated in a rather arch fashion by the previous speaker to his brother. He looked closely at Miller.

'You look familiar. Do I know you?'

'I don't think so,' replied Miller. 'My dad is Daniel Miller. My brother was also called Daniel.'

Charles 'Wag' McDonald registered both the name and the use of the past tense. He didn't have to ask why. He'd left his role as a gangland leader in 1914 to sign up for the army. He nodded to Miller, recognising the catch in the voice as he'd spoken the name of his brother.

'You're Daniel Miller's boy. Looks like you've not carried on the family tradition.'

'In fact,' interjected Kit, 'Harry did follow the family tradition. I managed to persuade him to consider an alternative path.'

'Really?' said 'Wag' McDonald looking from master to servant and back again.

'He saved my life.'

Wag McDonald studied the small Londoner before him. It had taken pluck to come into the home of south London's most feared gang leader.

'Looks like he was trying to do it again.'

Kit smiled and glanced at Miller.

'Yes, rather a bad habit of his. It could get him hurt someday. Harry, this is Mr Charles McDonald, although I'm sure you guessed this. The gentleman standing is Mr Wal McDonald. And the kind gentleman who let you in is 'Haymaker Harris' who I had the great good fortune to see fight ten or twelve years ago.'

'How did he get on?' asked Wag McDonald, genuinely curious.

'Sadly, it wasn't his night,' replied Kit to the guffaws of the McDonald brothers and the great discomfort of poor 'Haymaker'.

As Kit said this, the door opened. Into the office walked two women. The taller woman glared at Miller and then looked at Kit. Wag McDonald smiled and leaned back on his chair.

'Couldn't have timed it better, my love. Gentlemen meet Alice Diamond. She is…' He paused for a moment and shot Miss Diamond a look. She raised her eyebrows and smiled.

'An associate,' continued McDonald. 'An associate of the hoisting variety. Alice, do you want to tell Lord Aston, and his man, why he's here?' As he said this, he took a photograph from his desk drawer. He handed it to Alice Diamond.

For a moment she seemed overcome. She looked hard at the photograph and then handed it to Kit.

The image shocked Kit. It showed a young woman. Naked and dead. The wound around her throat was clear. So, too, were the markings on her stomach. It took Kit a moment to register what he was seeing.

'Good lord,' he said before fixing his gaze on Alice Diamond.

'Who is she?'

'Enid Blake,' replied Miss Diamond. Her voice was deep, and she spoke slowly. Kit remained silent so she continued.

'Enid was part of our group. Some of us do shops, others find work in houses and then, well, you know.'

Kit nodded and looked, reluctantly, at the dead woman.

'When did this happen?'

'They found her body last night.'

The next question was on Kit's lips, but he stopped himself just in time. He looked at the grim face of Wag

McDonald. The gangland leader seemed to read his mind.

'We have our sources.'

'I think I've met him,' replied Kit, thinking of Sergeant Wellbeloved.

McDonald nodded but did not offer any more information on their source. He regarded Kit closely. He could see Kit's eyes were on the photograph.

'What do you see, Lord Aston?'

Kit returned his gaze to McDonald. Unlike the photograph that Churchill had shown him, the shape carved into the stomach of the young woman was all too clear. For some reason, Kit sensed that McDonald knew what they were dealing with here. The murder had little or nothing to do with the frequent internecine wars between the gangs. This was of a wholly new character and even more unsettling for being so.

'Do you recognise this symbol?' asked Kit. McDonald merely nodded.

'Do you?'

'Yes, it's a pentacle. Inverted. If this means what I think it means, then you're dealing with a cult. A cult dedicated to Satan.'

'Can you help us find who did this?'

Kit had suspected this was coming but one question remained unanswered, although he suspected he knew.

'Why me?'

The Medium Murders

McDonald glanced up at Alice Diamond and smiled grimly. The answer was provided by the tall, utterly compelling woman with the expressionless grey eyes standing by McDonald's desk.

'Because it was your lot who did it.'

11

'Really quite roomy,' said Kit, sitting somewhat squashed between Wag McDonald and Alice Diamond. They were in a car driving towards Stepney. In the front sat the driver, 'Haymaker' Harris, alongside Miller and the diminutive associate of Alice Diamond who had been introduced as Maggie Hill. The latter young woman spent most of the journey staring at Miller. There was something manic in her eyes that suggested either a psychopathic disposition or that she had fallen in love.

Sadly, for Miller, this was true on both counts.

'Who are we going to see?' asked Kit after he had been told of their destination: a church hall in the east end of London.

McDonald allowed himself a smile and he replied, 'As we're dealing with the "Old Nick", I thought it made sense to visit a priest.'

Nothing else was added to this rather enigmatic, albeit logical, remark. The rest of the journey took place in a rather odd silence. Particularly odd, in fact, from where Miller was sitting.

The journey to the East End took Kit through some of the most deprived areas he'd seen in a long time,

The Medium Murders

certainly since a trip to India the previous year. He caught Wag McDonald's amused glance at him.

'A bit different, ain't it?'

Kit nodded. It was. It looked like civilisation had ended several minutes previously. They pulled up outside a church hall in the middle of hell. A crowd of children quickly gathered around the car. All of them were dirty. They were not quite dressed in rags, but many had no shoes. A land fit for heroes, thought Kit bitterly.

'Haymaker' got out of the car and was about to administer a few clips around the ear before Wag McDonald cautioned him.

'Leave it. Here, which one of you lot is the oldest.'

The tallest boy stepped forward. He seemed no more than ten or eleven. His sallow face emphasised a large nose. He looked underfed but there was no mistaking the burning pride in his eyes.

'What's your name, son?' asked McDonald.

'William, sir. William Hill.'

'Can I call you Billy?'

'Most do.'

'Right, Billy. One of the men over there is going to give you some money. Make sure the car is clean when we get back.'

Billy Hill turned to Kit and Miller. Kit smiled at McDonald's cheek as well as his shrewdness. Meanwhile, Miller stepped forward and handed the boy several shillings. With a nod from the boy, several of the children ran off to get buckets of water.

'Thanks, Billy,' said Kit. McDonald contented himself with waggling the boy's hair.

The two men walked alongside one another into the hall.

'How long will it be before young Billy is a rival of yours?'

McDonald smiled at Kit and replied, 'It'll be his only way out of this, your lordship. Might even recruit him myself. The kid's a natural leader.'

Miller, meanwhile, found himself accompanied by the two women. Alice Diamond began to engage Miller in conversation, rather like a father would a young man come to take his daughter out for a walk.

'So, you were a burglar. How'd you end up with 'im?'

Miller gave a very edited version of their meeting that significantly reduced the extraordinary heroism he'd shown in rescuing Kit from No Man's Land during the War.

'Where do you live?'

Miller glanced at the Amazonian 'hoister'?

'You fancy paying us a visit, darling?'

He smiled as he said this. It always worked. The cheek. As ever, the reaction on Alice Diamond's face told him he'd hit his target.

'Get out of it,' laughed the huge hoister. 'Just curious.'

The Medium Murders

Miller grinned and told them a little bit more about his life in Belgravia, although he didn't mention the address. They followed Kit and McDonald into the church hall. It was crowded with men and women. All had tried to dress for the church: suits and dresses held together by prayer. All were poor. All hopes had been crushed by the reality of life and the fear of sin. They were being fed in the makeshift soup kitchen.

'Nice place,' said McDonald spying the man they had come to see. He was small, powerfully built and a priest. His grey hair peeked out from the sides of his hat. He was sitting with a group of destitute women.

The man in question noticed the arrival of McDonald and the others. His face remained impassive but the anger in his eyes was unmistakeable. He excused himself from the group and walked over towards the new arrivals.

'If you've come to confess, McDonald, I don't think there's long enough in the day.'

'Don't worry, Father Vaughan. I need your help, definitely not His by the looks of this place.'

Father Bernard Vaughan glanced around him before replying with barely disguised anger, 'We all need His help.'

'Where is He then?' replied McDonald. His head jerked up a fraction and he waved his arm around him. Both he and Vaughan glared at one another like two fighters a few seconds before the bell rings. Finally, the priest registered Kit and looked him up and down. Kit saw that Vaughan was probably around seventy years old. His beak-like nose and bearing seemed almost noble. In fact, he had been born into a wealthy family.

'As Mr McDonald seems in no rush to introduce me, my name is Aston. I believe I may have met your brother.'

The priest listened to Kit. It was clear he came from another world than the gang leader. The question to Kit was in his eyes, but it was McDonald who answered.

'I think explanations as to why we are here and why Lord Aston is associating with the likes of me should be answered somewhere private.'

Even Father Vaughan could not argue with this logic, although the fiery chaplain would dearly love to have done so.

'Follow me. I'll give you five minutes.'

Vaughan spun around and walked in the direction of a door at the back of the hall.

'Haymaker' Harris stood outside keeping a watchful eye on the boys surrounding his car. Strictly speaking it wasn't his car, but he felt a degree of ownership that bespoke a man who took pride in his job and had a high degree of loyalty to his employer. Wag McDonald had always looked after him. The very least he could do was return the favour.

The Medium Murders

He was pretty sure that he couldn't trust the gang of boys as far as he could throw them. To be fair, this would have been a considerable distance. Billy Hill recognised the lack of trust. After directing his 'men' on operations, he sidled over to 'Haymaker' to keep the powerful-looking man on his side.

'How'd you join this gang, mister?'

'By minding my own business,' replied 'Haymaker'. Oddly this was true. Towards the end of his career, when he was losing more than he was winning, he ignored those moments when wins that should have been losses were wins. He kept silent when he saw his opponents leaving the dressing room with a few more readies in their pocket than he'd earned for the previous three fights. Strangely, he was never asked to take a dive. He had just about enough self-awareness to know that it probably wasn't necessary in his case.

The answer upset young master Hill.

'C'mon, mister. Only asking.'

'Haymaker' suggested that he shouldn't, thereby providing young Billy Hill with an early lesson in how to manage staff loyalty. The boy nodded and then walked away to ensure his team were doing a good job.

The office was crowded. Alice Diamond and Maggie Hill turned down Kit's offer to take the two seats in front of Father Vaughan. As soon as they were all seated, McDonald spoke.

'Look at these.'

The two photographs Kit had seen earlier were put on the table causing the priest to inhale noisily. He shook his head, genuinely upset by the image. He looked up at McDonald and then at Alice Diamond. She stared back at him impassively but remained silent. This wasn't just out of respect for McDonald; something in the intensity of the elderly priest made her nervous. Out of the corner of her eye she saw McDonald glance up at her. This was her cue to speak.

'She was one of my girls. Enid Blake.'

'Is this the medium murder I read about earlier?'

'Probably,' replied McDonald.

The priest pointed to the pentacle carved onto her body. He looked at the two men seated in front of him.

'You know what this is? What it means?'

Kit nodded and replied, 'I knew a man in France. Hodgson. William Hope Hodgson. He wrote a bit about the occult.'

Vaughan made a face at the mention of Hodgson.

'Cheap thrillers. I'm surprised that you read such rubbish, Lord Aston.'

'I do not read the genre, Father Vaughan. I heard the stories directly from Hodgson while we were sitting in a trench waiting to attack the Germans.'

The Medium Murders

McDonald glanced at Kit and felt like cheering. He'd never seen Vaughan taken on like this before. There was an unmistakable note of respect in the look. He'd been there. He'd felt what Kit would have felt sitting there with the men, guts churning. Anybody who could sing or tell a story was esteemed, cherished even.

Vaughan nodded and accepted the mild rebuke.

'Why do you think the murderer has used this symbol?'

Rage flared into the eyes of Vaughan. His face seemed like it would explode.

'I'm glad you said murderer, Lord Aston. Make no mistake, you are dealing with people who have murdered many times before in this way. The blood sacrifice is as old as man. It was practiced in Egypt, Mexico. Even Abraham would have performed it.'

'Why?' asked Kit.

'Power. To show they had the power or, perhaps, to gain some sort of magical power if the sacrifice was performed under certain conditions: a ceremony, within a pentacle.

In this case I think that they are trying to dress their evil acts as part of some ritual to Satan, but they are nothing more than murderers. They are impotent frauds. Ninety-nine percent of them. Their beliefs are a sham. Be it the occult, spiritualism; it's all the same. Fakery. And you have fools like Doyle going around legitimising this fakery.

Kit was taken aback by the vehemence of the attack on Doyle, however one question burned through the tirade.

'Sorry, Father Vaughan. May I interrupt for one second? You said "they". If you don't mind me saying, it implies you know who they are.'

Vaughan looked at Kit. The rage in his eyes died immediately. In its place there was only sadness. A deep well of desolation.

'I wish it were so. I cannot prove it is a group, or indeed the same group. I am convinced, however, there are some amongst them who have perpetrated the vilest of crimes on young women. They have been doing so for many, many years. I first saw this type of crime fifteen years ago. I've heard of similar. The authorities have never spoken of it probably because they fear panic may set in.'

'Or, indeed, others copying these despicable deeds.'

'True, but there is one other reason.'

Kit looked at Father Vaughan and for those few moments there was silence inside the office. Finally, it was McDonald that spoke.

'You think the murderers are amongst them, don't you? The authorities. The toffs.'

Vaughan glared at McDonald.

'As if you can speak.'

'Not my game padre.'

The Medium Murders

Kit held his hand up and removed from his pocket one of the photographs given to him by Churchill. He placed it on the table alongside the picture provided by McDonald. Aside from the indistinctness of the markings on the dead body, they seemed enacted by the same hand.

Both Vaughan and McDonald were in shock. It was Alice Diamond who reacted first.

'Who is she?'

Kit looked at her and replied, 'I don't know. I've been asked by someone to find out who she is and who…' He left the rest of the sentence hanging. Then he added a question that seemed superfluous.

'It's difficult to see the young woman's stomach, but it seems there are markings on it. Do you think it could be the same person who did this?'

Father Vaughan stared reluctantly at the second picture. He placed his finger on what looked like the apex of a star.

'I cannot say for certain but her age and what is visible of the marking makes me think it is the same hand. When did this murder occur?'

'1908. I know you will see this as a sign of the rich covering the tracks of their crimes but I'm not at liberty to say more on the subject. I will confirm that all evidence, and there is precious little, suggests it was perpetrated by rich people in a druid ritual.'

'When in 1908?' asked Father Vaughan.

'August, we believe.'

Vaughan sat back in his chair. He seemed confused. Then he saw Kit looking at him with a frown on his face.

'It seems strange,' said Vaughan. 'Dates are important for these madmen. Druids revere the summer and winter solstice. Satanists, on the other hand, venerate St Walpurgis Eve and, All Hallows Eve. Both dates are important for their ceremonies. All these dates can involve human sacrifice for their neophytes who wish to attain higher levels of enlightenment within the group. If the sacrifice happens on a day outside their traditional calendar, then it leads me to suspect that it is simply a case of murdering someone who may reveal who they are.'

'Are you saying that the killer can be anyone in the group?' asked McDonald.

'The whole group is complicit. I understand it's usually a designated High Priest who performs the actual sacrifice. I believe the blood is used as part of the ceremony for the neophyte. I cannot bring myself to say what I have heard but these are truly depraved individuals, and they must be brought to justice. Is this why you are involved, Lord Aston?'

Kit was aware that all eyes in the room were on him. His face was set, his heart heavy but he felt an anger burning inside.

He nodded in confirmation.

The Medium Murders

It was night, closer to nine than eight. Vaughan was true to his word and ended the meeting after five minutes. Kit returned to the Elephant and Castle to discuss with McDonald his thoughts on how they should proceed. Throughout the meeting, Miller stood uncomfortably aware of the lovestruck gaze of Maggie Hill. Had their day not been shrouded in such a desolate subject, Kit might have made great sport of the romantic feelings provoked by his manservant. 'Haymaker' drove Kit and Miller back to Belgravia accompanied by Alice Diamond, who was curious to see where they lived.

'I say 'Haymaker', can you stop over there for a second?' asked Kit, spying a flower seller as the car approached Grosvenor Square.

This brought a smile from Alice Diamond.

'In trouble, are we?'

'I rather suspect I am.'

A few minutes later the large car pulled away from Aunt Agatha's mansion in Grosvenor Square. Kit stepped up towards the front door. It was answered by Natalie. After a few pleasantries Kit walked towards the drawing room. Natalie opened the door for him.

Inside he found Aunt Agatha and Betty Simpson. There was no sign of either Cavendish sister. Kit felt somewhat foolish clutching the flowers. He looked at the two elderly ladies. They were sitting in front of a book with newspaper cuttings.

'Hello ladies. What are you cooking up?'

This question seemed not to find favour with Kit's aunt. Noting the reaction, Kit decided to ask what was really on his mind.

'Where are Mary and Esther?'

'Good question. Apparently not with you it seems.'

'Apparently not.' Now it was Kit's turn to feel irritated. He threw the flowers onto the chair.

'So, while you've been off detecting with Betty…' said Kit angrily.

Agatha stood up which stopped Kit in his tracks. There is something about an aunt approaching you, anger in her eyes, that can reduce even the most heroic of men to a quivering, fearful wreck inside.

'There's no use in being angry at me. You're the one that disappeared for the day. No telephone call, no interest in sharing what you were doing. I may no longer be a young woman in love, but my memory of the experience was a strong desire that I not be kept at arm's length.'

All of which was true but hardly fair. Kit was tempted to point out he'd been effectively kidnapped. However, he, too, was angry and he certainly did not want to be seen to be making excuses. This left him with precious few options. None of them good.

'Goodnight,' said Kit and left the room, then the house in search of a taxi.

The Medium Murders

Betty looked up at her friend and said, 'Well, part of me is glad to see he's not perfect. He'd be a bit boring otherwise.'

Agatha smiled but, in truth she was upset. Not with Kit, however. All men were fundamentally children to her. Eggshell egos housed within powerful bodies made for a catastrophic cocktail sometimes. She was woman enough to make allowances for good looks and a sense of humour. Kit had both in abundance. 'Useless' had too, once upon a time. No, her worry concerned Mary.

After Betty had left, Agatha sat by the window, the flowers lay heavily on her lap. It was as dark inside the room as it was outside. An hour passed. Then another. Finally, she saw a car pull up outside the house. The Cavendish sisters emerged from the car; both laughing. They said goodbye to two young men in the car before dancing up the steps of the house. Agatha heard the front door opening.

'Sssh, Mary,' said Esther. She was one stop past squiffy but not quite stewed to the gills. Mary had been careful to drink less but certainly had shipped enough to be unusually courageous. This was to be tested in a moment.

Mary whispered back, 'I suspect Aunt Agatha is…'

'She is,' said Agatha emerging from the room. Oddly, and more worryingly, her tone was not angry. In fact, an astute mind would have detected a base note of sadness. Mary had such a mind and instantly sobered. She looked down at the flowers in Agatha's hand and knew what was coming next as sure as she knew that tears were less than a broken heartbeat away.

'From Kit,' said Agatha, handing the flowers to Mary. 'I hope you know what you're doing.' She turned and left the two girls standing in the entrance hall.

Alone together.

12

Esther wisely stayed in bed the next morning to nurse a hangover and avoid the inevitable post-mortem from Aunt Agatha. Mary, on the other hand, went to face her five-foot destiny with a combination of pluck and no little dander. If you were to ask her what she was feeling, she would have been hard pushed to put a finger on it, but she was feeling something, and Aunt Agatha was not going it all her own way. Nor, indeed, Kit, for that matter. Such were her thoughts as she stepped lightly down the stairs towards the dining room for a breakfast that she had no hunger for.

As she reached the room, Natalie approached her with a telegram. All at once Mary's spirit rose several and a half fractions. She tore open the envelop and read the note.

'Oh.'

A frown crossed her face. Mary inhaled deeply then she entered the dining room. Agatha was sitting by the table drinking tea. Eyes straight ahead, Mary went to join her. Agatha looked at her strangely, at least if one eyebrow raised could be so described. Mary sat down and waited for Agatha to say something.

Oddly, at least for Aunt Agatha, she was silent. Mary frowned a little bit more. Then she heard a light cough emanating from the direction of the window. Mary turned to see Kit sitting in an armchair. There was a newspaper on his lap.

They looked at one another for a few moments in silence.

'Good morning,' said Kit.

Sergeant Wellbeloved put the morning paper down and looked at Detective Inspector Bulstrode. The Detective Inspector's grin was wider than the Thames. The colour of his teeth certainly resembled London's famous waterway. Bulstrode lit another cigarette and looked at the paper his sergeant had set down.

'Good news, I say. This is going to be a big one. I'll let his highness deal with it.'

Wellbeloved smirked at this. A smirk, even at the best of times, ranks lowly in the food chain of bonhomie. It's certainly preferable to a leer, but only marginally so. Perhaps it is the suggestiveness that offends. The smirker is either giving the deliberate impression of being in possession of knowledge that the beholder is unaware, or he is being slyly conspiratorial. Neither situation is likely to present the smirker in the best light.

Such was the man that Bulstrode was addressing. Neither man took much joy in the appearance of the other, but they had formed a brutally effective partnership. Their methods required less high-profile cases to reap the success they had enjoyed this past decade or more.

'So, everything is sorted then?' asked Bulstrode.

'So, I understand. They even took Aston to see some priest yesterday.'

Bulstrode shook his head. He didn't know what the game was there, and he no longer cared. It was someone else's problem now and not before time. He picked up the case file and handed it to Wellbeloved.

'Can you bring it up to Jellicoe with my compliments?'

Wellbeloved's smile turned into a cackle so repugnant that even Bulstrode recoiled. The laughter was brought to a temporary halt by the sudden onset of coughing as he left the office. Just after Wellbeloved departed, the phone rang. Bulstrode answered it and listened for a few seconds. A smile spread over his face. Awaiting Wellbeloved at Jellicoe's office would be an unpleasant surprise.

'Sir, with all due respect, I must protest,' said Jellicoe in a manner that showed more passion than the Commissioner could ever remember seeing from the, normally, imperturbable Chief Inspector.

Commissioner and former Brigadier-General William Horwood put his hands up in the manner one does when one wants to convey that it is out of one's control. The fact that this proposal was not only within his command but had also been his idea was something he neglected to mention to the increasingly irate Chief Inspector. Apparently, a similar idea had been heading his direction anyway. Can there be a finer feeling in the world than equalising before the other team scores? Probably, but at that moment the Commissioner couldn't think of any.

'James, it is only temporary.'

Jellicoe's response was as succinct as it was explicit in conveying his dismay. The Commissioner felt his temper rising but fought to keep control. To be fair to the man before him, Jellicoe was not normally given to displays of insubordination. However, the last expletive-filled sally had stepped perilously close to mutiny in the former soldier's eyes and was long past the point of outright insubordination.

Commissioner Horwood remained silent. This effectively closed the subject. Jellicoe glared at him for a moment and stalked out of the office.

Kit walked over to the table and sat down on the other side of Mary. The relief Mary had felt at seeing Kit

The Medium Murders

slowly dissolved as she began to feel she'd landed in the middle of an inquisition.

'Thank you for the flowers. They were lovely,' said Mary. Her face gave no indication that she thought anything of the sort.

'I was feeling guilty,' admitted Kit.

'So, you should.'

'In point of fact, no, I shouldn't,' said Kit. His tone was sharp.

This stopped Mary in her tracks. She suspected that Kit had been forced to attend meetings to which he could not, realistically, invite Mary. It was hardly fair to blame Kit and yet she did. On the other hand, she'd had equally good reasons for her night out with Bobby Andrews. However, Kit was going to have to work harder to hear them.

'So, tell me where you are on the case.'

The word 'you' stung Kit. Mary could see the hit had landed and immediately regretted it.

Kit briefly summarised the day's events. Every sentence increased the feeling within Mary that she was being unfair. In truth, the problem she was facing went beyond Kit's control. It was a problem that she and every other woman faced. If Kit could have involved her, she suspected he would have. Albeit reluctantly. She thought about the telegram in her hand. This would be incendiary.

Jack Murray

After Kit had finished there was silence. He deliberately avoided asking her where she'd spent the evening and with whom. It was equally obvious Aunt Agatha had told him. The ball hadn't so much bounced into her court as exploded in it. Mary studied Kit's face.

'Have you that list with you? The one that Mr Churchill gave you?'

Kit looked confused, however he reached into his inner pocket and placed it on the table. Mary looked down at it and then took a pen that was sitting near Aunt Agatha and wrote one other name on the list.

Kit was astonished. He took the piece of paper in his hand and studied the list again. Slowly a smile spread over his face, and he looked at Mary. By now Agatha, whose patience levels were on a par with a hungry lion staring at a herd of antelope catching forty winks on the Serengeti, was ready to explode. Kit handed her the note before the pocket Vesuvius erupted. It took a moment.

'Oh.'

'Indeed,' said Mary, unable to keep a note of triumph in her voice.

'Clever girl connecting the Earl of Gresham to the Honourable Mr Andrews. What did you have to do to obtain the name?' asked Kit. There was a slow smile on his face. This caused an unspoken rebuke from Aunt Agatha, although she was too curious to scold.

'Nothing you need worry about my dear, but my feet are killing me.'

The Medium Murders

'He's a good dancer?'

'Wonderful.'

'I gather he's good looking.'

'His eyes flash. I kid thee not. In fact, he asked me to go dancing with him tonight again.'

'Did he? And what did you say?'

'I said I'd let him know. I'm waiting to see if I receive a better offer.'

Kit felt a stab of remorse. He knew that his day would require him to be away from Mary. Additionally, he felt ashamed that he'd not told Mary the full truth of his discoveries. He hadn't mentioned any connection with Satanism or the detail behind the recent murder of the young woman. As he desperately fought for a way to introduce the topic, inspiration struck.

'Aunt Agatha,' said Kit. 'What have you been up to? I saw you with Betty Simpson last night. This can only mean one thing.'

Aunt Agatha managed the improbable feat of looking innocent, offended, and sly, all at the same time. Even Mary marvelled at how she managed this. Years of practice, she supposed.

'I'm glad you asked, Christopher. I wouldn't go so far as to say we've cracked the case, but we're certainly a lot further ahead than what I've heard so far.'

It would be fair to say that Agatha was more than gratified by the surprise on the faces of both the young people in her presence. A brief 'that's-told-you' followed. She leaned forward, licked her lips, and began.

'As you know, Betty and I have, over the years, collected cuttings related to…'

'Gruesome murders,' interjected Kit.

This was met by a stare from the two women.

'Ignore him, Aunt Agatha.'

'I shall. Betty and I returned to unsolved murders specifically related to young women. I'm sad to report there are so many. It's heart-breaking. I'm not in any way attaching blame to you, Christopher, but your sex has committed an untold number of crimes against women.'

It would have been impossible for any man not to have felt intense shame. Mary looked at Kit sympathetically and held his hand.

'The cases date back at least twelve years but that is when Betty began to collect the details. This has, almost certainly, being going on for longer.'

'I'm sorry to ask, but did the papers provide any details on the nature of the murders?'

Agatha shook her head.

'No, this is what we found interesting. Normally there is some indication of murder weapon or cause of death.'

Kit looked at Agatha and then Mary. He hesitated before finally saying, 'This corresponds with what I know of the murder of Enid Blake. It seems likely her death was part of a ceremony.'

The Medium Murders

'A sacrifice?' said Agatha, incredulously.

'Yes. There were markings on her body associated with Satanic symbols.'

Kit could feel the pressure on his hand grow as Mary digested this news.

'How horrible,' said Mary. 'How can people...?' she left the rest unsaid. What rationale can one apply to murder? A crime of passion? Assassination? Revenge? Each had a twisted logic. The occult was another matter. Although the occult held no fear for her, she still shivered involuntarily. Premeditated execution or ritual slaying seemed to her another level of horror.

'What are you going to do now?' asked Mary.

Kit held his hands up apologetically, "I have to meet with Churchill. You don't mind?'

'Certainly not,' smiled Mary. 'I have a lunch appointment myself, as it happens.'

Kit's face clouded over. He looked down at a telegram sitting on the table. Mary pushed it forward. Kit glanced at her and received confirmation that he could read it.

Moments later he said, 'Good Lord.'

Mary smiled at him and raised her eyebrows.

'Would someone please tell me what is going on?' asked Agatha in the manner of someone who did not take kindly to telepathy as a form of communication.

'Are you really going to lunch with her?' asked Kit. He saw Agatha on the point of spontaneous combustion so added for her benefit, 'Mrs Rosling. Remember Mary's former employer from 'The Phantom' case?'

It was Agatha's turn to exclaim 'Good Lord' along with standard aunt-like questions revolving around the separation of the subject individual from their senses, and such like.

'I saw her yesterday. Briefly. And she saw me. I attended a meeting of Suffragists at Claridge's. She was not a speaker but was at the top table. Anyway, when will you return from Whitehall?'

'I think late afternoon.'

'So, I shall finally have you to myself then?' smiled Mary.

'Well, perhaps you would like to join me for another appointment.'

'With whom?'

'A priest.'

It was one of Mary's more interesting attractions that her eyes could convey so much in the space of split seconds. First, they widened hopefully in perfect synch with her smile before narrowing suspiciously with a frown. Once again, Kit regretted that their marriage would have to wait until after Esther and Richard's wedding and the anniversary of their grandfather's death.

'I neglected to mention, my visit last night with our gangland friends was to a Father Bernard Vaughan. He's

The Medium Murders

not exactly an admirer of your friend Doyle, Aunt Agatha.'

'I hope you don't think for one moment that it'll just be you and Mary going on your own,' said Agatha.

'I wouldn't dream of going without you and Betty,' said Kit nobly. He glanced at the clock on the mantelpiece. 'In fact, I'm rather depending on you being there. It should be quite a meeting. Now, I must be on my way.'

Mary walked Kit to the door. For once Agatha deemed it wise that the two lovers should be left alone. Thankfully they were both at an age where moments of resentment merely act as a justification for further declarations of undying love. At least on the part of the man, that is. For one must always conclude, in these situations, that it was he who erred.

Mary returned to the dining room to find Agatha scouring the paper.

'What are you looking for, Aunt Agatha?' asked Mary. After eight months together in the house, Mary had license to ask questions that might have been considered impertinent.

'I was expecting more news on the Medium Murders but there appears to be none. Tell me about yesterday. I haven't seen Millicent in years.'

'You've met her?'

'I knew her a long time ago,' replied Agatha enigmatically.

'You were a suffragist?'

'Had I been in the country more, I should have been. By the time I returned,' Agatha stopped for a moment. The memory of a man swum into view.

'I'd just lost Useless. I wasn't ready to face the world again for a while. She's around my age. I admire her tremendously.'

Mary nodded in agreement.

'I want to do more, Aunt Agatha. I have a feeling Mrs Rosling will ask me to join. I shall.'

'You should.'

'I haven't spoken with Kit about this.'

'Why should you? You're entitled to have your own interests. Anyway, he'll do as he's told and like it. I may be old and decrepit, but I've noticed how he looks at you. In this regard, men make dogs seem the very definition of impenetrability.'

Mary was less sure. A frown appeared on her forehead.

'You say that, but I wish I knew what he was thinking sometimes.'

'Not knowing is perhaps a lucky escape. My nephew may be best of breed, but that doesn't mean he has escaped completely from the limitations of the species.'

13

Mary felt nervous. Perhaps even more nervous than she'd felt on her first visit to Sloane Gardens. Then, she'd come in disguise as a prospective candidate for a vacancy on the staff. The memory of working undercover to find a jewel thief that she and Agatha had correctly believed would target the house brought a smile to her face.

She skipped up the steps and rang the bell. The door opened and she was greeted by the familiar face of Grantham, the butler. The passage of several months and the Phantom case had done little to dilute any sense of his own dignity.

It took a few moments for him to register Mary was the woman he'd known as Miss Tanner, the maid. Then the light of recollection shone briefly in his eyes. This woman had disguised herself and made fools of them all. Now, for reasons surpassing all understanding, she was the lunch guest of the lady of the house.

'Please come this way, Miss Mary.'

From this point on, Grantham was pious professionalism personified. He managed to make Mary feel that she was in the presence of someone who could rise effortlessly above her previous misdemeanours. The effortful ease with which he accomplished this amused Mary so much that she felt much more relaxed by the time she entered the dining room where she had served dinner to the lady that she was meeting. The lady, in question, was sitting at the head of the table. In front of her lay open face down a book, 'Aristophanes, Thesmophoriazusae'.

'Miss Mary,' said Mrs Rosling, rising to meet her guest.

'Mrs Rosling,' said Mary, stepping forward with more confidence than she would have hitherto imagined.

'I hope you will call me Isabelle,' smiled Mrs Rosling.

'Only if you call me Mary.'

They sat down; the atmosphere was relaxed thanks to the calm intelligence of the woman she was meeting. Mary asked after Mr Rosling and their good-looking, if somewhat aggressively romantic nephew, Whittaker Rosling. In turn, Mrs Rosling asked about Kit.

'You're to be married soon?'

Mary laughed and realised that she had confused Mrs Rosling.

'I wish we were. We've been engaged for most of the year.'

'Why such a long wait?'

'Oh, it's a long story. I met Kit when I lost my grandfather. At the same time, my sister met the man she will be marrying in a few weeks. Anyway, what with the grief, the trial...'

'Trial?'

'I told you it was a long story. Esther and I were grieving, so weddings were out of the question. As Esther is the eldest, we agreed she should marry first. I turn twenty-one on the first of November, a week before her wedding.

'Twenty-one,' laughed Mrs Rosling. It was a nice sound. 'Oh, to be young again. And in love.'

There was no arguing with this. It was rather wonderful.

'My sister and Richard will be on their honeymoon until Christmas. And Christmas is the anniversary of our grandfather's death. Anyway, long story short, Kit and I decided on a February date.'

'Not St Valentine's Day?' asked Mrs Rosling, with a smile.

'Yes,' said Mary, colouring slightly. However, this was greeted with a clap and a warm smile by Mrs Rosling.

'How romantic. If I may say, your fiancé is the very picture of a romantic hero.'

'You may,' laughed Mary.

As they were speaking, lunch was served. Mary glanced at her replacement and smiled a thank you. One lesson she had learned from her time 'downstairs' was that she would never ignore the efforts made by the staff. Mrs Rosling noted her smile and said after the maid had left, 'I suspect you have some empathy for their role now.'

Mary laughed and nodded 'yes'.

'What became of our Phantom?'

Mary avoided answering the question directly.

'I gather she avoided capture. But the diamond necklace was recovered, wasn't it?'

'It was,' said Mrs Rosling, a slow smile spreading on her face. It was clear she liked Mary. It was clear she wanted something, too.

'Forgive me for being too American, but I think I owe it to you to get to the reason why I invited you here today. Although, having met you properly now, I suspect I could just as happily spend the afternoon chatting about many other things.'

'I did wonder. I wasn't sure we'd parted on such good terms.'

Mrs Rosling smiled, 'Trust me, we didn't. I don't think Carlisle or Grantham have ever had to work so hard as when you two ladies bolted the corral.'

Mary was not sure she was quite so sympathetic to the housekeeper's plight but, on reflection, neither she nor Caroline Hadleigh had made her life easy. In fact, the mention of the housekeeper brought up an unexpected feeling of guilt.

'Perhaps I could see Miss Carlisle afterwards. I feel I owe her an apology.'

'Of course, but I'm not sure you need apologise. Anyway, to business. I was, naturally, surprised to see you yesterday. It was, I may say, a pleasant surprise. What brought you to the meeting?'

Mary paused for a few seconds. Where to begin? She came from privilege but had never felt comfortable with either this or the assumption that the direction of her life had been decided in the womb. It was the twentieth century. Change wasn't just what was happening around you, it was something to be moulded to your will. And then it crystallised in her mind why she had gone to see Millicent Fawcett.

'I resent the fact that I cannot be what I choose to be. A member of Parliament, a doctor, or a surgeon; a lawyer or a judge; a banker or a worker in commerce. Am I less capable than a man? I don't believe so. The simple reason that I cannot become any of these things is that the law of the land or social mores prevent it. This must change. The law, in this case, is an ass.'

'Many of these things are possible now.'

Mary raised an eyebrow at this which caused the older woman to smile and revise this thought.

'Theoretically, anyway.'

The conversation continued over lunch in this manner. Mrs Rosling continued to probe Mary to understand better her motivation. Both recognised the underlying theme. To what extent was Mary prepared to involve herself in the movement? The answer to this question was more complex than Mary was prepared to admit. On the one hand, she wanted to use her free time to support initiatives planned by others. However, her life with Kit represented an inconvenient counterpoint to the strong and genuine desire to be an agent of change. This was something she'd not discussed with Kit, and it seemed inappropriate to do so with Mrs Rosling.

In the end, Mary compromised by agreeing to attend meetings and events organised by the movement, but she stopped short at agreeing to join any steering committees or planning. Her rationale was accepted by Mrs Rosling: she was heavily involved in two weddings. This was true up to a point, but Mary was under no illusions that Mrs Rosling was neither wholly convinced nor entirely satisfied.

At the end of the luncheon, the door opened. Herbert Rosling stood in the doorway. It was a close-run thing to see who was more surprised. Mary or Mrs Rosling's husband.

'You remember Mary, Herbert?'

Rosling's eyes looked darkly on Mary, so much so that she almost shivered. It seemed to her that he hated her. Mary felt her spirit rising at this thought. Here was a man who had thought he could take liberties because of her position.

'Hello, Mr Rosling.'

'Miss Mary,' said Rosling bowing, 'So good to see you again. I trust you're well.'

The Medium Murders

At least he made no mention of the past. His expression softened and he looked to his wife.

'Recruiting?'

'You could say that Herbert,' replied Mrs Rosling.

'I shall leave you to my wife's persuasive ways unless you wish to make good your escape now?'

Mary smiled and said, 'Well it doesn't feel like I've been press-ganged yet.'

'Early days,' replied Rosling taking his leave. Mary noted that he seemed to be implying more than just what Mrs Rosling had said. She thought no more about it.

Mary declined Mrs Rosling's offer to accompany her down to the kitchen to see Miss Carlisle. They parted on the landing and Mary descended the stairs she had last visited on the night of the robbery nearly six months previously.

Arriving outside the kitchen, Mary found, to her surprise, that she was nervous once more. She knocked lightly on the door and heard a surprised voice say, 'Come in'.

Mary entered and found Miss Carlisle seated and Rose, the cook, by the sink. Miss Carlisle immediately stood and curtsied. Rose's greeting was more in keeping with outsized personality of the friendly cook. She strode over to Mary and embraced her.

'Oh, Mary, it's so good to see you again, my love.'

'Miss Cavendish, Rose,' said Miss Carlisle stiffly.

'Oh, shush you,' said Rose smiling.

'It's Mary, Miss Carlisle. I'm happy to see you both. I've wanted so much to see you again.'

Mary turned to Miss Carlisle and felt a wave of emotion surge through her that she could not account for and certainly could not control. Miss Carlisle looked at her in confusion. The face of the housekeeper remained as pinched as Mary remembered. A lifetime of service engraved into a mouth that had long since forgotten how to smile.

'I wanted to apologise to you both, but particularly you, Miss Carlisle.'

'There's no reason to, Miss Cavendish,' said Miss Carlisle. She wanted to add more but could not think of how she could explain what she was feeling. The space between her emotions and her capacity to articulate them was too great. It had always been so. Her default was to say nothing. To remain impassive.

In the silence that followed, Mary looked into the eyes of the housekeeper and what she saw finally swept away her defences. Tears stung her eyes and she fought unsuccessfully to hold them back. Rose embraced her again.

'I'm sorry,' said Mary finally. 'I misled you both. And...'

And what?

The Medium Murders

She paused, like Miss Carlisle, unable to understand what she was feeling. Why was she here? To seek forgiveness, perhaps? Out of guilt, probably. Her adventure had made a mockery of a decent woman. Its conclusion had left the same woman exposed in her job and likely undermined her trust in human nature. The tightness Mary saw around the mouth, the fixedness of the stare, the unwillingness to give a little of herself with people was a result of hundreds of such slights this woman had experienced in her life. Mary's was but one more contribution. Another grain of sand.

Mary nodded to both ladies in apology.

'I'm keeping you back. I'll go.'

She turned and went towards the servants' entrance. Miss Carlisle opened the door for her. The two women looked at one another again. Once more Mary felt tears appear like an unwelcome guest at a party.

'If ever you need anything. I mean anything, you will tell me. I'll help you in any way I can.'

The face of Miss Carlisle softened momentarily. She nodded but said nothing as Mary darted up the steps of the basement onto the street.

14

It was around four in the afternoon when Mary arrived back to Grosvenor Square. Natalie opened the door and smiled a greeting. In the background, Mary could distinctly hear jazz music. It wasn't very loud, but it did not seem to be coming from the direction of any room on the ground floor. She frowned in puzzlement and looked at Natalie for an explanation.

'Monsieur Fish has purchased a gramophone. It's for his bedroom.'

'Good Lord. What had Aunt Agatha to say about that?'

'She was down in his room earlier, listening to the jazz music.'

'Wonders never cease. You don't think they were dancing, do you?' asked Mary. The two women giggled conspiratorially.

When Mary entered the drawing room there were a few pleasant surprises awaiting. Dr Richard Bright had returned from his locum placement. Mary immediately made her way over to her future brother-in-law to give him a hug.

The Medium Murders

As she did so, she spied Kit sitting by the window. He was holding an enormous bouquet of flowers. Another large bouquet lay on the table, probably for Esther, who seemed to have recovered her energy after a morning that, at best, could only be described as foul. She was smiling with happiness at the return of Richard, only…Mary detected something else.

'Kit, you shouldn't have,' said Mary, smiling.

'I didn't,' replied Kit, with an even bigger grin. 'Look at the card.'

Mary didn't have to read the card to guess the provenance of the flowers. Then she caught sight of Aunt Agatha's face. If a face could be said to be like thunder, then this was closer to a South Atlantic storm.

'Ahhh, my secret lover,' said Mary.

'Not so secret now. Nor indeed Esther's,' replied Kit glancing towards the other bouquet.

'I could always go to Bournemouth and interrogate the Earl of Gresham.'

'Well, it's certainly a thought,' replied Kit who stroked his chin thoughtfully.

Inevitably it was Agatha who brought a halt to the subject.

'When you've quite finished your music hall repartee.'

In such situations there is only one thing in England that can aid rich amateur sleuths in the serious business of detection and uncovering the crimes of the remaining rich people in the country.

'Can you put the tea over there, please, Natalie,' said Aunt Agatha to the trolley-driving young French woman.

As Mary and Esther dispensed the tea, all eyes turned to Kit to hear of his meeting with the Secretary of War and Sea. Kit sat back in his armchair with a wry smile.

'Is Betty Simpson coming, by the way?' asked Kit.

'Late, as usual,' replied Agatha brusquely.

'This tea is frightfully good. Is it Fortnum's by any chance?' asked Kit, continuing to draw out the suspense with some relish.

'Get on with it, Christopher.'

Thus, ordered by Agatha, Kit relented and began a brief summation of all that had transpired, which turned out to be briefer than he'd imagined.

'I met Churchill in the corridor at the war office building on Horse Guards and went for a walk around the block, so to speak. I told him that we believed there was a connection between the young woman in the picture and a number of other murders that had taken place over the last decade and a half.'

'What did he say?'

'Naturally, he was appalled. Oddly, I think he was rather relieved. My sense is he's not in the least bit worried by any revelations around druidism as he just sees it as a social thing. Rather like fancy dress. The fact that this death is not solely connected with that evening probably helps him in a strange way although it's still a

The Medium Murders

horrible situation, clearly. Anyway, he agreed that we should share what we know with the police. You may have to control your emotions at this, but he would like me to work alongside Scotland Yard. In fact, he sent instructions immediately after I had seen him.'

'So, what else have you been up to today?'

'I sent word to that horrible man, Bulstrode that I would like to meet him to discuss these medium murders. The good news is that Jellicoe has replaced him. We're to meet him at five. I suggested he should meet Father Vaughan. He didn't have much time yesterday and he has agreed to giving us a little more information today.'

'Are we going to Stepney? We'll need to get a weave on.' asked Mary, quite intrigued by the idea of visiting a part of London that she'd never been to before.

'Certainly not, young lady,' replied Agatha, but there was something in her voice that was less officious. If Kit had been asked to put a name to it, he would have said it was sadness. He couldn't blame her. From what he'd seen of those streets, it wasn't a place for Mary or, indeed, for the poor souls forced to live in those conditions.

'No,' replied Kit, 'In fact, Father Vaughan is rather close by. Just around the corner on Mount Street. We can walk. It should be quite a meeting.'

Mary looked closely at Kit, but it was clear by the half smile on Kit's face that nothing more would be said on the subject. Mary made a face at him which only made her fiancé's grin widen.

The arrival of Betty Simpson was never going to be a quiet affair. She bustled into the drawing room with all the focused energy of an irate customer about to complain of bad service. Moments later, a well-aimed throw saw her tweed shooting cap, which matched the tweed dress suit, nestling comfortably over the head of Canova's Helen of Troy. Not the original, of course.

Agatha rolled her eyes and made a decidedly loud 'Tsk'. This was greeted with smiles around the room although the two ladies in question appeared oblivious to the impact of their music hall routine.

'Sorry I'm late. Just managed eighteen as it was such a nice day. Don't ask me how I got on.'

'We shan't.'

'Poisonously bad putting. The greens were an utter disgrace, of course. If I catch that greenkeeper, he'll get a piece of my mind.'

'I'm sure he'll find that as elevating as we all do, dear.'

Post-mortem of the round complete, Betty marched over to the chair beside Agatha and sat down. She placed a large scrapbook on the table between the two ladies.

'Shall we start?' asked Betty, ready for business. Agatha rolled her eyes once more.

The Medium Murders

Kit led a rather large delegation on the short walk to the 114 Mount Street residence of Father Vaughan. Walking alongside Kit was Mary. Behind them, Agatha and Betty Simpson walked in silence. Betty was carrying their leather-bound scrapbook.

Parked outside were two cars. One was large and seemed to be filled to the brim. The other was smaller and contained only two people. Kit nodded to both as he passed them.

They arrived at a four-storey red brick house with a large black door. It was connected to the Church of the Immaculate Conception, a vaulted Gothic-style building run by Jesuits. They walked up the steps to the door.

A housekeeper opened the door and led the party through to the dining room. Waiting for them was Vaughan. If he was surprised by the number of people who'd come with Kit, he did not show it. Instead, he acted the perfect host and shook hands with everyone.

The dining room was large, dark, and austere. It seemed, unaccountably to Kit, Catholic. This was not solely because of the large wooden crucifix on the wall or the painting of Our Lady of Perpetual Help. Nor indeed was it the painting of Pope Benedict XV looking like the artist had just interrupted him reading Wittgenstein. The room had a spiritual dimension, a seriousness that Kit rarely encountered elsewhere. He wondered for a moment if there really was a 'something 'about the room or whether it was merely his expectation that it should be like this.

On the sideboard there was a small, framed photograph of Father Vaughan standing beside a biplane wearing flying goggles. He'd flown over to Flanders to meet the soldiers during the War. Father Vaughan caught Kit staring at the picture. They looked at one another for a moment but no reference was made to the trip. Then the priest surveyed his guests with a welcoming smile.

'I suspect there are more to come,' said Vaughan knowingly to Kit.

'May I get you a drink?' asked the housekeeper to Agatha and Betty.

'Yes, a brandy would be just the thing, my dear,' said Agatha.

The housekeeper stopped and stared at Agatha and then glanced mournfully down at the jug of water sitting on the table. Her eyes met Father Vaughan who wore an amused expression. He nodded to her, and she left to the room to prepare brandies for the ladies.

Kit replied to Father Vaughan that more were expected. As he said this, the sound of knocking echoed down the corridor and into the room. A few moments later, Chief Inspector Jellicoe and Sergeant Wellbeloved entered the room. The latter was a surprise to Kit. Not a pleasant one, either. He exchanged looks with the Chief Inspector. If Jellicoe looked unhappy about having a partner such as Wellbeloved then it was unlikely anyone would be able to recognise the difference from his normal disposition.

Introductions were made. Jellicoe looked at Kit and said with what might have been a wry smile, 'This is somewhat unusual, your lordship.'

Kit nodded but there was no smile. This meeting was more than unusual. It was probably unprecedented. There was another rap on the door and the housekeeper, Mrs Tring, gave a loud sigh that prompted amusement in the room to all who heard it. Even Father Vaughan, a man who made the Chief Inspector seem positively jovial by comparison, allowed himself a smile.

The door to the room opened a minute later. Wag McDonald and Alice Diamond entered. There were no handshakes, no introductions. The new entrants merely nodded to those assembled and sat at the large dining room table. Alice Diamond's attention was instantly drawn to Mary Cavendish. The two young women sized one another up like gunfighters in a saloon.

'Excellent,' said Kit rising to his feet. 'We're all here.'

He looked around and was immediately struck by the thought that this felt like a moment from that most elevated of literary forms.

'In the penny bloods that my aunt is so fond of reading, this is normally the end. The moment when the killer is revealed. Alas, we're not quite in this position yet. However, we are all holding pieces of a large and rather disturbing jigsaw puzzle which means that we all, no matter how we may feel towards one another in the general way of things, must work together. There is a common enemy. A dangerous, malicious and murderous enemy.'

Kit paused and again looked around. Wag McDonald and Alice were sitting across the table from the two detectives. The two sides looked at one another, neither prepared to give an inch in the intensity of their gaze.

'This is, possibly, an unprecedented moment when, one might say, the two sides of the law must work together. Do I have your agreement that, for the moment, whatever hostility you are feeling will cease for the duration of this investigation?'

All eyes turned towards Chief Inspector Jellicoe. He nodded. Kit looked at Wag McDonald. He gave a curt nod.

'Not sure it'll hold up in court,' continued Kit. 'But a contract of sorts.'

Kit walked over towards his aunt and Betty Simpson and stood behind them. This somewhat disconcerted Agatha as it meant she could not see her nephew. It was not her way to disguise irritation when it was possible to communicate it to the world. There were a few smiles from both sides of the table at her reaction.

'My interest in this case began a day or two ago. It comes from His Majesty's Government.'

'Who?' asked Wag McDonald.

The Medium Murders

'I can't say Mr McDonald although as you had someone follow me this morning, I'm surprised you don't already know.'

'You lost him.'

Kit smiled and shrugged modestly.

'I've had occasion to do this sort of thing before. I only mention it as this case, whilst tragic in its outcome for so many young women, has wider implications which could result in our country being blackmailed by either a foreign power or…' Kit paused for a moment and tried to think of the best way of describing ORCA, an organisation he had encountered in previous cases.

'Or some other organisation dedicated to terror and anarchism. The minister in question is aware that the threads of this case are intertwined with other cases that date back quite some time. I told him that this is not the beginning of the end, merely the end of the beginning. We have much to do and it begins this afternoon. We must share what we know. We will listen to our host, Father Vaughan, who has some knowledge of the area we are dealing with. Specifically, the occult or Satanism. Call it what you will. These people are dangerous and must be stopped.'

Kit looked towards the two detectives.

'Chief Inspector, how many cases do we believe are connected to this recent murder?'

Jellicoe had a file sitting on the table in front of him. He turned to Wellbeloved.

'Sergeant?'

Wellbeloved did not need to look at it. Instead, he gazed back at Kit before answering.

'Thirteen.'

There was almost a collective gasp at the number. It was unimaginable that so many women could have been murdered without so much as a word in the press connecting the deaths. Even the Chief Inspector, noted Kit, seemed surprised by the number. This was for another time, as was the reason why several murders had remained unconnected for so long.

'They were all young women. All murdered in a ritual manner with the same markings on the body. The first recorded case was in Bournemouth in December 1907. There was at least one every year until 1914 and then none until earlier this year when they recommenced. Enid Blake was the second one this year.'

'Which is where Mr McDonald and Miss Diamond come into the picture,' said Kit, taking over. 'Enid was a friend of Miss Diamond and Mr McDonald. Once again, I'm sorry for your loss.'

Mary looked on, fascinated by the mix of personalities around the table. At the mention of Enid Blake, she became distinctly aware of the look that Alice Diamond gave Sergeant Wellbeloved. There was no anger or antagonism in the look. If anything, it was sympathy.

'Her death, the first of Miss Diamond's associates…'

'The second,' said Wag McDonald.

The Medium Murders

Once again there was a stunned silence. McDonald raised his eyebrows to Jellicoe, but it was clearly news to the Chief Inspector.

'Liza Shepherd. 1913.'

The mention of the name caused a flurry of activity from Betty Simpson, whose fingers leafed through the scrapbook with a nimbleness and a speed that belied her seventy plus years. She found the page just as Jellicoe spoke.

'We weren't aware that she was one of your associates.' Jellicoe opened the file, found the page referring to Liza Shepherd and made some notes on the page.

'Liza and Enid were both working the maid game. They'd find work in a big house, get to know the layout, what was worth stealing. Then they'd leave for some reason or another. A few weeks later the house would be visited by someone like your manservant, your lordship.'

There were a few wry smiles at this, but they lasted momentarily. The atmosphere was too heavy, the subject too serious and the cause too urgent.

'We'll need the names of the last places Miss Blake worked,' said Jellicoe.

Alice Diamond nodded. The transition from suspicion to business happened almost without anyone realising. Kit moved away from Agatha and stood near Father Vaughan.

'Before we hear from Father Vaughan, I think we should hear more about the involvement of Eva Kerr.'

'Must we?' said Father Vaughan. This brought a ghost of a smile from Jellicoe.

'Yes, Father,' replied Kit. 'Whatever you may think of this woman, medium or whatever she may be, the plain fact is she has led the police to the scene of two murders. There's no suggestion that the first murder is connected to these ritual killings, Chief Inspector, is there?'

'None, the victim was male,' replied Jellicoe.

'I see. Can you tell us what manner of medium she is?'

'A fake,' whispered Father Vaughan.

Jellicoe turned to Wellbeloved. The sergeant cleared his throat and began to speak.

'Miss Kerr claims to have an out-of-the-body experience. She does speak to the other side in a séance, as far as we understand, but not on these occasions. She claims not to know how she sees these visions. They come to her sometimes, but not always, when she is in a meditative state.'

'Astral travel is bunkum,' announced Father Vaughan. Kit frowned and looked back towards Wellbeloved.

'These visions,' pressed Kit, 'How accurate were they?'

'She did not provide names and addresses, your lordship,' said Wellbeloved, which caused a ripple of amusement. 'However, her description of the people and the locations where we found the bodies was remarkably accurate.'

'May I meet her?' asked Kit to Jellicoe.

'If I may, I would like to talk to you in private about that,' replied Jellicoe.

Kit turned to Father Vaughan. The priest, thus far, had confined himself to just a few remarks around his scepticism towards the medium. He looked up at Kit.

'The floor seems to be mine. Very well. I won't add anything further to my remarks on Eva Kerr. Instead, I wish to speak about Satanism as we understand this cult. Specifically, I will address the role of sacrifice. I repeat, this cult has no spiritual basis. They can no more call upon the powers of Satan than a medium practicing necromancy can call upon the dead to ask them how they're enjoying life on the other side.'

There was no attempt to disguise his hostility to the practice. Vaughan was a sceptic and he wanted everyone in the room to share his scepticism.

'These people are well-versed in folklore. They are serious students of the Occult. Their activities often find expression in Black Magic or the Black Mass. This is a parody of the Roman Catholic mass dating back to the Middle Ages. It's merely an excuse for practicing the very worst sort of depravity. On certain occasions such as the two Solstices, All Hallows Eve and St Walpurgis's Eve, on April 30th, it can result in murder of young, unmarried women. I suspect not many of the victims had reached the age of twenty-one.'

'Do any of the dates of the other deaths or ages tally with Father Vaughan's evaluation?' asked Kit.

Everyone looked at Jellicoe but, oddly, it was Betty Simpson who spoke first. Her eyes were glued to the scrapbook in front of her.

'My goodness, most of them seem to be around either All Hallows Eve or St. Walpurgis's Night. There are one, no, two that took place during the summer solstice. Some other dates, too, by the looks of things. Nothing about the ages, I'm afraid.'

Betty looked up and directed her attention towards the two policemen. Jellicoe nodded to Betty and then spoke.

'There are only two exceptions, but, yes, all of the deaths are on or around the dates mentioned by Father Vaughan. We can only speculate as to the other murders, but it may have been to silence troublemakers or some initiation. From what I can remember, few of the victims were as old as twenty-one'

Agatha had been following proceedings with a keen eye levelled at each speaker. If either the police or Wag McDonald were wondering why there were two old ladies in the room these questions were finally put to bed when Agatha spoke.

The Medium Murders

'I don't understand why the murders are related to either solstice. Surely this relates to druids. They worship a much older god, the sun.'

Father Vaughan held his hands up and acknowledged the truth of this statement.

'Yes, but Satanism and druidism have no original scripture surviving in the way the monotheistic religions have. They are entirely modern constructions using texts created in the Middle Ages. In fact, the vogue for Satanism may have been prompted by a recent French book by Huysmans, La-Bas.'

'French? I should have known,' said Agatha. 'I doubt the French Satan is any way repelled by garlic.'

Father Vaughan allowed himself a smile.

'I doubt the real Satan would be put off by any of the charms and devices these old texts believe fend him off.'

'So, if we may conclude, Father Vaughan,' said Agatha, 'These practitioners are performing ceremonies of their own invention. We are, in no way, facing anything remotely spiritual or occult.'

'We are not.'

Agatha leaned forward. This was always a prelude, in Kit's experience, to a question of unusual perspicacity.

'But do the practitioners believe this?'

Father Vaughan leaned back and smiled. He nodded an acknowledgement to Agatha.

'I cannot say for certain, Lady Frost. Faith is a strange and misunderstood idea. There is no reason to suppose that many of the neophytes are not true believers. However, once you reach more senior levels of, and I use the word guardedly, enlightenment, who knows what you believe? This order is called Ipsissimus. At this level you are, theoretically, free from limitations. I daresay they believe themselves free of morality. The men, and we must assume they are men, committing these crimes, will be, I am certain, at the level of Ipsissimus.'

'And it is always women who suffer.'

Mary's words stunned the room. Not just because it was Mary. Not just because it was clearly the voice of a young woman. It was also because it was a statement rather than a question. Until this point, she had been silent. However, the words themselves, the suppressed anger in the voice and her youthful innocence brought everyone back to a sense of what was at stake.

'And it is always women who suffer,' repeated Father Vaughan in confirmation.

A sense of despondency fell on the room. Anger, too.

'Towards the end of the 1880's,' continued Vaughan, 'there was an organisation formed called the Hermetic Order of the Golden Dawn. It was devoted to the study of the Occult. It was rather like the Masonic order in its hierarchy and initiation practices. Many people who you will have heard of were members. The poet Yeats, Doyle probably, the actress Florence Farr. The intention was not, I believe, malevolent. They sought spiritual enlightenment. The source documents were probably fake, however. My point, though, is that the Order broke up at the start of the century and its followers splintered into various groups. I believe the murders we are seeing may have been perpetrated by a member of one of these splinter groups.'

Silence.

The implication was clear to everyone. Kit, finally, gave voice to the thoughts circulating around the room.

'We have a number of murders of young women, committed by people from the highest levels in society, covered up by those same strata and a two-decade old police investigation that has made little progress. Thank you, Father Vaughan. I think that just about covers where we are now. It gives us several avenues for inquiry. The next question for us to decide is how we shall work together.'

Kit turned towards Agatha and Betty. Both looked as if they should have been taking tea in a drawing room. In fact, they were both, at that moment, finishing off their respective glasses of brandy with some relish. Agatha nodded her approval to Father Vaughan.

'I have had some thoughts on how we approach, well, to be more accurate, my aunt has suggested some of this. Aunt Agatha?'

'Ah yes. Speaking with my nephew earlier...' She paused for a moment, aware that Mary was looking at her askance.

'You were in bed, my dear, otherwise you would have been welcome to join us.'

Kit shrugged as Mary looked at him archly. Agatha continued her train of thought.

'Where was I? Oh yes. It's clear that these vile acts are being perpetrated by people who are in the higher social echelons, aristocracy, even. As a member of this class, I can confirm that their ability to close ranks is without equal. The police are unlikely to make much of a dent on the walls of this citadel. To continue the analogy, we need a Trojan horse. My proposal is simple. Betty and I will seek to become members of groups who are involved with spiritualism under the guise of wishing to communicate with our husbands. This will provide, we believe, a possible opening to identify potential practitioners of the dark arts referred to by Father Vaughan.'

'What makes you think that the spiritualist groups are in any way connected to Satanists?' asked Chief Inspector Jellicoe.

Moments later, something landed on the table on front of him, thrown by Kit. Taken by surprise, Jellicoe glanced up at Kit and then picked up the object. After a few moments of examination he asked, 'Where did you find this, your lordship?'

He held the object up so that everyone present could see. It was a small collar. Something you would put on a pet. Attached to the collar was a silver star.

The Medium Murders

'But this is an inverted pentagram,' said Father Vaughan, leaning forward suddenly.

'I know,' said Kit. 'And it's been under my nose for the last day or two. The collar was worn by a cat named Simpkins. He belonged to the late Countess Laskov. Simpkins appears to have moved into my flat. A remarkable coincidence which I doubt any penny blood writer would ever get away with, but true all the same.'

Jellicoe stared down at the cat collar. From the moment he'd entered the flat of Countess Laskov he'd sensed an atmosphere. The walls whispered as they often did for him at a crime scene. Yet no crime had been committed. The death of the countess had been from natural causes. Now this would have to be checked.

For the moment, he was struck by the situation he was in. Madness, really. Sitting with the aristocracy on one side and known criminals on the other. All of them seeking a common enemy. He shook his head.

'Chief Inspector? Is there something you wish to add?' asked Kit, observing Jellicoe.

'What you're proposing is, with respect of course, madness.'

'Do you have an alternative plan?'

Jellicoe looked up sharply at Kit. The tone had been harder than he deemed appropriate given the company they were in. It was clear that Kit was in no mood to apologise. It was equally clear that there was no alternative plan.

Jack Murray

The room was silent. All watched in fascination at the battle of wills between the two men. It was Father Vaughan who spoke next.

'It's a fair question, Chief Inspector. I think that the police should consider accepting help from whatever source is available. Especially if it means ending these vile crimes.'

Jellicoe finally nodded. His reluctance was evident. Unspoken, however, was the inevitability of his giving way. Kit was working for the government in a matter that was potentially of national importance. Jellicoe knew there was little choice but to cooperate.

'Then, if we are all in agreement, a cease fire will be in place. What we discuss going forward will not be used in the future against one another. Yes?'

All around the table there were nods of agreement. Kit turned to Wag McDonald and Alice Diamond.

'Your role will be pivotal in terms of information gathering.'

The head of the Elephant Boys and the leader of the forty thieves looked at one another and then at Jellicoe. Alice Diamond cleared her throat. Looking directly at the Chief Inspector, she said, 'With no come back on us. Right?'

Everyone turned to Jellicoe. He nodded before adding a question.

'How will you obtain this information?'

The Medium Murders

Alice Diamond smiled. It would be fair to say the smile lacked a certain sunniness one associates with the smarter sex. The eyes were too shrewd, too knowing, too hard to allow such light to enter the dark, uncertain world where she lived.

'Some of my girls are working in houses now. My girls have friends, sisters, cousins in service. Quite a lot of people.'

She looked up at Kit, who took over at this point.

'Miss Diamond will be able to find out if any of the rich families where her associates have connections are exhibiting, shall we say, strange behaviour. This will be communicated directly to you, Chief Inspector.'

'If I may ask, your lordship, what will your involvement be?'

Kit smiled and replied, 'Of course you have a right to know. I have a list of people. High ranking people. They may be able to shed light on one of the murders from 1908. As you will appreciate, I am not at liberty to say more than that. Anything that can be used to expedite this case will, naturally, be communicated to you immediately.'

This was not a comfortable message to communicate. It felt too much like Kit was buttressing the conspiracy which had prevented news of these killings reaching the public.

'As you may have surmised, Chief Inspector,' said Kit, 'we'll need to understand more about the Hermetic

Order of the Golden Dawn, their members, what became of the splinter groups. I am certain Kell at MI5(g) will be able to help on this.'

The meeting had reached a conclusion, albeit one that Jellicoe was visibly uncomfortable about. There were no farewells between the two sides. They left in silence. Only Kit and his party remained.

The housekeeper appeared and asked if there was anything, she could bring the guests. Betty Simpson picked up the brandy glass and raised her eyebrows hopefully.

'I think you've had quite enough, Betty, my dear,' said Agatha.

15

The group arrived back at the Grosvenor Square residence around eight o'clock. The sound of jazz music danced up the stairs. Agatha and Natalie exchanged knowing looks which intrigued Kit. He glanced towards Mary who raised her eyebrows.

'It sounds as if the party is underway then,' said Kit. 'Are Lady Esther and Dr Bright here?'

'No, your lordship, they went out an hour ago to dinner.'

'Shall I go down to Monsieur Fish and ask him to turn down the volume of the music?' asked Natalie.

Agatha shook her head and said, 'No, I shall.' The tone was soft, not harsh, or condemnatory.

This surprised Kit and Mary somewhat. Moments later they were alone in the room. They listened for a few seconds to the sound of Agatha's footsteps descending the stairs.

'Strange,' said Kit.

Moments later he felt a pair of arms around his neck. In such a situation, there is only one way for a gentleman to respond and Kit was nothing if not a gentleman. Duty required a prolonged display of his devotion although, in truth, Kit discharged his obligations with an equal if not greater enthusiasm than the object of his affection.

'I was particularly interested in Father Vaughan's point around the age of the women,' said Mary some minutes later.

'Picked up on that myself.'

'Interesting, don't you think?'

'The only conclusion one can draw is that I am in a wonderful position to provide you with protection against all manner of evil spirits and wrongdoers.'

'It will require a great forfeit on your part,' said Mary.

'You have my assurance that I would not be thinking of myself. Your safety is paramount.'

The conversation was brought to a premature conclusion by the sound of the front door opening and footsteps outside in the hall. Richard and Esther entered the drawing room arm in arm, laughing.

'You can't stay out of trouble, by the sounds of it. Either of you, in fact,' said Bright, smiling.

Kit shrugged and acknowledged the truth of this. However, he was more interested in hearing about Bright's plans.

'I doubt I will be fixed up with anything before the new year. I've had my fill of being a locum. I'd like something more permanent now but definitely not Harley Street.'

'I'm sure you could find a hospital to take you on.'

The Medium Murders

Bright looked uncertain. The idea of working in a hospital had some appeal but it was a treadmill. He wasn't sure if he was ready for the politics either and said as much.

'I don't want to sound like Mr Micawber, but I'm sure something will turn up.'

In fact, the next thing to turn up was perhaps not what Micawber had in mind. Aunt Agatha bustled into the room. The music downstairs had stopped.

'I say, Aunt Agatha, you didn't have to ask Fish to stop listening to his gramophone,' said Kit.

'Oh, I didn't. He's taken to reading some of my detective books of late.'

'How very elevating,' said Kit with a grin.

Agatha fixed him with a glare but did not deign to honour the slur with any form of reply. Instead, she returned to the business in hand.

'What's happening next?'

Kit looked somewhat unhappy; a fact picked up by Mary.

'Is something wrong?'

'I'll let you know tomorrow,' replied Kit somewhat grimly. I must be away first thing but then I thought we would head down to Bournemouth to see the Earl of Gresham. We can catch the midday train from Waterloo.'

Agatha shook her head and said, 'You and Mary will have to handle that. I want to stay here and get things going with Betty.'

Kit and Mary looked at one another. This was something of a surprise and, if Kit read Mary right, which he certainly had, it presented all manner of considerations.

'Of course, Natalie can accompany you,' added Agatha, a heartbeat later.

This put an end to the delightfully inappropriate train of thought that was travelling at runaway speed through the minds of the soon-to-be-married-but-not-soon-enough couple.

'Great idea,' said Kit with as much enthusiasm as he could muster which caused a coughing fit in Bright as he fought to contain his laughter.

'Will you be able to cope without Natalie here?' asked Mary, more in hope than expectation.

Agatha's expression was an exquisite combination of derision matched with no little sense of having been affronted.

'Fish and I coped well enough this last decade. I see no reason why we can't manage another day or two.'

Having made her point, Agatha did what aunts tend to do in these situations. She spun around and made a grand exit.

'And that's told you, Mary,' said Esther, wagging her finger. Then her face became more solemn. There was

The Medium Murders

so much going through her mind and to utter what she was thinking would have seemed, at best, petty and, at worst, callous.

Mary sensed the conflict within Esther and held her hand.

'Don't worry Essie. With Kit's help I'll have this case cracked and we can have a wonderful time enjoying your last few weeks of freedom.'

'I hope that I can give you the support you need,' said Kit nobly to his friend, Bright.

'I'm sure you shall, old man,' replied Bright. 'However, I hope these last few weeks of freedom, as you call it, does not necessitate further nights out dancing at Dalton's.'

'You went to Dalton's?' The question from Kit was more accusatory than the tone or the smile that accompanied it.

Mary smiled and shrugged innocently to Kit.

'Maybe we'll run into my new beau down in Bournemouth.'

'I think the Honourable Mr Andrews would be best advised to stay clear,' replied Kit. 'I had Harry make some reservations at Highcliffe Mansions for us. We can use it as a base to see Gresham and the other name you managed to extract from Andrews, Mary.'

'Well done, Mary,' said Esther.

'Who is the other person in the area you're going to see?' asked Bright.

Mary and Kit exchanged glances. The answer lay heavy on Kit's heart.

'The Earl of Hertwood,' replied Kit. His face looked distant for a moment.

'His name is familiar,' said Bright. 'Why do I know him?'

'He's Olly Lake's father.'

16

'You knew and you didn't tell me,' said Kit, making no attempt to hide his anger.

Mansfield Smith-Cumming smiled a disingenuous smile. He seemed genuinely amused by Kit's reaction.

'Of course, I knew. It's my job.'

'So why not tell me? Why have me waste my time?' He was leaning over the table, glaring at "C".

'How else was I to know if you were the right man for the job?'

This took the wind out of Kit's sails somewhat. A problem of Kit's, since childhood, had been his ability to hold both sides of an argument simultaneously in his head. The advantages tended to outweigh the disadvantages except in situations such as this. In fact, he genuinely felt at a loss on how to respond to the wily head of British Intelligence.

Finally, for want of anything more intelligent, he said, 'So this was a job interview?'

'I suppose that's one way of looking at it. I must congratulate you, though. You pieced it together within two days.'

'We've lost two days you mean.'

'There's been no further contact with our rather worried Secretary of War, so I'm unconcerned about any delay. Anyway, I gather that not only have you demonstrated some impressive powers of deduction; you seem to have assembled a rather unusual coalition. '

'How did you know that? Are you having me followed?'

Smith-Cumming shrugged benignly.

'I understand I wasn't the only one who had this idea,' said Smith-Cumming.

'I lost him.'

'So, I gather. Thankfully, our man applied himself a little more assiduously to the task in hand.'

This topic of discussion was now exhausted. The next topic was obvious.

'May I ask what else you haven't been telling me?'

"C" handed Kit a folder. It was thicker than the original one. Kit picked it up and quickly leafed through it. Inside were all the victims. The full horror began to soak through to Kit as he saw name after name. All young women. Some had photographs attached. A quick scan of their birthdates confirmed all were under the age of twenty- one. It looked remarkably like the one that Jellicoe brought the previous day.

'How was something like this kept a secret? It dwarfs what Jack the Ripper did.'

"C" removed his monocle and wiped it. Replacing it, he studied Kit.

The Medium Murders

'An obvious analogy. Perhaps, there is some comparison, I warrant. As to why it has been kept secret, Kit, do you really need me to answer that?'

Kit shook his head grimly. The answer was all too clear. Ostensibly there were practical considerations. A desire to avoid creating panic. An even greater desire to discourage copycat killings or the usual collection of fools wanting to confess. However, a more objectionable reason had long since risen in Kit's mind.

There was silence in the office. A bird landed on the windowsill and squawked. Both men turned to the bird and then back to one another. Smith-Cumming, like Kit, came from the upper reaches of society. His father was a banker. He'd married an heiress. The crimes they were investigating had been committed by people like them.

'God forbid the lower orders should get wind of the fact that their betters are making a sport of their murder,' said Kit.

'Not quite how I would've put it, Kit,' said "C", 'but essentially correct.'

The two men regarded one another again. Mansfield Smith-Cumming made Russian dolls the very epitome of transparency. Evidently, Kit had been given all he would be given from "C".

'What is your plan?'

Kit rose and walked towards the door. He stopped and turned around.

'I'm going down to Bournemouth. Both Gresham and Hertwood live relatively close by.'

'Hertwood,' said "C" grimly. 'That could be an awkward conversation. I gather he hasn't shown his face at Sheldon's since the beginning of the year.'

'Can hardly blame him.'

'Are you sure he's not in league with his son?'

'You tell me,' replied Kit.

Smith-Cumming laughed. It started as a bark but became more of a chuckle. He looked up at Kit warmly.

'We don't know if truth be told. I think it unlikely. We have a man keeping tabs on him, of course, should Olly Lake reappear. I'm not sure what sort of welcome you'll have, given that you unmasked his son as an anarchist.'

'As it happens, I was thinking along similar lines. To this end, I do have one request to make.'

'By all means. If I can help you, I shall.'

It was one of Mansfield-Cummings great qualities that no one, even those with whom he disagreed, could ever feel angry with him for long. His reaction to Kit's request was to laugh for several minutes. He was not alone in his laughter.

On his way down the stairs, Kit called in on 'Spunky' Stevens. His friend was gazing idly out of the window down onto the park. Kit walked up behind him and

The Medium Murders

noted what his friend was staring at. The young lady in question was walking her dog.

Accompanying her was a formidably forbidding older woman dressed in battle tweed. Her glare had already sent two men scurrying for cover having committed the heinous crime of doffing their hats.

'I see her quite regularly at this time,' said Spunky, sensing Kit's presence.

'Well defended, I see.'

'Heavy armaments. I don't think a frontal assault will yield success.'

'It may need a flanking attack.'

'Working on it,' said Spunky turning around as the young lady and her mother-aunt-guardian disappeared.

Kit showed Spunky the file "C" had given him. A few unSpunky-like words followed which confirmed all of this was news to him. Kit believed him. It was entirely probable that "C" would have kept this information from Spunky. Kit mentioned the test "C" had put him through. This made Spunky laugh.

'You know what the old boy is like. Wheels within wheels.'

'I know too well,' said Kit. 'I'm surprised Dawn didn't mention anything to you.'

'Yes, well, that's all finished now. She returned to her fiancé. The wedding's in January.'

Jack Murray

It would be fair to say that Spunky was bearing up manfully to the end of his love affair, so Kit decided there was little point in showing sympathy.

'Did you get an invitation?'

'Funnily enough, no. I say, old chum, what have you got Aunt Betty working on? I called up yesterday evening and she tells me that she's hand in glove with you on this case. Wasn't exactly forthcoming on what. I have to say, old chum, you should really give a chap a bit of advance notice on these things. I felt like a damn fool.'

'Are you concerned?'

'No, far from it. She and your aunt have probably forgotten more about this sort of thing than we'll ever know.'

Kit was surprised by this but had other things he wanted to speak to his friend about. He stayed for another ten minutes before heading downstairs and out onto Holland Park. He noted with some amusement that the object of Spunky's attention was walking towards him. She was still accompanied by their Labrador and the older lady, who Kit judged to be a welterweight.

For amusement, Kit nobly raised his hat to them both and was rewarded by a sweet smile and two scowls: one from the older woman and one, for good measure, from the dog. As they went by Kit glanced up to the third-floor window of the Secret Intelligence Service villa. Spunky smiled down at him and saluted. Kit gave his friend the thumbs up, laughing as he did so.

The Medium Murders

Waterloo Station was still a building site for the most part. The station was situated on Waterloo South Bank, near the Thames. As he walked towards the entrance, Kit marvelled at how such a busy station could operate in what seemed to be chaos. The construction of the victory arch entrance was still incomplete forcing Kit to take another route into the main station.

Arriving on the main concourse, he spied Mary standing with Natalie underneath the large, newly installed clock with four faces. A few other people had the same idea of using the position directly underneath the new clock as a meeting point. It was not difficult to spot the two young women. Both were attracting the attention of many passers-by. Mary was dressed in a camel-coloured coat. Each wore a cloche hat. Natalie was dressed head to foot in black. At their feet were two small overnight bags. Although Natalie was slightly taller and Mary slimmer, from a distance they might have passed for sisters.

Mary waved and smiled when she saw Kit coming. That smile. He never tired of seeing it. As he considered his manifest good fortune a dark shadow crossed his mind. Thoughts of the young, murdered women rose unbidden. He felt a cold chill for a few moments. Long enough for Mary to see the change. Her eyes narrowed momentarily.

'Is everything, all right?'

'Yes darling,' replied Kit, unabashed at telling a fib. He smiled and pointed in the direction of their platform.

'Shall we?'

Mary did not look like she believed him, but another thought entered her mind.

'Isn't Harry coming with us to Bournemouth?'

Kit held up the second suitcase and smiled enigmatically.

'He is, but he'll meet us there.'

This was suitably ambiguous and obviously designed to irritate a curiosity as immense as Mary's. It did. Just as Mary was about to beat a confession out of Kit with her umbrella, she saw a half smile on his face. Mary contented herself with aiming the point of her umbrella at Kit's chest.

'No prizes for guessing where this will go if you don't tell me what's on your mind when we're on the train.'

The train journey lasted two and a half hours. Kit, Mary, and Natalie sat together in a carriage with a vicar, a governess and what looked like a retired army officer. It didn't take a psychic to work out what was on Mary's mind regarding their travel companions. At the end of the journey Kit asked her.

'Which one was the murderer?'

'The man pretending to be a vicar.'

'How so?'

'His hands.'

'I noted there were two of them,' said Kit. 'Did I miss anything else?'

'They were not the hands of a vicar,' said Mary.

'Which are?'

'More delicate. Refined. Those were the hands of strangler. Or a workman.'

'Is there a difference in your world?' said Kit, as they exited the station. Outside, Kit hailed a cab.

Mary smiled at her fiancé and said, 'Sometimes you can be sorely lacking in imagination.'

'I've found that evidence tends to work better in the conviction of our criminal classes.'

'Imagination is to evidence as the stars were to ancient sailors,' replied Mary primly. They were both giggling as the cab took them away from the station. The journey to their hotel was only a few minutes.

Highcliffe Mansions overlooked the golden sands of Bournemouth. It was perched at the top of the cliff with a view that encompassed everything from the pier and the beach to a horizon of blue sea. In summer.

Mary stood as close to the edge as she dared and scanned the horizon. Wind blew into her face. She had to hold onto her hat as a gust threatened to blow it away. Her laughter rippled through the air like water bubbling in a brook in mid-summer.

She turned and looked up at the whitewashed walls of the hotel standing starkly against the cloudless early afternoon sky.

'Shall we check into our room?' said Mary, a suggestive smile on her lips.

'Rooms.'

'Ah yes, I was forgetting Natalie.'

Kit raised his eyebrows as he watched his fiancée make her way towards the hotel entrance.

'I'm sure you were,' said Kit to himself as he followed the two women inside.

After they each received their keys, Kit and Mary walked up the stairs hand in hand.

'What time is the Earl expecting us?'

'Seven, I believe.'

'When will we see Harry?'

'I suspect it won't be until around this time tomorrow.'

They reached their floor and ambled along the corridor. Mary looked at the carpet. The design was a hideous deep red shield and gold leaf. She found she wasn't very interested in it. Glancing upward, she noticed the paintings on the wall were a mixture of landscapes and equestrian art. These held no interest for her, either.

In fact, her entire focus was now on her breathing. Unaccountably, it was becoming something of a challenge. This may have had something to do with the fact that her heart was beating like the bass drum in a brass band. She felt a slight draught on her face which gave her a slight chill all over her body.

The Medium Murders

They reached their respective rooms.

'I expect Natalie will be along soon with your bag,' said Kit, brightly.

Mary smiled up at Kit.

'I think she may be a while.'

Kit's frown was an attractive mix of amusement and curiosity.

'Why?' he asked.

'Because she's French.'

17

The motorcycle clipped along the empty country road at fifty miles an hour. Miller was tempted to go faster but decided against it. The risk of meeting a heifer strolling lazily onto the road was too great. The ride down from London had started very early in the morning and taken him through parts of London he was glad to have left behind.

Now he was in the country and his spirits rose in direct correlation to every mile he was further away from London. The sky was cloudless. The stars glimmered brightly, and the moon acted like a giant spotlight.

Whether it was the dark or the emptiness of the roads or something yet indiscernible, the journey was a chance for Miller to think. As much as he enjoyed being with his lordship, he wondered what the future would hold. The wedding would take place in February. However, no mention had been made of how or where they would all live.

It was not that he was ready to leave. Far from it. He enjoyed the job too much. How could he not? And then he thought again about tonight. No, the job had proved to be the best thing that had ever happened to him. The gut-wrenching fear he had felt that night three years ago when he had crawled out into No Man's Land had changed two lives forever.

The fresh country air and the lack of people appealed to Harry Miller, born nearly twenty-seven years previously in Peckham. The smell of the air was different. Miller found he couldn't drink enough of it. It seemed to be tinted blue or green. An independent life form just like the trees, the cattle, and the crops he was passing by.

At this moment Miller felt as content as he could remember feeling. Happiness is fleeting though. You should kiss joy as it flies, wrote the poet. Miller remembered his lordship quoting a poem by a man called Blake. Miller agreed with the sentiment. The moment we feel happiest is the moment the first cloud usually appears.

It did so with Miller. The image of Ida came into his mind as it did often these days. Those days in Paris seemed like a lifetime ago. Miller forced his thoughts away from her and back to the road. Riding a motorcycle was fun albeit a tad dangerous. He had to keep his mind on what was in front of him.

Around twenty minutes later, three hours after he had set off, Miller saw the first sign that he was nearing his destination. On the crest of a hill, he saw some large stones standing upright. Miller slowed down to get a better look at Stonehenge. He'd heard of it, of course.

His basic schooling had given him some history. When his lordship had told him of the new mission, he'd gone to the library and found out a little more.

He pulled over to the side of the road and climbed off the bike. Moments later he was clambering over the low perimeter fence and walking up the slight incline to the stones. He could see a few pilgrim lamps in the distance. He stopped and sat down on the grass around fifty yards from the outer perimeter of the prehistoric circle. It was now around three forty in the morning. A low mist had descended shrouding the base of the stone monoliths.

As the sunrise approached, the number of the people carrying lamps gradually increased. There was a mixture of men and women but no more than thirty or forty in total. Most were clad in overcoats. A small group of around five people wore white robes. Their faces were hidden by what Miller guessed were false beards. He looked at them and felt like laughing. Overall, he decided it would not be a good idea. Rising reluctantly from the grass he walked slowly towards the pilgrims.

With each step forward he felt a queer, sickening thrill pass through him. He put his hand in his pocket and felt for the reassuring presence of metal, the keys of his motorcycle. Miller noticed a few other stragglers like him approaching the stone circle. This was a relief.

The five robed figures were now in the centre of the henge. Miller sensed that the light was beginning to change. Night was beginning to give way to the day. A light wind rose from nowhere. The only sound he could hear was the clicking of the lamps against the poles and the rustle of leaves in the trees. No one looked at him as he joined the circle. All eyes were fixed on the priests.

The oddness of what he was witnessing was made more eerie by the utter absence of noise. It gave him a sense that something inhuman was impending. He felt a prickling sensation on his skin and his palms began to sweat a little despite the chill. In truth, if he could have run, he would have, and he was not a man easily given to fear. But his legs were rooted to the spot even if his heart was not.

As the first rays of sunlight broke through the stones one of the druid priests let out a cry which caused Miller to jump halfway out of his skin. He crouched immediately ready for a fight, flight, or both.

The autumn equinox had begun.

Several of the others in the crowd joined in the chant. Miller glanced at a man standing near him. They exchanged looks. Beside him was a young and not unattractive woman with long golden hair, dressed in Saxon costume. Unlike the man holding her hand, she was chanting with the others. The man noticed that Miller was as perplexed by the whole business as he was. His mouth formed a half smile, and he rolled his eyes in the way chaps do when they know their better half is probably right but for the life of them, they can't see how. A mixture of duty, uncertainty and a desire for an easy life forbade further enquiry on the part of said chap.

Miller nodded and mouthed, 'Good luck.'

The man grinned back and mouthed a thank you.

The chanting reached a climax, quite literally if the look on the faces of some people was anything to go by. The level of excitement in the crowd was at a pitch and some of the pilgrims started dancing as the sun appeared into view. This had the odd effect of relaxing Miller who was able to focus his attention on the apparent leaders of this eccentric group of sun worshippers.

After an hour of excruciating singing and incomprehensible chants, the revellers began to disappear. Whether through exhaustion or, more likely, the whittling away of their audience, the druid priests decided to end the ceremony.

Miller followed them at a distance. Luckily, he was one among many. It appeared that the modern druid relied less on being carried by celestial spirits than they did on the modern motor car. And chauffeurs. Miller watched them disrobe at their cars, capturing to memory as much as he could of the individuals as well noting details of their cars.

He watched all the druids leave in a convoy before retracing his footsteps towards the henge and then onwards to where he had hidden his motorcycle. A few stragglers remained at the monument, but the plain was mostly empty. Within a few minutes, Miller was on his way again.

His journey took him south towards Salisbury. The spire of the cathedral hove into view. It was around seven in the morning and the town was still sleeping. Miller parked his bike in Choristers Square and sat in the grounds of the cathedral. An hour later the Bell Tower Tea Rooms opened, and he was able to have breakfast. Although replenished, the lack of sleep was getting to him. By nine he was back on his bike and heading towards his next destination: the estate of the Earl of Hertwood.

The journey took around half an hour. Part of the large estate encroached into the New Forest. Miller had been given specific instruction by Kit on where to go and rest up. It was clear from the directions provided by Kit that he was very familiar with the area. Many summers had been spent there with his friend Olly Lake. Miller had no problem locating the small hut in the middle of the forest. According to Kit, it had been built nearly two decades before by him and his former friend.

The hut was around six feet square and leaned against one of the large oak trees. Miller wheeled the bike to the other side of the oak and made a small fire using sticks and leaves. He had a long wait ahead. He knew there was no point in trying to deny himself sleep. Having warmed himself sufficiently, he put the fire out.

Ambling into the hut, he settled down into a bed of leaves and made himself comfortable.

Sleep came easily. A deep, dreamless sleep.

It was the crack of twigs that woke him up. He sat up startled. In the doorway was a man gazing down at him. It was difficult to tell with the sleep in his eyes, but it looked to Miller like he was holding a rifle.

18

'This looks like it here,' said Agatha pointing to a large townhouse. The two ladies had just driven through Regent's Park and up through the tree-lined streets of St John's Wood. On each side of the street were large, well-made houses.

'I gather this area is supposed to be improving.'

'Really?' replied Betty. 'You could fool me. I imagine it's full of artists, writers and actors and the like. Which is all very well, I suppose.'

Agatha glanced at her friend and assumed that it meant nothing of the sort.

Betty Simpson slowed the car down as they drove past the house spotted by Agatha. They could see a few people arriving at the entrance which further confirmed to them that they had the right place.

'Over there,' said Agatha, pointing to a car parking space.

'Yes, I'm not blind dear.'

'Just trying to help. You don't have to be like that.'

'I know you're just trying to help but perhaps if you could assume a modicum of intelligence on my part it would be a tremendous comfort to me.'

Agatha looked at her friend of over sixty years and shrugged her shoulders. This was part of their daily discourse. She reached into her handbag and pulled out a small silver hipflask. It was slightly larger than her hand and it glinted in the light. Agatha held it up for Betty to see.

'Dutch courage.'

'Good idea.

Betty parked the car and pulled out of her handbag a matching silver flask. They clinked flasks and prepared themselves spiritually, emotionally and, it must be said, liberally for battle. Duly fortified, they debouched from the car like two aunts going to a séance which, in this case, they were.

As they approached the house Betty whispered, 'Don't you think it has a certain atmosphere about it?'

'No, dear.'

The house was a low-built mansion with a carriage driveway and iron railing fence. There were four well-dressed people chatting outside. None of them was younger than forty. The group comprised three women, two of whom were at least as mature as the two aunts and an equally mature man.

'I don't recognise any of them,' said Agatha in a whisper.

'I don't either,' agreed Betty.

The two ladies were greeted with smiles from the group outside the house. Agatha and Betty put on their sunniest faces for the group and soon all were ascending a handful of steps towards the house.

Betty gave the door a vigorous rap which might have rocked a less solidly constructed house to its foundations. She received a nod of approval from Agatha. No point in keeping their arrival secret. This approach had stood Betty in good stead for many decades and worked a treat once more. The sound of feet running to the door was distinctly audible to the amused onlookers on the doorstep.

'Never fails,' confirmed Agatha, nodding to the others. The importance of establishing from the outset who was in charge was an article of faith for Agatha.

'Have you done this before?' asked Betty of one of the party as the door was opened by a butler.

The man and two of the older women nodded. The younger one looked a little sheepish and nervous. Clearly a first timer.

They stepped into the house. The hall was decorated, floor to ceiling, in the current art deco style. Agatha did her best not to look appalled. Failure was inevitable and she was unable to stop herself saying, 'Good lord.'

This is not to say that Agatha was in any way antithetical to the art deco style. In fact, there were quite a few pieces of furniture at Agatha's Grosvenor Square residence that any discerning eye would have happily labelled as part of this movement without fear of reproach from their host. However, confronted with such a singular lack of variety, the impact of the décor was overwhelming, probably vulgar, and certainly lacking in taste. One look from Agatha to Betty reinforced the impression both felt that the investigation was unlikely to move very far forward.

The butler led them through to a large drawing room. They were greeted by a man and a woman who introduced themselves as Rupert and Dorothy Bell. The couple were at that indeterminate age of forty to sixty. If they were the former, things were going downhill fast. If the latter, they were well-preserved.

'I say, so jolly good of you to come,' said Rupert Bell to his guests. The older couple were obviously known to the hosts suggesting they had been before. Everyone else appeared to be new.

'Can I offer anyone a drink?' asked Rupert Bell, clearly keen to make a good impression with his guests or, at the very least, desensitise them. His wife, meanwhile, remained slightly distant from the group and no one sought to speak to her. Agatha feared, correctly as it turned out, that she was the medium.

One is always warned not to judge a book by the cover. Agatha had never subscribed to this rule and never would. Much like books, one's appearance was a window to the content therein. It could be exciting, inventive, and intelligent or it could be dull, derivative, and superficial. Dorothy Bell had already made a poor impression with her taste in interior décor. Her sense of dress, as far as the two ladies were concerned, merely added to the impression that Mrs Bell was of the second category.

The medium was dressed in a long black smock with a gold headband embellished with a feather of such exuberant dimensions, that it was entirely possible an ostrich was wandering around London Zoo, at that very moment, shivering in the late September chill.

She smoked, not without some flourish, it must be said, a cigarette joined to a cigarette holder of remarkable length. Dark makeup had been applied around the eyes with such demonic intensity it would have had Theda Bara calling for soap and water.

Agatha glanced towards Betty. Her friend was either a psychic herself or of a like mind. A few minutes later, supplied with brandy, the party sat down. With a nod from the host, the butler turned off the lights.

The séance was to begin.

The group put their hands on the table. Except for the sound of breathing there was silence for fully two minutes. Then Dorothy Bell spoke. If her appearance had done little to inspire confidence in the credibility of the gathering, her next words all but shattered any remaining hopes.

In a kind of quivery shamanic intoning as if she were summoning the dead which, to be fair to her, she was, the medium said, 'I have the consciousness of some presence here.'

Jack Murray

Of chumps, thought Agatha. Complete chumps.

'I don't know what your friend Doyle was thinking of in sending us there,' said Betty, afterwards, as they walked back towards the car.

'Complete waste of time,' agreed Agatha, stopping in the middle of the street. 'I'll tell Doyle. Admittedly he hasn't seen the Bells personally, and it was all he could arrange in the time available. We have another séance tomorrow in Chiswick.'

A car turned onto the street and drove towards her. It tooted its horn which was just as well. The noise woke Agatha up and she hurried forward again.

'What are you looking at, dear?' asked Betty, aware of Agatha's gaze which was set to disapproval.

'Do you want me to drive?'

'Of course not.'

'That third brandy was rather large.'

Betty looked in no mood to debate the subject further and they both climbed into the car. It was dark now; the evenings were beginning to draw in.

'What is Kit doing today?'

'He's gone down to question Gresham in Bournemouth with Mary.'

Betty glanced at Agatha and smiled.

'Yes?' asked Agatha, noticing her friend's reaction.

'Was that wise?'

The Medium Murders

19

Wessex Mansions was home to the 6th Earl of Gresham. The country house was built in the Jacobethan style of the 18th century. The gardens, unlike at Cavendish House, were designed by Capability Brown, rather than a distant relative. Set in four thousand acres of countryside, the house was surrounded by forest, and it was only after a few minutes of entering the estate that the imposing house came into view.

'So, this is the home of Bobby Andrews,' said Mary, looking up at Kit with a wry grin.

'Not bad if you like that sort of thing.'

Mary did not reply. The couple looked at one another and grinned conspiratorially. The cab deposited them at the front entrance where they were greeted by the Earl and his wife, Countess Gresham.

Both the Earl and the Countess were in their fifties. While he was unexceptional but kindly looking, his wife was a beauty. Granddaughter of a Spanish nobleman, her skin retained a hint of olive while the eyes were night black. The ladies exchanged kisses while the men gave one another a brief handshake.

'Pleasure to meet you, Aston. Lady Mary,' said Gresham, nobly kissing her hand.

They went inside and Mary had something of a shock when she reached the drawing room.

'Hello, Mary,' said Bobby Andrews. His dark eyes seemed even darker than Mary remembered. She wondered if he was angry with her. He had every right to be. He bent down, for he was as tall as Kit, to kiss her on the cheek. Mary accepted this with an embarrassed smile. She wondered if he'd said anything to his parents.

'Hello, Aston,' said Andrews. There was little warmth in the greeting, which worried Kit not a jot. More troubling, however, was the incontestable fact that Andrews was a good-looking man. He held eye contact with Kit as they greeted one another. The two men were standing by the fireplace. On the mantlepiece, Kit spied a photograph of an army battalion. He glanced at it and then back to Andrews.

'That was taken just before Amiens in eighteen,' explained Andrews.

The men in the photograph looked worn down. The face of Andrews was drawn, and he seemed a shadow of the man before him. Kit nodded to Andrews but said nothing. They joined the others for pre-dinner cocktails. The conversation was light and inconsequential. No mention of druids, no mention of the War, although the progress of the Suffrage movement was given an airing.

The key business of the evening would be for later.

Dinner was fully five courses. Fully in the sense that Mary was full up by the second. Kit, meanwhile, had built up quite an appetite following his afternoon and enjoyed each course immensely. Wisely, he declined drinking too much wine. He wanted to keep his mind clear for later.

It was an enjoyable two hours. Gresham was a humble man and happy to leave the floor to his wife and son. This gave Kit time to assess the Honourable Mr Andrews. What he saw, much to his disappointment, he found himself liking. His expectation had been of a ladies' man. In this he was not disappointed. However, it was clear there was more to the young man than mere good looks and charm. It was more difficult to read Mary now. She seemed uncomfortable. Kit suspected a guilty conscience.

Dinner came to an end before ten. The countess signalled its end by rising from the table and suggesting that Bobby and Mary join her in the drawing room. This would allow Kit and Gresham time to chat over a brandy. Kit smiled towards the countess and nodded his gratitude.

Inside the drawing room, the countess, sensing that her son desired to be alone with Mary, made an excuse to go and speak to the staff. She smiled and left the room to Mary and Bobby Andrews.

'Bobby,' started Mary.

'You don't have to say anything, Mary,' replied Andrews.

'I do and we both know it. I behaved disgracefully and I'm sorry.'

'You didn't behave disgracefully, Mary. I knew your situation and I pursued you anyway.'

'Even so, Bobby,' said Mary shamefully. She felt wretched. The evening had been pleasant, and Andrews had proved to be both an amiable host and now a true gentleman. Perhaps in another time this would have been enough. Was it always the case that we hurt those who least deserve to suffer? It seemed so to Mary at that moment. Both Kit and Bobby Andrews, in different ways, had been wounded by her actions. Once again, it occurred to her that investigating crime had emotional consequences she had not realised would affect her so much.

'Even so, Mary, nothing. Let's speak of this no more. Yes, I was a little hurt. I'm certainly quite jealous but I'm also relieved. If Kit had been anything other than the man, you deserve then I should have been angry. I know from others because, believe me, I've asked, that Kit is the finest of men. I hope he realises how lucky he is.'

Mary's attempts at preventing tears from falling were in vain. She felt Andrews hug her and gently kiss the top of her head. After a few moments he released her, and they regarded one another for a moment. The darkness in his eyes could not hide some of the pain he was feeling. She felt some of that pain too.

The door to the drawing room opened signalling the return of the countess. The three sat down and waited for Kit's interview with the Earl to finish. It was not a long wait. Mary was grateful for this. She felt ill at ease now. Guilt and curiosity make for uncomfortable bedfellows. She was impatient to return to the hotel. Very impatient.

The door opened and Kit entered followed by Gresham. Kit looked angry. He hid it well, but Mary knew the signs. As they left a few minutes later to take the taxi back to the hotel, Mary turned to Kit and said, 'So go on. What happened?'

'Winston called me a couple of days ago to warn me you'd be coming down,' said Gresham, as he sat alone with Kit.

This was the first thing Gresham said after the others had left.

'Did he say anything else?' asked Kit

This seemed to confuse the older man and he shook his head.

'He didn't tell me to lie if that's what you're driving at,' said Gresham. There was a smile on his face which lessened any barb contained within his comment.

Kit laughed and said, 'I'm relieved to hear it, sir.' Following this he removed from his pocket two photographs. One showing Churchill amongst the druids. Then he showed the other where the young woman was standing to the side of the group.

'Do you remember seeing this woman?'

Gresham took a few moments to look at the photographs. Then he looked up at Kit and shook his head.

'I'm afraid I have no recollection of this woman. In fact, I have no recollection of any women in the group. I must confess I was a little bit drunk.'

Kit studied the face of Gresham as he said this. He seemed a trifle embarrassed by the whole thing. Or, perhaps, that he had been a little the worse for wear.

Further probing by Kit on this subject proved fruitless. It confirmed his worry that many of the people at the ceremony were unknown to one another. More worryingly still, the druid priests never revealed themselves at any point. They remained a mystery.

Gresham confirmed the presence of Kit's father and the Earl of Hertwood. None had stayed after the ceremony concluded. All had joined Churchill back at Blenheim Palace for more refreshment. Gresham raised his eyebrows at the word refreshment to indicate they were, probably, getting even more intoxicated.

'The druid ceremony was a bit of a damp squib. I think Winston thought it would be more fun. Instead, it was all a bit ridiculous. The chaps in the costumes seemed to take it all a bit seriously. In the end we were glad to get back to the main business of the evening.'

'Which was?'

'Celebrating Winston's impending engagement.'

'I gather he proposed the next day.'

'Yes, damn lucky too. Sonny Masterson got him out of bed in time otherwise Clemmie would have been on her way home. I'd say he was suffering a bit of a hangover when he popped the question. Still, if she did notice, she obviously didn't mind.'

Sadly, Gresham could not add to the names on the list. He studied the photographs once more and shook his head in frustration. He pointed out the people he did know.

'Did Hertwood come back to the palace with you?'

Gresham thought for a moment about the evening twelve years ago. It was obvious he was having difficulty remembering and admitted as much.

'I don't believe so. In fact, I'm not so sure he really knew Winston that well. I have no recollection of them speaking to one another.' He looked again at the group photograph before adding, 'He's not in the main group as far as I can see although he appears in this one. Isn't that him standing near the woman you mentioned.'

Kit looked again at the picture and realised that it was. He was looking away from the group which meant it would have been difficult to identify him.

The Medium Murders

'So, aside from those people you've identified, you're sure there's no one else in the photograph that you recognise?'

'Well, of course there's the photographer chappie, let's not forget him.'

Kit's eyes widened for a moment. He had forgotten him. Churchill had claimed that he did not know the chap.

'What is his name?'

'Hanley. Philip Hanley. I wouldn't have remembered his name had it not been for the ghastly murder.'

'Which murder?' asked Kit, genuinely confused.

'The one in Yorkshire. You know. The first medium murder. D'you remember? During the summer.'

The *first* medium murder. It had been a man. Kit realised he'd discounted it for this reason. Now there was a possible connection with the murders of the young women. Kit felt a wave of anger rise inside his stomach. Anger with himself but also with someone else. Wheels within wheels. The next question came through gritted teeth.

'Have you told anyone else about this chap Hanley?'

'As a matter of fact, yes. The other chap who came.'

20

Harry blinked and tried to focus his eyes on the man in the doorway. Lying on the ground, his clothes had become damp, and he shivered involuntarily. He rubbed his eyes. Then, with no little alarm, he realised there was a blackbird beside him. It had wandered silently into the hut.

'Harry Miller?' said the stranger. He was about Harry's height, maybe slightly taller. He was probably over fifty, well-maintained and spoke in a voice that suggested he was not from Miller's class. He let go of the long branch he was using as a walking stick and stepped forward into the hut. The twigs cracked underneath his feet.

Miller leapt to his feet and grinned. This caused the blackbird to fly out of the hut in a blur of feathers.

'Raven Hadleigh?'

The man nodded. Harry extended his hand which was firmly grasped by the other man.

'I've heard a lot about you, Harry.'

'Mr Hadleigh, this is an honour.'

The Medium Murders

Miller and Hadleigh sat on the edge of the forest and watched evening descend on the Hertwood House. They were eating sandwiches prepared by Miller.

'Very good,' said Hadleigh, nodding down to the sandwiches.

'I used to sit with my dad like this when we were about to pull a job. He always insisted on having a full stomach,' replied Miller by way of explanation.

'Can't have a rumbling tummy giving the game away.'

'Exactly.'

The lights were on in several of the rooms but, overall, the mansion seemed quiet. There were three floors according to the plan Kit had made. Hadleigh and Miller looked down at the large piece of paper that Kit had drawn on.

'I wish I'd had this when I was working,' said Miller.

'Yes, I always found it a great help to know the interior well. When you've only seconds between jewels or jail, it can be all the difference in the world.'

Miller smiled at the man known as 'The Phantom'. Miller had not had the opportunity to meet him earlier in the year. Back then, Kit had been working on a case where Hadleigh's daughter was a suspect in a series of jewel robberies in London.

'If it's just the old man and his wife, I suspect they'll be in bed soon. If we give the staff an hour to clear up, we should be ready to go around midnight. Do you know if there are many dogs?'

'I gather,' said Miller, 'there is an old sheepdog but apparently he's half deaf. Kit hasn't seen the old boy since his son was exposed as an anarchist.'

'Can't say I blame him. Would be a devilishly awkward conversation, I imagine.'

'That was his lordship's view,' agreed Miller.

They waited until just after one in the morning. The time passed quickly as they chatted about their 'profession'. It helped take their minds off the chill that had descended like a curtain from an overcast sky. It seemed to infect both men. Or perhaps it was something else. Both felt nervous. Neither mentioned it.

'I much prefer when it's some rich woman's diamonds. Hunting for Satanic temples never held much attraction.'

Miller's taut laughter betrayed how he felt.

'On the plus side,' continued Raven Hadleigh, 'We know there's only the Earl and the Countess there tonight, aside from the staff. We won't be stumbling into any Black Mass with any luck.'

'Yes,' agreed Miller, 'I don't fancy becoming some sacrifice to Lucifer.'

Hadleigh gave Miller a long look up and down.

'Unless you're a young virgin in disguise, Harry, I think your chances of avoiding this fate are pretty good.'

With these words of encouragement, the two men stood up and circled around towards the back of the house. Their reconnaissance confirmed that the household had retired for the night. There was no sign of any potential canine presence either.

They studied the map once more using Hadleigh's flashlight.

'The safe is a Mosler,' said Miller. 'Hertwood had it imported from America, apparently. It's behind the Munnings in the library. There's only one. His lordship said you'd know which one.'

Hadleigh nodded confirmation.

'I will go to the odd-looking turret to the side. His lordship never went there in all the time he visited. If anything's untoward then it's likely to be up there.'

Both men were startled by a sound above them.

Hadleigh shone his torch upwards. An owl looked down from the branches. The light caused it to fly off. The bird's journey was accompanied by a stick thrown by Hadleigh and a few whispered words of farewell from Miller that were unlikely to be used at a social gathering in Mayfair.

'Let's go,' said Hadleigh, laughing nervously. 'This place is giving me the colly wobbles.'

'You and me both, sir.'

'Shall we synchronise our wristwatches. I have seven minutes past one.'

Miller nodded.

'Right then,' said Hadleigh. 'I'll go directly to the library. It's around to the right.'

'I'll enter via the cloakroom,' said Miller.

'Meet back at the bikes at twenty minutes past one,' said Hadleigh. They shook hands and wished each other luck. Seconds later Hadleigh had disappeared into the night.

Miller sprinted in the opposite direction. Arriving at the house, Miller used a screwdriver to lever open a narrow-arched window. It was old and gave way easily. Moments later he was inside the cloakroom. It was then he encountered his first problem. The door was locked from the outside. He shone a torch and saw it had a simple latch.

Removing a file from his pocket, he slipped it in between the door and the frame and flicked the latch open. He was now in the corridor. It would have been pitch black without his torch. He crept down the hall and found the back stairs that led up to the strange turret at the side of the house. Miller flew up the stairs and reached the door at the top.

Pressing his ear to the door he checked for any noises from within. All was silent. He used two metal picks to unlock the door. It took a couple of minutes before he heard the lock click. He opened the door.

The Medium Murders

Miller's flashlight shone around the interior. It was a largish room. On the walls hung paintings. All had a similar theme. His eyebrows shot up at the same time as a smirk appeared on his mouth. On the table in the middle of the room were some books. He glanced at them. The content could, at a stretch, have been described as esoteric. His smile widened.

'Dirty devil,' he whispered.

He walked over to a large cupboard. Opening it, he found a variety of implements that would have been used by Torquemada some four hundred years previously. Curiouser and curiouser thought Miller. The only other cupboard was across the room. He opened it and nearly exploded in laughter.

The dresses, to his untutored eye, looked very much of the current fashion. On a shelf above was a collection of Venetian masques. Hanging from the back of the door were some handcuffs and a cat-o-nine-tails. Buried deep in the wardrobe, he recognised several birches of the type he would have had first-hand experience of around fifteen years previously at school.

One thing was certain, thought Miller. The Earl of Hertwood, on this evidence, had some unusual interests but Satanism was not one of them.

It was then Miller heard the alarm. It started at the other side of the house but soon others took up the baton. Before long, the whole house was in uproar. He restricted his reaction to string of oaths made in a passionate whisper. A split second later he was leaping down the stairs, several at a time. Half a minute later, he was out through the window he'd entered and running around to the front.

He was greeted by quite an extraordinary sight.

Raven Hadleigh tested a few windows on the ground floor to see if they were open. It often amazed him the lack of caution in houses that had much to be cautious about. Once more his faith in human stupidity was rewarded when a large window opened easily to the merest hint of force. Seconds later he was in.

The room was dark until he drew the curtains. Then it was still dark, only slightly less so. The flashlight revealed that he was probably in the drawing room. He opened the door and crept across the corridor to the room that Kit's map suggested was the library. Thankfully, Kit's map was still up to date. He shone his torch around the room and saw floor to ceiling books in what was by any standards a rather impressive collection. He wondered idly how many of them had been read.

The few gaps in the walls were filled with paintings. Equestrian art mostly. He spotted the Munnings on the far side. Had there been time, had it been a decade previously, he would have considered taking it. It was a rather fine painting. Small, colourful, and done with the

The Medium Murders

slapdash joie de vivre of a master. Hadleigh carefully lifted the painting off its hook. This action coincided with the letting loose of all hell.

The room immediately exploded into noise. The sound of the bell, if not deafening, was certainly sufficient to raise those twin enemies of any cat burglar: Mr Hue and Mr Cry. There was no time to inspect the contents of the safe. He glanced wistfully down at the painting and made straight for the window. Already he could hear barking.

-

Nathaniel Robinson was a former infantry man with the Black Watch. Former because after his demobilisation he had been taken on by the Earl of Hertwood as a footman. This recruitment was less to do with Robinson's skills in the art of service than his physical scale, strength, and penchant for violence.

The end of the war had in no way diminished his proclivity for meting out punishment. A chance introduction to the Earl at an exclusive location in London visited by a privileged clientele with singular predilections had provided a new, permanent, and paid outlet for a onetime hobby that had now become his profession.

The alarm could only mean one thing. Nathaniel Robinson leapt into action.

'What's happening?' asked Daisy Winthrop, a parlour maid in the Hertwood estate.

'Burglars,' said Robinson, through gritted teeth.

Opening a cupboard in his bedroom, he took out his old Lee Enfield and raced through the door.

'But your clothes?' pointed out Daisy, wondering how the pursuit of dangerous criminals could in any way be aided by an absence of clothes. However, as men went, and Daisy Winthrop's experience was fairly limited in this regard, it did seem, her inexperience notwithstanding, that Nathaniel Robinson was a magnificent example of the breed.

Raven Hadleigh was not a man to hang around when a burglar alarm was ringing. Nor was he going to retrace his footsteps back to the drawing room. He had seconds to play with. Before the alarm was seven seconds old, Hadleigh had drawn back the curtains and opened the window of the drawing room which, from the map, lay at the front of the house. Hadleigh's slim frame was through the window and darting into the night before you could say, 'Stop thief'. Which, coincidentally, was the first thing he heard from behind.

As he had been crunching through the gravel pathway, he'd been vaguely aware of a front door being opened. He didn't look back. He tore ahead hoping that his old fleetness of foot had not deserted him. The noise of gravel behind told him someone was giving chase. He risked a glance behind.

The Medium Murders

It was nearly his downfall.

The sight of a naked six-foot-tall man running towards him was as bizarre as it was, naturally, compelling. For a moment the two men locked eyes then Nathaniel Robinson's training kicked in. He stopped and knelt.

Hadleigh speeded up.

The first bullet went whistling by his ear principally because Hadleigh had deliberately weaved at the last moment. This was worrying, to say the least. He had another twenty yards to cover before he was in the forest.

In the background he heard the voice of an elderly man shouting at him to stop. Given he was currently the target of a naked man with a rifle, the advice was always likely to get short shrift from the escaping cat burglar. All things considered, Hadleigh was a worried man. If the naked oaf was as good a shot as his first effort suggested, this was a sticky situation. His lungs were exploding as he sprinted forward towards safety, expecting at any moment to….

-

The sight of a naked man chasing a burglar was not one Miller had come across often in his brief career as a robber. A few things struck Miller immediately. The man was well over six feet tall and impressively made. Furthermore, he was waving around an army Lee Enfield. In fact, this wasn't the only thing waving around in the night air. Miller knew well how the cold could impact one's extremities. In one regard, he found himself doubly impressed by the goliath who, it appeared, was about to take a pot shot at his partner-in-crime.

Moments later he knelt and fired off a round. Miller glanced towards Hadleigh and was relieved to see him still running. Glancing towards his partner meant that he missed the arrival on the scene of a middle-aged man wearing a nightshirt.

'Stop thief,' shouted the man.

His arrival managed to distract the naked man momentarily as well as providing cover for the noise of Miller who, instinctively, was sprinting directly towards the shooter on his blindside.

It wasn't until he was within a few yards that either of the members of the household were aware of him. The kneeling man swung around.

Too late.

Miller's flying kick knocked the man to the ground and the Lee Enfield out of his hands.

There was no time to engage with the other man who was loudly inquiring as to who the blazes Miller was. Miller rolled over and grabbed the weapon and pointed it at the naked man as he rose. His confident manner of handling the weapon quickly disabused Nathaniel Robinson of any foolhardy notions.

Miller slowly backed away from the two men who were now joined by a woman. She was probably in her early fifties and very striking. Miller guessed that this was the Countess, Olly Lake's mother. Miller jerked the rifle upwards. All three immediately put their hands up.

'Stay where you are,' ordered Miller as he retreated. Once he was twenty yards away, he turned and ran towards the forest. No one following him.

'Who on earth was that?' exclaimed the Earl of Hertwood, putting his hands down. As he did so, he became aware that his man, Nathaniel, was conspicuously unclothed. The countess had long since noted Robinson's lack of attire and had positioned herself accordingly to enjoy the spectacle fully.

Robinson's hands came down to his sides. It was at this moment; he became aware of the rather distracted state of his employers. As the cold night air bathed his skin, realisation dawned that he was, quite literally, exposed to the elements. The big manservant immediately covered himself as best he could, apologised for his unclothed state and inquired whether Lord Hertwood wished for him to give chase.

In the distance they heard two motorcycles roaring to life and driving off. The look on the faces of the Earl and the Countess suggested that not only were they desirous that he should not give chase, but his night was also a long way from over.

21

The dining room at Highcliffe Mansions was ideally located to give diners a stunning view across the English Channel. Today there was barely a cloud in the sky. The bright sun glistened on the sea and the sky was a crisp blue. Sitting by one of the large bay windows were three gentlemen enjoying their breakfast. In fact, the atmosphere at the table went beyond mere enjoyment; it was a positively jovial affair. The three men could barely talk to one another as each additional comment was greeted with yet more laughter. Finally, Kit managed to string a few words together.

'I can't believe it. To think I used to spend every summer there.'

This caused more merriment among the group. The news that Hadleigh had failed to break into the safe was accepted with equanimity as the revelations of the torture chamber replete with dresses somewhat undermined the Earl's credentials as a murdering Satanist. His tastes, on the evidence presented by Miller, lay in a wholly different, albeit no less iniquitous, direction.

The Medium Murders

'Have you made much progress, sir?' asked Miller. Under any normal circumstances such a question from a manservant to his master might be considered a case of borderline insolence and deserving of a good thrashing. Kit pointed this out to Miller and then the table descended once more into hysterics.

They were just coming up for air when Kit spied the arrival of Mary in the dining room. Her entrance, it must be reported, was also noted by many of the diners with varying degrees of admiration if the wave of kicks under the table administered by the many women to their male partners, was anything to go by. Kit waited until Mary was just at the table before replying.

'We've been at it non-stop. I'm exhausted.'

Mary's eyes widened in alarm. She looked at Kit questioningly.

'They were just asking me how our investigations were going.'

The men stood up to greet Mary and she sat down. Kit continued to update the others on what they had found out. When he'd finished, Raven Hadleigh gave a heavily edited account of his adventure with Miller. However, the smirks from both Kit and Miller and the suppressed laughter eventually angered Mary enough to force a more unrestricted account. Thankfully the story about the poor manservant sufficed and a discreet veil was drawn over the predilections of the Earl and the Countess.

The conversation turned back towards 'the Phantom' and his plans. With a grin he made his big announcement.

'I'm a free man.'

Congratulations were immediately forthcoming from all. Kit was delighted by the news as he was aware that Hadleigh's daughter and the young detective Ben Ryan were to be married in the South of France before Christmas.

'Yes, I'll be going down to France as soon as I can. Please thank your aunt once again, Kit. She's been so kind for looking after Ben's brother and family.'

'I shall but there's no need. Anyway, wait until Aunt Agatha goes down there and stays. You'll change your tune, believe me.'

'I'm sure she's not that bad,' laughed Hadleigh.

The looks on the faces of the other three breakfast companions suggested otherwise, which only amused Hadleigh even more.

'She does have many good points,' said Kit loyally.

Kit, Mary, and Miller took the train back to London, arriving at Waterloo mid-afternoon. As they trooped off the platform, Mary turned to Kit.

'What did you think of the old woman in our carriage?'

'Seemed nice enough. I suppose you're going to tell me that it was really a man. The vicar who accompanied us down.'

Mary stopped on the platform causing an elderly couple almost to collide with them. After a few half-hearted apologies, Mary said, 'Are you mocking me or were you being serious? That's what I was going to say.'

Kit smiled and shrugged,

'I looked at the hands this time.'

'Why didn't you say anything?'

'To you or to him?'

'Well, both, actually,' said Mary, laughing.

'I have a feeling he was on our side,' replied Kit, enigmatically, before moving forward and causing Mary to aim a gentle slap on his rear with her umbrella. This was accompanied by a subtle warning about where the next one would be aimed if he was not more forthcoming in future.

Mary was dropped off at Grosvenor Square where they picked up Sam. He'd spent the night at Aunt Agatha's mansion in the company of Fish. It was an arrangement that suited neither very well. He leapt up into the Rolls and barked happily at the return of his master. Miller drove the Rolls directly to New Scotland Yard.

It was around four in the afternoon and the blue sky of Bournemouth had been replaced by the leaden grey of London. After a short journey to New Scotland Yard, Miller parked the car on the Victoria Embankment outside the police headquarters.

The building housing the Metropolitan Police looked like one of the many apartment blocks that had sprung up in the last twenty years. It was certainly a lot less imposing than the buildings in Whitehall but a vast improvement on the relatively meagre pickings given to the Secret Intelligence Service. Kit stepped up into the building and was led straight through to the office of the Chief Inspector.

Jellicoe was alone in the office, and he greeted Kit warmly. The two men sat across the desk from one another. Kit regarded Jellicoe for a moment. There was no question he liked the Chief Inspector. In addition, he trusted him. There was something about his solemnity; the utter seriousness in the way he went about his job. His integrity was incontestable. It was there on his face and in the aura surrounding him.

At that moment, Kit needed to talk to someone and there was no better someone than Jellicoe. The case had spun off its axis. The trip to Bournemouth had raised more questions than it had provided answers. The questions posed led to avenues of inquiry that suggested Kit had been misled right from the start. He expected nothing less from Smith-Cumming. He expected more from Jellicoe. But Kit had to be sure he could still count on the Chief Inspector.

'Why can't I speak to Eva Kerr?' asked Kit, getting down to business.

'She has disappeared.'

Kit raised his eyebrows at this. This was an invitation for Jellicoe to explain more about what he had first revealed the previous day.

'She was never under arrest, and we don't have the manpower to post a guard on her. Quite simply she has vanished into thin air.'

'You don't seem that surprised, Chief Inspector,' said Kit, 'Or worried, I might add.'

This prompted the merest hint of a smile from the policeman.

'We don't think she's been kidnapped. She called Wellbeloved and told him that she was leaving her hotel. She refused to say where she was going.'

'Is it not possible to go to her home address?'

At this point Jellicoe's smile widened and he almost laughed. This was a rare occurrence. The smile, however, was a brief one. Then his face resumed its normal gravity.

'My apologies, Chief Inspector, I'm sure this was the first thing that you did. My guess is that not only did you not find her address, but it also transpires that neither the address nor, indeed, Eva Kerr, actually exists except as a stage name, for wont of a better description.'

Jellicoe nodded in approval.

'May I ask how you reached this conclusion?' asked Jellicoe.

Kit smiled grimly.

'Chief Inspector, if what I believe is true, then we're both being played for fools.'

It was clear that Jellicoe had reached a similar conclusion. He leaned forward on his desk.

'Can you tell me, your lordship, what you believe to be the truth?'

'Only some suspicions. I'm certainly no nearer finding a killer of these young women, sadly.'

Following his interview with the Chief Inspector, Kit asked to borrow an office from which he made two brief phone calls. Then he bid farewell to Jellicoe and rejoined Miller who was waiting in the Rolls.

'Where to now, sir?'

'The apartment, please. We're finished for today, Harry.'

The two men trooped into the apartment. Sam skipped happily into his home and hopped up onto the Chesterfield beside Simpkins, who had left Kit's seat for the time being.

'Hello,' said Kit to the black cat.

The cat glanced up at Kit before shutting its eyes.

The Medium Murders

'Well, I'm sure you're glad we're back, anyway,' said Kit. He stroked the cat behind its ears and was rewarded by rather loud purring.

'He doesn't seem to be missing his collar,' said Miller.

'I'm sure he's delighted to be rid of it,' agreed Kit. 'Beastly looking thing it was.'

Richard Bright arrived back to the apartment half an hour later. Kit looked up in surprise at his entrance.

'Oh, I thought you'd be with Esther still.'

'No, she kicked me out of the house when Mary arrived back. She wanted to hear about the case. I'm not quite sure why that necessitated my departure but there you go. The girls have their ways I suppose.'

Kit smiled and nodded in agreement without saying anything. Bright sat down opposite Kit and looked at Simpkins in surprise.

'Yes,' said Kit, 'For the time being, anyway, I have my seat back.'

Just as he said this, the telephone in the apartment rang. Miller picked it up on the third ring.

'Lord Kit Aston's residence.'

Moments later Miller looked at Kit.

'Sir, it's the Chief Inspector.'

Kit went over to Miller and took the phone. He listened for a minute and then said, 'I shall be there directly.' He replaced the phone and looked at Bright.

'There's been another murder.'

22

The chamber was dimly lit. Five black candles were positioned at the edge of a circle. Inside the circle was a floor decoration. A star. The candelabra stood at the point of each star. A raised concrete slab lay in the middle of the circle. It was around two feet high with a black cloth draped over the top.

It was dressed like an altar.

Lying on the altar was a young woman. She was unclothed and unconscious. Standing inside the circle were a dozen men and women. All, bar four of the congregation were dressed in thin white cotton shifts. Standing at the head of the altar, dressed in white robes, were four people. One was holding a large ancient leather book and murmuring an ancient language. Another older man was holding a knife.

Music wafted around the chamber, but no musician was present. The melody was as compelling as it was discordant. It echoed around the walls but did not drown out the sound of the ritual taking place. The robed figure holding the book faced the altar, back to the congregation. The ceremony continued as the priest read words from the book. There followed a murmured response from those present.

The priest reached the end of the reading and turned to face the congregation. The book was held aloft, and all bowed before it in awed silence. After a few moments of quiet supplication, the book was lowered and handed to a neophyte from the congregation. Another neophyte stepped forward and handed the priest a chalice.

The priest intoned a prayer while holding the chalice. Then, turning to the other robed figure, bowed. The congregation began to chant an ancient petition. It began as a slow murmur. But with each canto the volume increased. The voices grew louder and louder. The chant beat like a steady pulse. They were no longer a congregation of individuals. The pulse was of a single organism. Their voices, their breathing, their excitement, and their fear were one.

The throb of voices grew louder and began to reach its crescendo. As it did so, it lost its cohesion, and the individual components became more distinct. The noise from the neophytes was now no longer a chant. They were screaming. A blood lust bathed their eyes. And then they saw the glint of a knife raised.

The screams grew louder and then all was quiet.

-

Chief Inspector Jellicoe stood with Sergeant Wellbeloved overlooking a ditch. Below them lay the dead body of a young woman, half submerged. They were in Hyde Park, near the Albert Memorial. The night's chill permeated through the layers of clothing they were wearing. Around them half a dozen police constables created a cordon around the area.

'What's keeping French?' asked Jellicoe with more than a trace of irritation in his voice.

'We couldn't locate him, sir,' replied Wellbeloved. 'We've sent someone to his house.'

Jellicoe nodded and looked behind Wellbeloved. The sergeant turned around and saw Kit walking towards them accompanied by another man that Jellicoe half recognised. They arrived a minute or two later and Jellicoe shook hands with them both. Kit introduced his friend as Dr Richard Bright. Jellicoe remembered who he was now.

'We're waiting for Dr French,' explained Jellicoe. He looked at Bright. The man before him was obviously from a privileged class but, based on the suit he was wearing, the youngest son. Jellicoe remembered he was to be married to Lady Esther Cavendish. They would make a handsome couple. Impatient to move ahead with the investigation, a thought struck the Chief Inspector as he regarded Bright.

'Perhaps Dr Bright might do an initial inspection of the young lady?'

Bright nodded in agreement and stepped down to the edge of the ditch. He heard the Chief Inspector urge him not to disturb the area around the corpse.

'Can you shine a couple of those torches on the body, please?'

Two of the constables did as they were requested.

'I would say no older than thirty, probably younger.,' said Bright, kneeling. 'I can't see any signs of a struggle. There's no bruising visible. He lifted her arm and then replaced it. Given the cold and the state of rigor, I would say that she's been dead no more than two to four hours. It might be more, but I doubt it. Without moving the body, I would be surprised if the cause of death isn't the wound to the neck. I think the marks on her stomach were added after she was killed. Is there anything else you want me to add, Chief Inspector?'

There were no questions from either Jellicoe or Wellbeloved. Kit helped Bright back up onto the pathway.

'Thank you, Dr Bright. Sorry for pressing you into service. We're having trouble locating our coroner, French.'

'He of the whiskers?' asked Kit.

'The very one.'

'Who found her?' asked Kit.

Jellicoe pointed to a park attendant standing near one of the constables.

'We've taken a statement,' added Jellicoe, 'but he did not see anyone in the vicinity. The murderer chose the location well. Visibility is poor, particularly at this time of night and there are never many people around except maybe a drunk or a tramp. We have a few policemen looking for anyone that might have seen something. I'm not optimistic.'

Fifteen minutes later, Dr French and his whiskers made it to the crime scene. Underneath his overcoat, the good doctor was wearing a dinner suit and wellington boots. He gave a cursory nod to Jellicoe, ignored Wellbeloved completely and stared at Kit with a puzzled expression before carefully climbing down towards the ditch.

'Young woman. Twenty-five or so. Cause of death? Probably a knife to the throat. Been dead no more than five hours. I presume you've taken all the photographs you need. She's fine to be collected.'

With that he jerked his arm at one of the constables who descended a few feet to help up out of the ditch.

'Anything else I can help you with? My wife will give me merry hell for this,' said French, with no effort to disguise his irritation.

'No, Dr French, thank you,' said Jellicoe.

'Good,' replied French. 'I had to borrow these boots and they hurt damnably.'

With this revelation he limped away from the scene. Jellicoe looked at Kit and then Dr Bright. There was nothing more to say about the crime or about the short-tempered doctor for that matter.

'I'll call in with you tomorrow,' said Kit. 'I may have some things to tell you.'

The Medium Murders

Jellicoe nodded absently. His attention was now back with the young woman and the need to carry out a more detailed inspection of the area. He waved as Kit and Bright walked back towards the exit.

'Horrible,' said Bright grimly. 'We need to catch this vile beast.'

Kit couldn't agree more. However, at that moment the only things that made sense to him made no sense at all. His heart was heavy but there was anger there also. Anger at the role played by his sex, his class in these deaths. Now there was another element of frustration. This would be resolved tomorrow when he saw Smith-Cumming and Kell.

They had some explaining to do.

23

Vernon Kell, head of MI5(g) gave his spectacles a wipe and glanced towards his opposite number in MI6. Smith-Cumming took out a pocket watch and looked down at the face. It was a Patek-Phillippe he'd picked up for a song in France. He turned to Kell and shrugged.

'It's not like Kit to be late. Usually set your watch by him.'

Kell looked unhappy. He'd cancelled two meetings to attend. He was a busy man. Had this been any other topic and a request from any other man, his response would have been brief and unlikely to involve words of more than one syllable.

The two men were sitting in Green Park. The mood of Kell was probably not helped by the undoubted nip in the air and the presence of a crying baby nearby. Smith-Cumming looked at Kell and smiled. Such lack of patience. The deep furrow running vertically on his brow was there for a reason that went beyond solely mother nature playing a joke.

"C" turned his attention towards the child who was around four years old. The hell-child was in the middle of an epic tantrum. He smiled sympathetically towards

The Medium Murders

the mother. She seemed embarrassed. Smith-Cumming pointed to the child and by a hand signal, suggested he come over.

Kell looked on in horror as the child stopped crying for a moment and stared at the two men. Then Smith-Cumming took out a sixpence and brandished it to the young child. The boy turned to its mother and, after receiving a nod, ran towards Smith-Cumming to receive what, by any standard, was an ill-deserved reward. With each step closer, Kell's horror of the hell-child grew.

From a distance he'd merely seemed unspeakable. With each step closer, the child's dirty face and the nose was now revealed in its full horror. Kell looked away unable to stomach the sight of so much unwiped mucus. It was at this point he caught sight of Kit Aston walking slowly toward them. He was swinging his walking stick. The free, almost joyful, swing of the stick was at odds with a face that was set to stone.

The child ran off just as Kit arrived at the park bench.

'Shall we take a walk?' suggested Smith-Cumming affably. He could immediately see the rage on the young man's face. Kell rose and the two men walked either side of Kit.

There was no greeting from Kit. He went straight to it.

'When were you planning on telling me that Eva Kerr was one of yours?'

Kell looked as startled at the intensity of Kit's glare as at his directness. Both could hear Smith-Cumming chuckling beside them.

'I don't see what's so funny, Cumming,' said Kell waspishly.

'Don't you?' replied Smith-Cumming.

The three men walked in silence for the next minute or so then Smith-Cumming spoke again.

'Why don't you tell us what you think, and we'll confirm how much it tallies with the facts.'

Kit was not happy about this and said as much. However, he recognised that this was likely to be the only way to get the two heads of Britain's Secret Intelligence to admit anything.

'Eva Kerr is an alias or a stage name for someone who claims to be a medium. She is probably with MI5. She is implicated in the murder of Philip Hanley if only because she told the police where to find the body. This potentially means that MI5 has murdered a man who was in possession of photographs of our Minister of War associating with modern day druids. For reasons that I cannot be sure of, although I can hazard a guess, MI5 and MI6 are collaborating in the blackmail of one of His Majesty's cabinet ministers. I have lost count of the number of laws that have been broken so far, but I suspect there would be enough to put both of you in prison for a long time.'

'Good lord,' said Kell.

The Medium Murders

Smith-Cumming laughed again and seemed genuinely entertained by Kit's remarks.

'Well Kit, I must congratulate you on a fascinating, albeit flawed, theory.'

'Flawed?'

'It's true that Miss Kerr is a stage name of sorts. I shan't go into who she is but suffice to say she is innocent of any crimes and has played her role remarkably well. As to the murder you described, and blackmail…'

Smith-Cumming paused for a moment and wiped his monocle.'

'Both are true, but the finger does not point towards us. Which is not to say that we have not tried to take advantage of the situation. Shall we stop over there?'

Smith-Cumming pointed to a low standing wall which curved in a manner that would facilitate a face-to-face conversation. They went over to the wall and sat down.

'Let me explain,' continued Smith-Cumming. 'Some months ago, Mr Churchill was sent the photograph you have in your possession. The photograph is a cropped version of the original which shows a rather larger group. Dozens, according to Churchill. Written on the back of the photograph was a promise that further communication would follow. This is the point at which my friend Kell, here, enters the picture. He ascertained from Churchill who might have taken the photograph and sent people to speak to this man. Unfortunately, when they arrived, he was already dead. Murdered, in fact. A search of the premises revealed no more plates related to the original.'

'Do you have any idea who might have done this?'

'We believe it was either Russia or, more likely, our friends at ORCA,' replied Kell.

'So how, or more to the point, why, did you dream up this medium angle.'

The two men glanced at one another rather shamefacedly if Kit's intuition was correct. Kell answered the question.

'The body of Hanley was found by one of my people operating in the York area.'

'Eva Kerr? Or whatever she is called.'

'Correct. She contacted me. At this point I let Cumming know of the latest development in the blackmail. As the man was dead, we decided to leave the scene of the crime. Obviously, we made a thorough search of the house.'

'But why a medium?'

Smith-Cumming's grin grew wider. Kit had to admire the gall of the man.

'Eva Kerr is a medium. At least she claims to count among her talents the ability to have out-of-the-body experiences as well as necromancy. I would add she has several clients who come to her on a frequent basis. Quite a lucrative career these days, I gather.'

'Is she really a medium?'

The Medium Murders

'Who knows?' replied Smith-Cumming, clearly amused. 'As a way of interrogating people, however, it is remarkably effective. I must congratulate you, Kell, on finding her.'

Kell bowed his head. The two men seemed to be relaxing, although Smith-Cumming never seemed anything but in control. Kit remained frustrated by what he was hearing.

'So, Eva Kerr reports the whereabouts of a dead body in one of her séances. Fine. I understand the mechanism. What I find difficult to grasp is why? And why have you brought me into this? And, I might add, wasted my time on a wild goose chase?'

Smith-Cumming took over from Kell, sensing Kit's growing irritation.

'Both of our departments have suffered significant cuts in our budget, Kit, since the end of the war. This is one of the reasons we moved to our Holland Park address. We, that is Kell and I, have been looking for an opportunity to remind the government of the necessity of retaining a fully resourced Intelligence Service. We have merely connected a separate problem, the murders of the young women, to the existing one involving Churchill.'

Kit remembered Jellicoe's surprise at the number of murders revealed by Wellbeloved.

'Does this mean the young woman in the photograph with Churchill was actually added afterwards. Or to put it another way; the murder photograph was staged.'

'Yes. The young woman is alive and well, working in a private club that I can assure you I've never been to. We have Sergeant Wellbeloved to thank for this.'

'Can I take it that Wellbeloved is one of your men?' asked Kit looking at Kell. The head of MI5 smiled but did not answer. Kit continued, 'But I thought Churchill was a supporter of the Intelligence agencies.'

'Oh, he is,' agreed Smith-Cumming, 'None bigger. Quite rightly fears communism. He's a good man to have on your side. We intend that he stay that way.'

Wheels within wheels. Kit shook his head and, briefly, was grateful that "C" was on his side.

Smith-Cumming continued, 'I'm sorry that we had to make use of your abilities on what appears to be a side project. However, you must see, Kit, that there could be a connection between the murders of the young women and the sort of people who meddle in druidism and, dare I say it, Masonic lodges. We're fishing in the same pool. We're convinced of this.'

'And my involvement in what, we all agree, is the bigger issue?' asked Kit.

'As I say, Kit. These dreadful murders are being committed by someone or people from the upper echelons of our society. The police have made no progress in a decade. The Commissioner came to Kell and asked for you specifically. It was felt that your undoubted capabilities as well as your access to the very highest society in the land could bring the success that has eluded the police. I must say, Kit, you've certainly brought new impetus to the case. We're all dreadfully impressed by your progress.'

Kit shook his head. The sense of frustration still burned within him.

'I've made no progress and, thanks to the sophistry I've been listening to, I've wasted days on a wild goose chase.'

Smith-Cumming shrugged but the smile did not leave his face. Criticism was like rainwater off a mackintosh to him.

'Hardly a wild goose chase, Kit. Both Gresham and Hertwood would have been suspects anyway. Gresham because he is involved with spiritualism. He lost his middle son in the War; Hertwood for reasons that we all know. You've managed to piece together an extraordinary coalition of interests which certainly would not have occurred to the police. It seems no avenue of inquiry is being ignored. Actually, you are to be congratulated on your progress.'

The mention of the Elephant Boys reminded Kit of something else that had irked him.

'How did Eva Kerr know of the death of Enid Blake?'

It was Kell who spoke. There was no denying the sadness in his voice.

'Miss Blake was one of ours. We have, shall we say, placed people in various organisations to keep a check on who they are associating with. I'm not terribly worried by racecourse bully boys in the normal way of things but if they were to connect with foreign agents or ORCA, then it is clearly a problem. Miss Blake saw something at a house which she thought we should know about. Her note said it was connected to the killings. We didn't get to her on time so know nothing of who or what she saw.'

'And Eva Kerr?'

'The agent running Miss Blake found her dead in the room she was occupying. Naturally this was distressing. Once we knew what had happened, we had to be practical. We contacted the police. Eva Kerr immediately travelled down from York to claim knowledge of the whereabouts of the body.'

Kit could see Smith-Cumming nodding in agreement.

'And you can't or won't tell me where Miss Kerr is now?'

Smith-Cumming looked at Kell. Kell barely moved his head, but this still seemed to be enough by way of communication for Smith-Cumming to speak.

'Miss Kerr remains involved in the investigation. Whatever one may think of necromancy, she can still help us in several ways. For the moment we see her working independently of your investigation.'

This was far from satisfactory, but Kit guessed the two men had their reasons. He had long since given up on trying to comprehend the mindset of high command.

The Medium Murders

'Did your manservant and Hadleigh find anything connecting Hertwood to ORCA or Satanic cults?' asked Smith-Cumming.

Kit looked at Smith-Cumming quizzically. He judged that the spymaster really had no idea about where Hertwood's interests lay.

'I don't believe Hertwood is connected to these crimes. Gresham either, but I was not speaking to him about spiritualism because I knew none of what you've just told me.'

'Why do you believe Hertwood is not part of this.'

To the amusement of both men, Kit told them why.

24

'It was good of you to come here at such short notice, Lady Mary.'

The 'here' in question was a church hall near the south bank just a few hundred yards from Waterloo Station. Mary looked at Isabelle Rosling and smiled. There was something compelling about the older woman. Her wide-set eyes suggested an intelligence that was confirmed every time she spoke. The words rarely came quickly. Instead, they were evenly paced and obliged the listener to follow them on a journey which weaved ideas and facts together in a narrative which engaged the heart as much as they fed the mind.

Mary realised that the older woman was becoming her guide in the world of women's suffrage. Perhaps even more than that. Being with such a powerful personality was inspiring. Even liberating.

As fanciful as it seemed to Mary, it felt like Mrs Rosling saw her not only as a kindred spirit, but also, potentially, as someone who would carry the fight forward in the future. Mary realised she was a little in awe of this woman. As much as she did not want to admit this to herself, Mrs Rosling was beginning to fill a gap that had lain empty since the passing of her mother.

The two women rose from their seats in the small office and stepped outside into the hall. All around them were women from the streets: homeless, on the run from abusive husbands, prostitutes, and thieves. There were young children running around screaming, crying, and laughing. The centre was a playground, a refuge, and a haven. Sanctuary for women who needed protection from the elements, from men and from themselves.

Mary looked around the room almost paralysed with shock.

'I didn't realise places like this existed.'

'They don't,' replied Mrs Rosling grimly.

'What can I do?' asked Mary as she felt tears sting her eyes and fear slowly engulf her heart. She felt desolate and inadequate in equal measure. Incapable of answering the questions posed by her presence among the abandoned, the abused and the abhorred.

'Help us,' said Mrs Rosling, simply.

'These women, children need medical help,' said Mary looking around, her feelings of helplessness growing.

'We have a doctor who helps us out from time to time. I'll introduce you if he comes later. But Lady Mary, I seem to remember you've had some experience in these matters.'

Mary reddened and looked at Isabelle Rosling in surprise. The surprise was not that this lady knew of what she had done during the War. Rather it was the feeling of pride that she had mentioned it. It was the surprise she felt that it *mattered* to her what this woman thought.

Mary nodded to Mrs Rosling. A moment later her coat and hat were off. A quick survey of the scene identified who was most in need of immediate attention. Then she left Mrs Rosling and went into the Hogarthian scene in front of her.

When Mary returned to the house in Grosvenor Square later that afternoon, she found a large bouquet of flowers in the entrance hallway. She raised her eyebrows in a question to Natalie. She desperately hoped they were not from Bobby Andrews. In the background there was music, but she barely noticed the sound of it now. It had become a permanent and welcome addition to the madness of living with Aunt Agatha. Natalie, meanwhile, tried and almost succeeded in hiding her smile.

'They are from Monsieur Lewis. He delivered them personally.'

'Xander,' exclaimed Mary with a laugh. 'My goodness, he's persistent. I'll give him that. Has Lady Esther seen them?'

The Medium Murders

'No, mademoiselle. She went out with Monsieur Bright earlier,' replied Natalie in a tone of voice that suggested it had been a close shave.

Mary grinned at the maid conspiratorially. Then she went over to the flowers and inhaled deeply.

'They're beautiful. Pity to see them thrown out. I'm not sure that Lady Esther needs to know about them and certainly Richard doesn't. I dread to think what he might do to Xander. Why don't you take them down to your room, Natalie?'

This was an eminently sensible solution to an awkward problem of the heart that, frankly, only a member of the practical sex could have conceived. Natalie smiled. She was genuinely grateful to be considered in this way. Naturally she was not so unromantic, which is to say, French, that she would not have preferred flowers intended for her. Perhaps one day a young man…

Natalie thanked Mary and curtsied. Moments later she had removed them from the vase and was hurrying downstairs. Mary watched her go before entering the drawing room. Agatha and Betty were deep in conversation.

'What have I missed?' asked Mary.

The two ladies looked up from their conference. In front of them, taking up a goodly portion of the table, was the large scrap book used by Betty to capture cuttings from the newspapers.

'Well, you missed that ridiculous young man attempting to court Esther. I hope you've both learned a lesson from this,' replied Agatha, tartly.

Betty rolled her eyes, however. In the oft expressed worldview of Betty Simpson, anything that helped advance a case was within the rules. Rule number one, of course, was not to endanger yourself. That was out of bounds. Everything after that was in play. You could go for the green or lay-up. Your choice. The object was still to sink the putt in as few strokes as possible. It would be fair to say that Agatha had long since lost patience with the comparison between sleuthing and golf.

Both ladies listened to Mary's recounting of her morning's activity. Agatha nodded her approval. Was that a moistness in her eye, wondered Mary? Betty, meanwhile, gave her a hearty pat on the back which nearly knocked Mary clear across the table.

'Well, we're waiting to hear from that young man of yours. In the meantime, Doyle has struck gold for us,' announced Betty.

'Really? How so?

'This weekend, he's organised for us to attend three séances. Imagine! One in Kensington, one in Knightsbridge and one in Sloane Square.' said Betty excitedly. 'Isn't that near where that banker lives where you pretended to be the maid?'

'Yes,' said Mary. 'That's the Mrs Rosling I was with today.'

The Medium Murders

Agatha seemed less overwhelmed by the news.

'More opportunity to spend time with the feckless, the foolish and the fatheaded if our first two séances were any guide.'

'Ignore your aunt's cynicism,' replied Betty.

Mary wondered for a second if 'your aunt' was appropriate. But only for a moment. Aunt Agatha was becoming as much her aunt as Kit's. Only the humbleness of Mary would have caused her surprise had she realised to what extent those feelings were reciprocated.

'They are being preyed upon, I agree,' said Mary, wisely taking a middle course.

'My point exactly,' said the two older women in unison, therefore confirming in each of their minds that they were right.

Kit arrived at that point in the afternoon when it's trying to decide to become evening. All three women listened eagerly to the latest developments and with dismay at the news of another murder.

'I didn't see anything in the morning newspaper,' said Agatha.

'The police won't release any details until they find out the name of the poor victim.'

'That's the second murder in a week. I wonder why?' said Mary.

'It does seem strange,' agreed Kit. 'The date has no significance. According to Father Vaughan this could be because she found out about the activities of the killers. It's a ghastly thought, but it may have been part of either an initiation into their circle or some sort of repulsive graduation to a higher level of enlightenment.'

Mary shook her head, but Kit could see the anger in her eyes. Only through the abuse or violence against women could these men acquire power. Mary felt Kit take her hand.

'It's repugnant, I know. I'm sorry.'

'And this Eva Kerr is really with the police?' asked Agatha.

'Well, certainly with MI5. I have the feeling, though, they think there is something to her. Don't ask me to define what that something is. Neither Kell nor Smith-Cumming were prepared to declare her a fake.'

Agatha had already made up her mind on that score and rolled her eyes. Mary merely smiled at Agatha's reaction.

'How was your morning with Mrs Rosling?' asked Kit.

'Sad and inspiring, I would say. She took me to a refuge for women near Waterloo Station. I tried to help. They need so much though. It's difficult to know where to start. These women have escaped bad marriages or families. They've nowhere to go. And then there were the children. What hope have they?'

The Medium Murders

There was silence in the room as she spoke. All felt her pain because they were all feeling it too.

'We should do more to protect vulnerable people in our society,' said Mary at the end.

There was no argument from anyone in the room nor any answer to the problem. For Mary the heartbreak of her morning was not eased by returning to the privilege that formed her everyday life. She wanted to enjoy the adventure of being a detective, but reality had an annoying habit of butting in and leaving her with a feeling of guilt rather than elation.

'The books make it so much more glamorous. Thrilling even,' said Agatha. 'It's not always so.' Her voice trailed off. Her mind drifted to another country, a lifetime ago.

The arrival of Esther and Bright towards the end of the afternoon picked everyone's mood up. They agreed that any discussion of the case would cease for one evening. Kit felt relief at this. For the moment there was nothing that could be done, at least by Kit and Mary. The baton was very much with the police on following up on the movements and the people who associated with the last two victims. Aunt Agatha and Betty would not be able to move forward with their attendance at the séances for a couple of days. Kit wondered what progress was being made by, quite literally, their partners in crime.

25

A couple of evenings previously, two men met at the site of a former prison. At least this is what Wag McDonald told Sergeant Wellbeloved. The sergeant looked around at the paintings on the wall and assumed that the head of the Elephant Boys was pulling his leg. He expressed this rather forcibly which caused McDonald, who was telling the truth, to laugh so loudly that it caused one elderly lady to shush him. The gangland leader and the policeman looked at one another like naughty schoolboys.

The National Galley, situated on Millbank, was home to a collection bequeathed to the nation by Henry Tate. They were not to the taste of Scotland Yard's finest, although McDonald professed liking a George Clausen painting of a melancholic young woman staring at the viewer. Life was hard. Why pretend otherwise? The muted colours in the painting and the expression of the young woman reflected a truth McDonald had learned long before he reached Flanders. He rose from the seat facing the painting and walked over to read its name.

'The Girl at the Gate,' said McDonald. 'Bloody good.'

The Medium Murders

Wellbeloved seemed less impressed, but, then again, he never was. The sergeant went through life with the permanent expression of a carnivore who has discovered a sprout beside his steak. He was one of those men whose chief characteristic was distrust.

McDonald's praise of the painting merely provoked the sergeant into eye-rolling impatience. He was keen to get back to the reason for the meeting. McDonald returned to his seat. Neither man looked like they should be there. Around them were school children and a teacher, a few elderly women, and a man of an artistic disposition.

'Have you got it then?' asked McDonald.

Wellbeloved handed him a piece of paper.

'These are the names and current addresses of all the people known to have been part of this Order. The ones still alive that is.'

'Maybe we can get in touch with the ones that have passed to the other side through your friend Miss Kerr,' said McDonald. Wellbeloved began to cackle. It was not the most attractive of sounds. Nor was the hacking cough that followed it. Moments later, the teacher corralled her children away from the detective towards the next room. She turned around and looked pointedly at Wellbeloved as she went through the exit.

McDonald looked at the list. There were at least twenty names on it. The addresses were all in the parts of town where neither he nor Wellbeloved would make dinner party guest lists. The paper was folded neatly and placed inside McDonald's wallet. There were a lot of other notes. Pound notes. This caused the policeman's eyebrows to rise a notch or two. The leader of the Elephant Boys noticed Wellbeloved's reaction which caused him to smile.

'Who says crime doesn't pay?'

'Not me,' said Wellbeloved rising to his feet. The meeting was over. The men parted. There were no farewells. Each went down the steps of the Tate building and headed off in different directions; just two art lovers after their trip to the gallery.

Sir Watkyn Snodgrass didn't like to answer his door at the best of times. Why else does one have staff? This not unreasonable thought struck him as he went to the door of his townhouse in Fitzroy Square. For some reason Bean, his butler, had asked for an hour off duty to attend to an urgent matter. The matter in question was the serendipitous news that he'd won a competition. That he, for the life of him, could not remember entering this competition was not a matter to trouble him when the princely sum of £500 was his for the asking. To collect his prize, Bean had to be at the statue of Eros in Piccadilly Circus at no later than nine thirty in the morning, and say to a policeman, 'You are Drew P. Dilberry, and I demand my prize'.

The Medium Murders

Bean would soon find out that he had been duped by a wholly fictitious letter which had arrived in the first post. It would result not only in his arrest but also in the arrest of butlers all around the city who had been deceived in a similar manner.

Sir Watkyn was wholly unaware of what lay in store for his unfortunate butler as he opened the door to a rather short man and a very tall woman. They were an odd-looking couple to say the least. In fact, it had been a long time since he'd seen anyone so peculiar.

The man was in his forties. His grey pallor emphasised the dark rings under his eyes. The man's mouth was even less promising. It did not seem to be large enough to cope with his teeth. The movements of the man's jaw were compelling. It looked like he was trying to polish off a tough steak. Equally unprepossessing was his dress. The brown coat had patches on the arms and stains that did not stand further investigation.

The man doffed his hat and smiled. Ye gods. The smile revealed a set of poorly fitted dentures. This explained the odd contortions his mouth broke into when he smiled. The lady standing with him beamed amiably in his direction. It was most disconcerting.

'Yes?' said Sir Watkyn with ill-disguised irritation.

'Good day to you, sir,' said the peculiar-looking man. 'My name is Reverend Henry Threepwood.'

The enunciation was like nothing Sir Watkyn had ever heard before. The provenance was geographically hard to pin down. It started out in West Kensington but appeared to end somewhere in the North Australian outback. The accent temporarily distracted Sir Watkyn long enough for the Reverend to seize the initiative.

'We're collecting for Poor Relief. We want to improve the condition of their lives. Could we have a few moments of your time to tell you more.'

Sir Watkyn certainly did not have time to hear more. He'd spent a lifetime avoiding the lower orders in society and he was damned if he cared a jot about their condition. He recoiled as the Reverend smiled again. It was diabolically compelling. Then there was the overly vigorous nodding of his head at each point made. The movement of the Threepwood's head was so hypnotic that before he knew what he was doing, the knight of the realm and fourth son of Viscount Spiers Snodgrass found himself nodding, too.

The diminutive clergyman stepped forward into the house much to the distress of Sir Watkyn who'd not quite regained his senses sufficiently to tell him where to go. He was followed by his Amazonian wife or assistant. Sir Watkyn hadn't quite worked out the relationship between them never mind its logistics.

'Is it this way to the drawing room?' asked Threepwood with a smile.

Sir Watkyn spluttered something in the affirmative, and before he could say 'Damn your eyes,' the three of them were sitting down.

'There's no need to give us a cup of tea,' said Threepwood to a man for whom tea was the last thing he wanted to offer. 'We've had so much tea on our rounds. Haven't we, dear?'

'Indeed, my love, we have,' said the Amazonian putting her hand on Threepwood's knee, thereby confirming the relationship in Sir Watkyn's mind but throwing up all sorts of other things that, frankly, did not bear thinking about.

'In fact, my dear, I rather think that the tea is beginning to have an effect, if you know what I mean.'

The timbre of the voice was not unattractive; her accent suggested a woman who had married well. Looking at the two of them together, Sir Watkyn wondered how they had married at all. He slowly became aware that they were looking at him expectantly. What had she said? In truth he hadn't been listening. Married chaps have years of training in not listening. The occasional nod of the head and general comment, at seven second intervals, gives the happy impression to the distaff side that they are hanging on every word.

'My wife was perhaps suggesting in a rather delicate manner that she has need of the ladies' room,' said the Reverend Threepwood.

Sir Watkyn glanced once more towards Mrs Threepwood. He could see nothing very delicate about her, in truth. He reckoned she would give Jack Dempsey a run for his money. Bare knuckle.

'It's up the stairs. Second door on the right,' said Sir Watkyn, slowly regaining his composure, if not his senses.

The two men watched Mrs Threepwood leave. One with his eyes full of love, the other with the sort of horror one feels when one knows it's a nightmare and you can't quite manage to wake.

Threepwood turned to Sir Watkyn again and smiled. Whatever the charity, the poor knight had reached a point where he would happily have contributed anything just to be rid of this awful man.

'I notice a picture of a beautiful lady over the mantelpiece.'

'It was my wife,' said Sir Watkyn, softening.

'Oh,' said Threepwood, 'I'm most terribly sorry if I have been indelicate. I'm a believer we shall all meet again in the future at His house.'

Aware that Sir Watkyn had temporarily lost the thread of his consolatory reflections, Threepwood put his hands together and looked heavenwards. The light of understanding reappeared in Sir Watkyn's eyes. Threepwood also recognised impatience when he saw it. He hoped Mrs Threepwood, better known to him as

Alice Diamond, would make the search in double quick time.

Upstairs, Alice Diamond was making a rapid search of the rooms. Each door was opened. Each door revealed a bedroom. All were empty. It was with a heavy heart that she closed each door and went to the next. There were rich pickings to be had and no mistake. For another time maybe.

She returned to the corridor and looked at the paintings on the wall. It occurred to her that she should educate herself on art. Where there was oil paint, there was money. Although quite why anyone would invest money in some of the hideous faces adorning this corridor only Christ, alone, knew.

There was another set of stairs at the end of the corridor. They were quite narrow, and Alice Diamond had to duck a little to avoid banging her head. She ascended quickly and arrived at a corridor with three doors. The first door was opened. Another empty bedroom. The second proved likewise. As she was about to open the third door, she heard sounds emanating from inside the room. These sounds were distinctly human and required no further investigation on the part of Alice Diamond.

The door opened to the drawing room a few minutes later bringing salvation for both the Reverend Threepwood and Sir Watkyn, who rose immediately to his feet and went to the door. This didn't so much suggest as shout that the meeting was over. Sir Watkyn was now back in command of his emotions; chief among these was ill-disguised irritation. The door shut behind Reverend Threepwood and Alice Diamond with an indecent haste. Under normal circumstances this might have offended the lady and the man of the cloth. However, what Sir Watkyn lacked in genteel good manners he made up for in the generosity of his desire to be rid of his guests.

'I'm beginning to like this detective lark' said the Reverend Threepwood waving three-pound notes in the face of his accomplice. They both laughed and went forward to the next address on the list. One down, sixteen houses to go.

Two mornings later, Kit sat in Wag McDonald's office listening to the gang leader recount how matters were progressing.

'Do you know 'Soapy' Smith by any chance?' asked McDonald.

'No, I can't say I've across the name,' admitted Kit to McDonald.

The Medium Murders

'Bert's a confidence trickster. Long cons, shorts cons. He does 'em all. He's been working the charity job with Alice.'

'Which is?'

McDonald explained the mechanics of the operation much to the amusement of his guest.

'I must warn Harry about this in case our paths should cross with Mr Smith's.'

'He's made good progress,' said McDonald.

'I suspect that's not all he's made.'

McDonald laughed but admitted nothing. Then he looked a little more serious.

'None of the houses have any temple that Alice could find. There's still four to do. Three of them refused him entry, so we're having to look at other ways of getting access.'

'Do you need Harry's help?'

McDonald grinned and looked thoughtful.

'Let's see how things go but we might have to consider something like this.'

'How will they manage to gain entry?' asked Kit.

'Well, he can always try the accident job. Leave it to Bert, he'll think of something.'

Kit rose and shook hands with McDonald.

'I think I'll need to rescue Harry now. Your associate, Miss Hill, seems very interested in him.

'Good luck to him,' said McDonald chuckling at the poor man's predicament. He rose and walked with Kit to the door. 'Might come along with you. Maggie has a bit of a temper. You'd never guess of course, what with all that red hair.'

The two men walked out of the office and then downstairs through the saloon bar. Up ahead they saw Miller sitting in the car. In the passenger seat was a young woman. Miller's face was a healthy combination of martyrdom and no little fear. His relief at seeing the arrival of Kit stopped just short of him bounding up to his lordship with his tail wagging.

Across the street, Kit saw a now familiar figure of a man. He was reading the morning newspaper. A hat pulled over his head made it difficult to discern his features. A thought struck Kit and he turned to Wag McDonald.

'By the way, I was wondering if I could ask a small favour of you? I'd be happy to pay.'

Wag McDonald nodded and smiled when he heard the commission.

Bert 'Soapy' Smith, otherwise known as the very Reverend Threepwood, stood with Alice Diamond across the road from a large house in Hampstead. It was a tree-lined avenue just a short walk from the heath. His patience was wearing a little bit thin. There was more than a hint of rain in the air. Not quite pouring but not a refreshing spit either.

The Medium Murders

Smith looked up at the leaden sky and gave vent to his thoughts in a manner that was distinctly ungodly. This coincided with an elderly pedestrian walking past. She stopped and looked aghast at the Reverend. If his language regarding the inclemency of the weather had been colourful it was as nothing compared to the next two words he uttered. Both were directed towards her. This achieved the desired result sending the old lady scuttling off in a state of shock.

'Was that necessary?' asked Alice Diamond, shaking her head although she was highly amused.

'Old baggage,' was all Smith could muster by way of justification.

'Look,' said Alice Diamond suddenly. Soapy Smith followed the line of her outstretched arm.

'I see it. Right. Looks like we're in business.'

Up ahead, a large car was driving at what can only be described as a stately pace. It was a Bentley and the silver gleamed, or at least, it would have, had there been even a ray of sunshine.

Soapy Smith crouched behind one of the cars parked on the road. A few moments later he walked out in front of the oncoming car. He slightly mistimed his sudden appearance. He was too early. The car stopped promptly forcing Smith to hurl himself forward onto the bonnet of the car. From inside screams of anguish and anger could be heard. Two people emerged from the car in great haste to see the none-too-greatly injured vicar. One was an elderly woman wearing a short fur coat and a pearl necklace. The other was a young, suited chauffeur.

'Oh, my goodness,' exclaimed the elderly woman.

Her chauffeur looked shaken although a lot less sympathetic. His suspicions were doused immediately by the arrival of Alice Diamond.

'Oh, my dear, speak to me, speak to me,' she cried dramatically.

'Is he alive?' asked the elderly woman.

Soapy Smith made some sounds that passably could have come from an injured man. They were vigorous enough to indicate pain but reassured, more importantly for the shocked onlookers, that death was not imminent.

'I'm fine,' said Soapy Smith in a voice that indicated he was anything but. He tried to get up off the ground. 'Please, it's just a scratch.'

The chauffeur looked at the elderly woman hopefully. The last thing he wanted was censure for an accident of which he had not the slightest culpability. In fact, he'd been moments away from pointing this out, rather forcibly, when he saw the collar worn by Smith.

'My own fault,' said Soapy Smith, accepting the arm of the chauffeur around his shoulders. He leaned heavily on the young man. Alice Diamond put her arm and considerably more strength to haul the stricken minister in the direction of the woman's house.

The elderly woman replied, 'You must come inside.'

The Medium Murders

It would have been rude to refuse. A minute or three later, Smith was lying on a sofa and the elderly woman ratcheted up the care of the injured man to the third highest level offered in Britain at that time, just behind a doctor attending or a surgical procedure; tea was ordered.

In a voice groaning with stoicism, Soapy Smith introduced himself to the elderly woman.

'My lady, I'm most terribly sorry to put you to this distress. It was entirely my own stupidity. My name is Reverend Threepwood. This is my wife, Mrs Threepwood. My good lady and I are collecting for poor relief.'

Alice Diamond smiled hopefully at the elderly woman and then said, 'I'm very sorry to ask, but all this excitement I'm most terribly in need of the ladies room.'

You're most terribly in need of acting lessons, thought Soapy Smith, but remained silent as the woman gave Alice Diamond directions to the bathroom.

'Collecting for poor relief, did you say?' asked the elderly woman reaching for her handbag.

A smile materialised on the face of the Reverend. His teeth appeared like a dozen grey dreadnoughts ready for scuttling. She handed him five pounds.

'You're too generous.'

He grimaced as he reached to take the pound notes.

26

'So, no wedding then?' asked Kit as he and Miller drove along the embankment. It was raining gently, and the Thames had a slight mist obscuring its grey, brown colour. It was a vast improvement, thought Kit.

'No, sir,' said Miller. 'I think the sooner you catch this killer the better, sir.'

Kit laughed but, in truth, he felt far from jovial. The conclusion to the case was as far away now as when he'd started. They badly needed a break. A mistake. Luck. Either would do right now. Up ahead he saw the Scotland Yard Building emerge from behind some trees.

A few minutes later Kit was sitting with Jellicoe and Sergeant Wellbeloved. The atmosphere between them was less charged than before. As much as he may have deplored the methods of Wellbeloved, there was no questioning his doggedness. Kit's suspicion that the sergeant was working extraordinarily long hours was confirmed partly by the look on Jellicoe's face as well as by the report from Wellbeloved on the number of people he had interviewed.

'We still, however, do not know the name of the most recent victim,' said Wellbeloved by way of conclusion.

'We've been through every missing person in the country now. Only seven matched the description and estimated age of the young woman.'

Kit rubbed his eyes although it was probably Wellbeloved who was the more tired of

the two.

'What will you do next?'

At that moment there was a knock on the door. A man entered or, to be more accurate, made an entrance. Had Kit not felt so despondent he might have been amused by the man's manner.

'Hello, Mr Watts,' said Jellicoe.

'Ahh Chief Inspector, so good to see you looking gay as ever,' said Watts airily.

At this point Rufus Watts, the chief artist at Scotland Yard noticed Kit. He stopped for a moment and made a point of studying him closely. He seemed to like what he saw.

'Who do we have here?'

Jellicoe did manage to smile at this point. He glanced at Kit and then back to the police artist.

'This is Lord Aston, Mr Watts.'

Kit felt that there was a degree of theatre in the way Rufus Watts exaggerated how impressed he was. The light clap of the hand, the brushing back of a stray lock of his rather long hair and his exclamation, 'Well, this is an honour.'

Kit wasn't quite sure how much Watts was honoured or how much the little man was making fun of him.

'I picked these up from the photographer.'

Jellicoe broke the seal of the envelope. He took out a thick pile of photostats and placed them on the table. Kit picked one up and looked at it. He felt his skin prickle. Two things were apparent to him immediately. He recognised the work of Watts from a pair of cases he'd solved earlier in the year. More importantly, there was something about the young woman.

Jellicoe had a sense of these things. Normally, these images were glanced at then ignored. Kit was staring at the drawing of the young woman. Finally, he looked up at Watts and then Jellicoe.

'I must congratulate you, Mr Watts. This is remarkable. Very lifelike.'

The artist waved his hand in a manner that suggested such compliments meant nothing to him when, in fact, they meant the world.

'Congratulations to you too, Chief Inspector,' said Kit. 'I think this makes much more sense than publishing a picture of a dead young woman. I dread to think what the reaction would be.'

'This image will be in the evening papers,' confirmed Jellicoe. 'The sergeant and a number of my men will visit some shelters for homeless women now.'

'Is there anything I can do to help?' asked Kit.

The Medium Murders

'I'm not sure that there is but take one of the images anyway. Who knows?'

This effectively ended the meeting. Kit left the office and negotiated the stairs down to the ground floor. As he walked, he studied the image. There was something familiar about her. He managed, more by good luck than good grace, to avoid any collision with a car as he crossed the road and headed towards the Rolls.

'Back home, I think, Harry.'

'What's that, sir' asked Miller, indicating the photostat.

Kit showed the image to Miller.

'May I?'

Miller took hold of the picture and looked at it intently. It was something in Miller's reaction.

'Do you recognise her, Harry?'

Miller shrugged in the manner of a man who is almost embarrassed to say what was on his mind.

'Well, you're not going to believe this, but I think she looks very much like Patty Tunstall. Countess Laskov's maid.'

Kit looked at the image again.

'Good lord, you're right,' exclaimed Kit. 'Of course.' He stared at the picture for a moment longer. 'We need to tell Jellicoe. Not a moment to lose.'

Jellicoe was silent for a moment as he studied Kit. It was not in his nature to be excited about anything. However, he had instincts about people. About things. The amateur detective was for the penny bloods. Jellicoe had always believed this. Yet here, now, once again, a case was potentially opening before his eyes. The way forward was clear. All thanks to a man who came straight from the pages of fiction.

He almost laughed. Almost. It was too serious a business. Instead, his mind turned to the case as it always did. The problem to be solved. It was the same every day of his working life. By virtue of his rank, his experience and his competence, the questions he had to answer were never easy. More than this, the problems he faced were as harrowing as they were heart-breaking. When he finished this case there would be another. Then another.

But for the moment it was just this case, these killings and the killer. More than one killer, probably. Almost certainly male. Ending the lives of young women. He felt a wave of anger course through his body. Of course, he would take help from whatever source he could. Didn't he always?

Finding the truth was more important to him than anything else. However, there were lines he would not cross. The faces of Bulstrode and Wellbeloved came into his mind. Yet here he was now, not only consorting with criminals and nobility, but *working* with them. He knew the world was mad. He saw the human misery caused by this madness. Was he going mad as well?

Perhaps.

For now, though, there was this. A young woman. Murdered before her life had really begun. Murdered in manner that ensured her last seconds on this earth were filled with terror and agony. Murdered by madmen. They had to be stopped.

'You're absolutely certain, sir?'

'Yes, Chief Inspector. I knew I'd seen her face before.'

The Chief Inspector sat back in his seat and turned to Wellbeloved. The sergeant's face retained that look of permanent scepticism which made him awkward company but an effective policeman. Jellicoe saw no point in asking his sergeant whether he believed they had now identified the young woman. He believed Kit. That was enough. It made sense. They had been unable to trace either Tunstall or the other servant, Bentham. In truth, they hadn't tried very hard. There were more pressing matters to attend to.

'Sergeant, you'll need to find Tunstall's family. Someone will have to break the news. Find out if she went to see them. If she didn't, find out what friends she may have had.'

'It sounds as if she was doing a runner, sir,' said Wellbeloved. 'Perhaps she stole something.'

'Or perhaps she was seeing things in the house that scared her,' added Kit.

'In which case she may not have had time to find somewhere to live,' said Wellbeloved.

'Try some of the homeless refuges in London,' suggested Jellicoe. 'She had to go somewhere. It'll either be there, her family or a friend. We need to know her whereabouts from the moment she left the countess and why she left. Get someone to check on Bentham again. Is Fletcher around? Take him off whatever he's doing; this is the priority.'

Wellbeloved nodded. Without saying anything else, he picked up the photostat copies and walked out of the office. Jellicoe and Kit watched him go. Then Kit turned to Jellicoe. There was a grim smile on his face. Jellicoe noticed this and raised his eyebrows by way of a question.

'Well, Chief Inspector, this may be the break we've been looking for. While your man is checking on the last whereabouts of Miss Tunstall, I have an idea of who I need to speak to now. It may help answer the question of why she left Countess Laskov.'

'Who do you have in mind?'

'I doubt you'll believe me when I tell you.'

27

The account of Patty Tunstall's murder was now in the news although no details had been provided that would connect it in any way with the other murders. The next day, Fallon Bentham, the former butler to Countess Laskov, had come forward. He'd been staying with his cousin in Birmingham. He was now at Scotland Yard helping the police with their inquiries. Jellicoe took the lead in this, fearful that Wellbeloved's interrogatory methods would not only be misplaced but probably counterproductive.

At thirty-five years of age, Bentham was probably a bit too young to have been involved in the earliest killings. In the Chief Inspector's mind this did not preclude a connection. However, his whereabouts, once checked, would probably confirm that he could not have had a hand in Tunstall's death. The key question to be answered was why he and then, Tunstall, had left the Laskov household.

'What led you and Miss Tunstall to leave?'

Bentham was sweating profusely. Jellicoe was unsure if this was because of guilt or, more likely, fear. The more he studied Bentham, the more he was convinced it went beyond fear. What he was looking at was terror. Pure, unadulterated terror. Nothing to do with any thought that he was a suspect in a crime. This man was in dread of something more sinister.

'That place was evil, sir.'

'Evil?'

'Yes, sir. After the Count died. Before it was strange but they're all a bit strange. But when he died, she went mad, sir. At first, we thought it was grief. Y'know, picking us up on little things. She'd never leave the house. Didn't want to see visitors. Then she seemed, one day, to change. It was as if she'd overcome her grief.'

'How long after the Count's death was this?' asked Jellicoe.

'Three months as good as.'

'What happened?'

'She began to go out more. I would take her out to the houses of her friends. She was happier, if you know what I mean, rather than happy. The visits to her friends seemed to give her a lift. Even Patty said as much. She became much nicer again.'

'But then she began to change?'

Bentham sat back in his seat. Having the opportunity to tell the police was beginning to help. The perceptible quiver of fear in his voice, the restless eye movement began to slow down. The calm, monotonous voice of the Chief Inspector was working to exorcise the demons that had submerged him. This was a catharsis.

The Medium Murders

'It wasn't a change in her. She began changing things in the house and she invited more and more her friends to visit.'

'What changes in the house?'

'Everything. Black curtains, black walls. Candles. It was strange but we thought it was just the grief.'

'And her friends?'

'This is what we, me and Patty, didn't like. At first, they were just a lot of 'nobs. You know the sort, harmless old rich people. But then we heard them in that room having these séances. Patty was really afraid.'

'Were you?'

'Not at that point. I've seen these people, these mediums before. Y'know, fairgrounds and the like. Crystal balls. I thought it was balls. I said as much to Patty.'

For the first time, Bentham managed a smile.

'But you changed your mind?'

'Not at first, as I say. After a few months, though, it began to change. The people we were used to seeing stopped coming. Then it was others.'

'Did you know any of them?'

'No.'

'But what was it about them.'

'I don't know. There was something dark about them.'

'Men?'

'Men and women. They were evil. I don't know how I know. Actually, I do. Simpkins didn't like them. At first when they came, he would hiss at them. Then the Countess told us to take him away whenever they came. I think she was embarrassed. Where is Simpkins, by the way?'

'He's being looked after,' replied Jellicoe, keen to move on, 'What did they do in the room?'

'I don't know. We just heard chanting. Not loud. Just low.'

'What were they saying?' probed Jellicoe. He knew any servant worth his salt would have had his ear pressed to the door. If he knew Bentham, and he was beginning to, he would have been far too curious not to have listened.'

'It wasn't any language I'd ever knew. From what I could hear it was like Latin or something, but I couldn't be sure.'

'What did Miss Tunstall think?'

'She stayed well out of it. She said they looked at her strange. The men. She didn't like them. She was an innocent girl, but she knew what they were thinking.'

'Did she have a sweetheart?'

Jellicoe looked closely at Bentham. He wondered if they were lovers.

'None. She was a good girl, Chief Inspector. This was her first proper job. She didn't want to make a bad impression. Cooking, cleaning. She was happy to be in such a nice place.'

Jellicoe nodded.

'You left before her. What made you leave, Mr Bentham? What made you leave before Miss Tunstall.'

-

She looked hideous. Like an old crone. Like? She was an old crone. Barking mad. There was a glint in her eye. Aye, barking mad, all right. The way she spoke to Patty. Do this, don't do that. It wasn't right.

The day I left I went into that room. It was dark, as usual. Those curtains didn't just stop the light coming in. They stopped life. Inside was the whisper of death, the smell of decay. I hated it. I hated her.

Here she was again. My god, couldn't she see how she looked? What was she becoming? Like a monster. Or worse.

'Tunstall, you haven't been in the sitting room, have you?'

'No, madam,' said Patty.

'Well don't. Do you hear?'

She's standing a foot away from you. Of course, she hears you. Old bag. Leave her alone.

'And you, Bentham. Why haven't you got a lock on this door? I asked you yesterday.'

'He's coming later this afternoon, madam.'

She's mad. Look at her. What has she drawn round her eyes? Mascara? Looks like wall paint. You'd see less rouge on a harlot in Whitechapel. Mad.

Jack Murray

'Get your coat, Tunstall. I'm going to the park. Come with me. You, Bentham. Make sure there's a lock on this door for when I return.'

'I will, madam.'

They go out.

The door. It's black now. It used to be a lovely rich oak colour. Old bag. Why does she want a lock on it?

The door.

The room is dark when I open the door. At least the lights still work. I see the chest that arrived the previous day. A wooden thing, like the pirates use. Doubt there's much treasure in there. It's padlocked.

Strange. Was that a noise?

I stay still. There it was again. Muffled.

I can hear blood rushing around my ears. My heart feels like it's the noisiest thing in this room. The sound stops.

Dong!

Bloody clock nearly gave me a heart attack. Four o'clock. Where is that bloody locksmith.

Then I hear it again. Whatever it is, it's coming from the chest. I go to it and looks down. At the side there is a grill. Can't see what's inside. The countess has left a key on the mantelpiece. I go over and then bring it to the padlock. I'm shaking like a leaf. The key fits and I hear the click of the padlock. I take off the padlock. The sound is more distinct now.

It's like a…

The Medium Murders

'A black cockerel, a white hen and what…?' exclaimed Jellicoe.

Bentham was crying.

Jellicoe gave him a few minutes to recover himself.

'I don't know. Just bones. But there was tissue on it and blood, feathers. A small animal I suppose. I don't know. How could there be a noise? I just shut the chest, put the padlock back on and ran out of the room. I wasn't staying there a second longer.'

'What about Tunstall? You just left her?'

'No. Yes. I warned her. I left a note in her room. I told her to pack her things and go.'

'Did you tell her why?'

'Yes. I said the countess was mad. That she was evil. I thought she would harm us. I mean, I told her to go. You must believe me.'

'Did you go back?'

'No, I went as far away from that evil bitch as I could.'

Bentham broke down again. This time Jellicoe left him. There was nothing to say to him. By escaping, he had, effectively, condemned the young maid to die. Jellicoe was certain of this. He was sure that Bentham knew this, too. Whoever was killing these young women had visited the house. He, or they, were known to Countess Laskov.

It would take a day, but Bentham would be required to trawl his memory for faces that he would rather forget. Try and remember names. Fragments of conversation. Anything that could generate a line of inquiry.

Jellicoe looked into the eyes of Sergeant Wellbeloved. He could see the contempt there. Contempt for Bentham's cowardice. Contempt for his weakness. He glared at the sergeant. This was not a time for coercion. He jerked his thumb at Wellbeloved. Outside he was saying.

In the corridor, Jellicoe whispered urgently.

'I want names. If he can't give us names, I want faces. I'll get Watts down here. I don't care if he spends the next twenty-four hours drawing pictures. I want Bentham's memory dredged. And what's more, sergeant, I want it done right. Do you hear? He's not under arrest. But hold him here. And tell no one who he is and what this is for.'

'Yes sir,' said Wellbeloved. He could have been talking to his teacher.

Jellicoe left the corridor and went in search of Rufus Watts. Frustratingly he was not in his office. He spotted a large, rather stupid-looking detective nearby and asked him for the whereabouts of the police artist.

A shrug of the shoulders confirmed that the detective in question was every bit as bovine as he looked. Muttering an oath under his breath, he walked along the

The Medium Murders

corridor checking in each office for any sign of Watts. Finally, one uniformed officer provided a potential location. He was with the Commissioner.

Jellicoe bounded up the stairs and went to the Commissioner's office. A middle-aged woman was sitting on guard outside. His secretary. There was a marked coldness on her face that suggested that not only were visitors unwelcome, but she also positively hated them and their families.

'Mrs Brook.'

'Miss Brook,' replied the guard dog.

Strange that you never married, thought Jellicoe fleetingly.

'I urgently need to see Mr Watts. I gather he is with Commissioner Horwood.'

'Does Mr Watts urgently need to see you?'

Jellicoe stared at the gorgon in horror. A slow smile crept across her face like a tiger contemplating its sleeping prey.

Which is about the moment that Jellicoe, for the first time in decades, lost his temper. Miss Brook was a bully. She had risen to the top of the secretarial tree within Scotland Yard. Commissioners came and went. She was immutable. With such longevity comes a certain standing, even if it's only you who sees it. At that moment, Jellicoe only saw one thing.

Red.

He walked slowly towards her. By this stage Miss Brook was uncomfortably aware that her attempts at intimidation had, for the first time, gone sadly awry. The look on the Chief Inspector's face suggested murder: if not the one he was investigating, then the one he was about to commit.

'Please tell the Commissioner I need Watts. And I need him now, please.'

Jellicoe's manner of communication was a far cry from his usual brisk enunciation. This was a slow growl rather in the manner of a demonic German Shepherd. The manner of asking impressed Miss Brook sufficiently to leap up immediately and go to the door.

Jellicoe, working on the principle that a hot iron needs to be struck, followed her closely. She knocked on the door and entered when she heard the call.

'My apologies for bothering you sir, Chief Inspector Jellicoe is rather desirous of seeing Mr Watts.'

Jellicoe walked into the room and saw Watts, Dr French and the Commissioner enjoying what looked like a whisky. A glance at the nearby cupboard confirmed the presence of a Glenlivet standing proudly atop some files no doubt containing details of various heinous crimes. Jellicoe was sure that the country would feel very reassured by the sedulousness of the nation's law enforcement commander.

The Medium Murders

'What do you want, Jellicoe?' asked the former Brigadier-General, amused by the expression on his Chief Inspector's face. 'Come on, spit it out, man.'

28

'Now, my dear, you,' said Rufus Watts pointing dramatically at a slightly alarmed Bentham, 'are going to describe to me all of the people you can remember. I will draw them on this beautiful piece of paper here and we will be great friends. Won't we?'

Bentham wasn't so sure he wanted to be. He gazed, awestruck, at the remarkable little man in front of him. Although he wasn't an expert on the forces of law and order, he was certain they did not wear red velvet jackets to work. He was equally sure that their hair was shorter than shoulder length. The cravat went well with the jacket, to be fair, but, once more, it struck Bentham that this was probably atypical for the police.

Watts placed several photographs of men and women on the table. There was a mixture of ages and genders.

'Now, handsome, look at these pretty pictures and tell Rufus if any of these lovely men and women have features that resemble people you saw. As much as I would have loved one of these people to be a devil-worshipping fetishist, they are all policemen and their spouses. Which is not to say they don't have esoteric interests, it's just highly unlikely if I know the breed. And

The Medium Murders

I do. Look at the hair, look at the noses, look at the shapes of their faces. Think of it as a jigsaw puzzle that we're going to piece together. It's going to be fun.'

To reassure the perspiring Bentham, Watts gave his hand a reassuring squeeze.

'There, there. It's time to make Rufus a happy boy.'

Watts arranged himself into a comfortable position and studied the former butler as he went through the photographs.

'Is this helpful?'

'A little, sir,' responded Bentham. 'It wasn't always easy to see the people's faces when they arrived. Many wore hats. One of them even looked a little like you, sir.'

'Did they?' said Watts with a smile. 'Handsome and well-dressed I'll be bound.'

Bentham seemed to be relaxing now and he allowed himself a smile.

'Yes, sir. Of course, he had spectacles.'

'Really? Did they look like these?'

Watts reached behind him and put on a pair of glasses. Bentham looked at Watts for a moment. A trace of nervousness reappeared on his face.

'Yes, a little like that, sir.'

'Excellent, Bentham. I'll make a start while you are perusing the other pictures. Don't be afraid to lift them either if you need a closer inspection. And remember - you can combine several pictures into one face.'

Six hours later, a relieved Bentham was escorted from the office of the police artist. Watts looked down at the pictures he'd created from the descriptions. He picked up the first and examined it. A smile broke out over his face, and he began to chuckle. He shook his head at the absurdity of it all.

Watts spent the next hour tidying up the drawings. Any stray marks were erased. The value of the shadows was raised or lowered in accordance with how it related to the overall harmony of the picture. He hated the meaningless jargon of modern art. Every time he created a piece of art, for his work was art, he started with one thought in mind. How would Whistler do this? What he sought was not mechanical accuracy, although he accepted this was the objective required of him by his colleagues. Watts was searching for something else.

That something else was nothing less than the inner life of the subject he was drawing.

-

It was after eight in the evening. The lateness of the hour was not something which bothered Watts particularly. He was a nocturnal animal. A bachelor. There was no family waiting for him by the hearth. This meant he could work late into the night quite happily. Afterwards there were a few places where his society was appreciated.

The Medium Murders

Rarely did Scotland Yard enjoy his company before ten in the morning. His talent bought him a degree of latitude that his sharp tongue often mortgaged. Despite his diminutive physical stature, it was a point of pride to him that many of the officers lived in fear of his artistic temperament.

He collected his sheaf of drawings into a neat pile and left his office. There was a police photographer who would be able to convert these into photostats for circulation. As he was walking towards the staircase that led to the basement of the building, he encountered a familiar face.

'Commissioner,' said Watts with a smile.

'Working late as ever I see, Rufus,' replied the Commissioner. 'How many people was this butler chappie able to remember.'

'Six in all. One of them looked a bit like me apparently.'

This was greeted with a guffaw from the Commissioner.

'If you think that's funny, look at this one.'

Watts turned the papers over so that the Commissioner could see better.

'Well, well, well.'

They walked together along the corridor. Then the Commissioner turned to Watts, 'Why don't I take those to Shepherd. Save you a walk. I'm going in that direction anyway. I left my pipe in French's office. Might even get the man to get a move on if he's there. If not, I'll write him a note. If he sees it's me, it might expedite matters somewhat.'

Watts handed over the drawings and bid the Commissioner good night. Outside in the night air, Watts considered his options. There were many for a man such as he. And he was not someone who would forego any pleasure available to him.

Commissioner Horwood walked down the stairs to the basement floor. He saw a light on in Shepherd's office. As he walked towards it, he saw a familiar face.

'Hello William, what brings you down here?'

Commissioner Horwood held up the drawings of the suspects identified by Bentham.

'I'm Rufus' errand boy these days.'

The two men had a good laugh at that.

-

Arnold Bentham scanned the hotel room that the police had taken him to. The single bed was unwelcoming. A brief peek at the sheets neither confirmed nor refuted the proposition that they had not been cleaned in a considerable time. The carpet had a distressing combination of holes, cigarette burns and stains that Bentham really did not want to think about. How the mighty had fallen.

Once upon a time, he'd lived in mansions, waited at the tables of lords and ladies. Now he was reduced to this. Staying at a tawdry hotel in Soho. It was almost enough to make a man yell.

Coincidentally this is what he heard in the next room. However, the sound was from a female and did not suggest that anguish was the principal emotion of the moment. Bentham sat down on the bed and put his head in his hands. He would find a way back. He had experience. He was capable. He had much to offer an employer of taste and discrimination.

The thought of the future inspired him to look beyond the dismal present. Tomorrow he would return to Scotland Yard. Hopefully this would draw a line under the nightmare he'd experienced with the countess. The horrible old crone.

As this thought and a few other equally unkind reflections drifted through his mind, he became aware of a gentle knock on the door. Perhaps it was the policeman again with some sandwiches. In all the clamour to question him, there'd been precious little by way of sustenance. Bentham leapt up from the bed and went to the door. Not the longest of journeys, it must be reported.

He opened the door and was in the process of saying 'I'm glad you're back' when the words froze in his mouth. The man before him was not the policeman who'd accompanied him earlier. By the time he'd registered who the man was, Arnold Bentham was already falling to the floor, his throat cut by a single swipe of an expert hand.

29

'It was good of you to see us at such short notice, Sir Arthur,' said Kit, sitting facing Conan Doyle.

They'd set off early in the morning by car with Miller driving. The first stop had been to Scotland Yard to collect the photostats of the people who may have visited séances in Countess Laskov's apartment.

From there it was a long drive into the heart of Surrey to a village called Windlesham. The journey would have been more pleasant had the weather been better.

'Stinking day,' said Agatha giving voice to the thoughts of Kit and Harry. Mary had stayed behind to visit Mrs Rosling. The thought of this slightly perturbed Kit but he avoided thinking about it too much for fear that his reasons were jealousy, or worse, an irrational disquiet about associating with the Rosling family. Sam had joined them on the journey and soon provided a welcome distraction from disquieting thoughts.

An hour and half later they were in the sitting room of Doyle's residence, Windlesham Manor. It was an impressive country house, very much to Kit's taste, located in the Surrey village. Inside, it was light, airy, and decorated without any desire to follow fashion other than the good taste of the owner.

'Nonsense, Kit, I'm only sorry I couldn't see you sooner. You don't mind if I call you Kit? Call it a privilege of old age.'

Kit smiled and replied, 'Of course, Sir Arthur.'

Agatha shifted uncomfortably.

'Can we get on with this. Even if Arthur isn't busy, I certainly have things to do.'

Doyle roared with laughter; a relieved Kit joined him moments later.

'You haven't changed, Agatha.'

Kit wasn't sure this was entirely a good thing. However, he noted that far from being offended, Doyle seemed to enjoy her, Kit struggled for a moment to find the right expression before settling for, restless energy.

'Nor you. You're too courteous. Always have been,' said Agatha, although only someone who did not know her would have missed a certain nostalgia in her tone.

'How can I help you?' asked Doyle, sensing it was probably time to get down to business.

Kit told him all he knew of the events leading up to the death of the countess including the departure of both Bentham and Tunstall. There was sadness in the eyes of Doyle as he listened intently. When Kit had finished, Doyle shook his head in sorrow rather than in anger for his friend.

The Medium Murders

'And the séances? Have they thrown up anything useful, Agatha?'

'We're attending three the day after tomorrow, so we shall see.'

'Were you aware that the countess's interests had moved further towards the occult than before?

Doyle pondered this for a moment. It was clear there was some awareness. Kit had no doubt that Doyle would not lie so he was content to let the great author find the right expression for what was on his mind. He looked down at Sam and picked the little terrier up. Doyle chuckled but Kit sensed the melancholy in the man.

'I was indirectly aware. I told you when I met you that I had attended one séance at her apartment. We met at a few others. In fact, Agatha, you will be going to two of them. But I had noticed that she withdrew a few months ago from attending any others. I did ask a friend about this. I remember seeing him shake his head. He said she was mixing with some of the Alpha Omega factions.

Kit leaned forward. He felt his heartbeat faster.

'Sir Arthur, am I right in thinking this group was once part of the Hermetic Order of the Golden Dawn?'

Doyle smiled but there was embarrassment in the smile, Kit could see.

'Yes. I thought they'd been consigned to history.'

'Sir Arthur, one of the reasons we came here today was to ask you about this Order. We think the killers may once have been part of the Order. Furthermore, they're responsible for more than just the murder of Miss Tunstall. We believe they have killed as many as thirteen young women over the last twelve years or more.

'Good lord,' exclaimed Doyle. 'But how is this possible? Why haven't we heard?'

Kit explained how and why the decision had been made to draw a veil over the connection between the killings. The political and social ramifications spanned party politics, social class, and issues such as suffrage. The decision to keep secret the murders came from the very top.

'It would be of value to know about the Order around the time that it broke up and which, if any, of the splinter groups may have had more extreme members.'

Doyle thought for a while. Neither Agatha nor Kit interrupted him. After a minute, Kit was genuinely worried the great man would fall asleep. A minute passed. The only sound to be heard in the room were birds outside before Agatha broke the silence.

'More tea?'

The two men nodded yes, and Agatha refilled their cups.

'I am convinced that medical science will one day make a connection between tea and improved brain function,' said Agatha.

Kit was tempted to point out that his aunt was proof positive there was absolutely no connection between tea

The Medium Murders

and having a patient, easy going disposition. The thought lay unspoken in his mind however as Doyle seemed restored by the imbibing of the miracle elixir.

'How much do you know about the Order?' asked Doyle.

'Anything you can tell us would be useful,' said Agatha, reaching for an Eccles cake.

'I would preface my comments by saying two things. It was a long time ago.'

The unspoken truth that one's memory tends not to improve with age was clear. Kit smiled sympathetically. Agatha finished the Eccles cake.

'Secondly, I was not part of the Order in the sense that I wanted to rise through the different degrees. For me, it was more a meeting of like-minded individuals keen to understand metaphysics and esoteric philosophy.'

The Eccles cake proved too much of a temptation for Doyle and he followed Agatha's lead in demolishing one. Then Doyle mopped the side of his mouth with a napkin and continued.

'The Order was founded by three men: William Woodman, William Westcott and Samuel Mathers. All Masons, of course,' added Doyle wryly.

'Westcott came into possession of Cipher Manuscripts which he deciphered and, with the help of Woodman and Mathers, developed them into a curriculum with rituals. The manuscripts themselves were a combination of Hermetic Qabalah and elements of basic astrology, tarot reading, geomancy and alchemy. In those days there was never any talk of Satan or God. I started attending meetings around 1890 usually with people who were very well known. My interest tailed off in the late 1890's after Westcott left. Woodman, I would add, died a few years previously. This meant that Mathers was very much the leading light in the movement. Was never quite sure of him.'

'Why not?' asked Kit.

'Something. He liked being leader. Anyway, by this time my interest was waning. Spiritualism was becoming a greater part of my life. After I left, I lost contact with many of the members. I heard through some friends that the Order began to break up around 1900. This was brought on by Mathers, I believe. He was high handed. Smart, I'll give him that. As the nominal leader of the organisation, he claimed to be in touch with the Secret Chiefs. No one knows who they are. They could be supernatural beings or little men from outer space for all we know.'

'You don't seem convinced, Arthur,' suggested Aunt Agatha.

Doyle raised his palms up, unwilling to commit one way or another. It was plain he didn't believe.

'After Westcott left, Mathers was the only one in touch with these beings.'

The Medium Murders

'Why did Westcott leave? I mean, if he was in touch with these special beings, it seems to me he would want to stay the course.'

Doyle smiled, 'One would think so. But life has a way of throwing pebbles at the window while you're trying to sleep. He lost some important documents that revealed his involvement with the Order. I would add Westcott was a Crown Coroner. Naturally his employers were none too happy. So, he left. I say, left, I think he was still involved. You don't ever stop believing,' said Doyle, more dismissively this time. He finished tea before looking back up at his guests.

'What became of him?' asked Agatha.

'He retired long before the War from his role as Coroner and went to live in South Africa. Still alive for all I know.

Kit and Agatha looked at one another.

'To finish off on the breakup of the organisation, Mathers fell in with a very odd chap named Aleister Crowley.

Doyle looked at Kit when he said this. Kit nodded; he was familiar with him.

'He was an occultist. Heard he was in the Secret Intelligence Service.'

Or Germany's, thought Kit. Spunky could never confirm which.

'Many of the members apparently objected to the way he was introduced. He was brought in at a senior level and it caused ructions. I believe they eventually led to the fragmenting of the Order. I'm afraid I don't know what shape that took. I do know that some of the people Westcott had brought in formed some temples which, I hear, dabbled in the worship of Lucifer. These were just rumours. Nothing more. I'm afraid I don't know who was involved. It was all so long ago I'm not even sure I can direct you towards who might know.'

'I know it's been a long time, Sir Arthur, but it would be a great service to us if you look at these photostats. Do any of them seem familiar from the séances you have attended?'

Kit reached down and withdrew a selection of pictures from his bag, placing them all on the table. There were five in total. Four men and one woman. Doyle did not have to ask what was required of him. He rose from his chair and went to a cabinet to retrieve his spectacles.

'Old age,' he sighed as he sat down.

He adjusted the spectacles and picked up each picture and looked carefully at the faces. Kit and Agatha glanced at one another but neither felt optimistic if Doyle's countenance was any guide. Finally, he looked at his guests with a look of sorrow.

'They are fine likenesses I'm sure, but I cannot put a name with certainty to any of them. This one and this one seems familiar,' said Doyle pointing to a man and the woman.

The Medium Murders

Agatha, to be fair, did try to avoid looking vexed at this. She failed of course.

'Oh, come on, Arthur. You're among friends. Look at them again. At this point even a vague likeness could be important.'

'You haven't changed,' smiled Doyle. He picked up the picture of the woman and studied it again.

'You're accusing no one, Sir Arthur,' said Kit.

Doyle nodded and continued to look at the picture.

'There is a passing resemblance to Beatrice Wolf.'

'Peter Wolf's wife?' exclaimed Kit.

'You know her?' asked Doyle.

'Well, I know her husband, Peter. I've met Lady Wolf once or twice.'

Doyle handed the photostat to Kit who, likewise, studied it closely. He nodded and looked at Doyle.

'There is something about the likeness. I didn't know she was a follower of spiritualism.'

'Oh yes. Many years. I don't know her husband so well. He doesn't appear to share her interest. I gather she lost family and was hoping to make contact again. I can't remember the details, however. I'm sorry.'

The interview drew to its conclusion with no further insights from Doyle. As they walked out of the room Kit stopped in front of a photograph of a young man in an army uniform. He was smiling. Life and confidence radiated from him.

'Kingsley,' said Doyle. He couldn't add anything else. Agatha took his hand and pressed it gently.

Kit looked at his aunt on the journey back. She seemed troubled by the interview. Kit asked her why.

'I'm not sure it's moved us further forward.'

'There were some things. We need to send a telegram to Westcott in South Africa. I'm sure Spunky can manage to find out where he is. He can tell us if there were any individuals that might have harboured a curiosity beyond the philosophic interests of the Order.'

Agatha nodded and agreed it was worth trying. However, her mind seemed to be on other things. For the remainder of the journey, she stared out of the window at the countryside as they passed through one rain squall after another. Whatever was on her mind, Kit knew from experience, would stay there until she was ready to share.

The silence on the journey gave Kit the peace and quiet to think through the next steps of the investigation. Then there was Mary.

And Mrs Rosling.

Try though he might, he couldn't fight the feeling that he was losing a part of Mary to the American. Losing? He hated to think of it in this way. Mary loved him. He knew this to be true just as he knew there was no one else for him. Their love was unconditional.

The Medium Murders

But love is never unconditional. It makes demands.

Kit not only accepted Mary's fierce independence, but he also loved her for it. Already he'd found, however, that it left him with little option but to accede to how this spirit would, on occasion, place her in danger. He'd never reconciled himself to this.

Why did it bother him, then, if she became more involved with Mrs Rosling? With a realisation bordering on shame Kit realised how little account he'd taken of the suffrage movement. He supported the right of women to vote. It seemed insane to him that there were educated, intelligent women like Mary who had no right to vote while men who were no better than thugs could exercise this right.

Over the years he'd been aware of the actions taken by the Suffragettes. The protests. The militant action against shops and buildings. The imprisonments. The hunger strikes. And, of course, the fatal protest undertaken by Emily Davison at the Derby.

It wasn't until later, through Mary, that he heard of the brutally repressive way these protesters had been treated. The beatings at the hands of the police and the prison warders; the forced feeding.

And yet these same women, during the war, had effectively dropped their protest and joined the effort to defeat Germany. Many women were recruited into jobs vacated by men who had gone to fight in the war. They worked in intolerable conditions in munitions factories, supporting the police, in transport as Esther had done and, of course, providing childcare.

Their reward at the end of the war was a half-hearted acknowledgement of their effort: the right to vote for women over the age of thirty. The right to vote, that is, if they lived in a property with a rateable value above £5, or if their husband did.

Kit shook his head. *Or their husband did*. What should have been a moment of reflection and atonement became yet another slap in their face. What had he done? Had he even thought about the movement over this period? Intellectual agreement was one thing, yet he'd done nothing in support of the movement's aims. In a moment bordering on epiphany, he realised his objection wasn't to Mrs Rosling so much as the light it cast on his own apathy.

This had to change.

After stopping off for lunch at a country pub, they made it back to London in the early afternoon. The rain continued to beat a dismal reminder that winter was coming. It did little to improve the mood of any of the passengers. Each, including Sam, seemed lost in their own world.

Kit joined Agatha as she made her way to the entrance of the Grosvenor Square mansion. There was no sign of Mary, or Esther for that matter. Agatha

The Medium Murders

passed a large bouquet of flowers in the hall and went downstairs. There was music playing. It was classical but Kit did not recognise it. Rather than wait, Kit decided to return to the flat in Belgravia.

'Hello, Richard,' said Kit as he entered the apartment. 'I thought you'd be with Esther.'

'No, not today. She's abandoned me to join Mary. I think she's with those Suffragist types.'

His voice was more lonely than amused or angry. Kit knew how he felt.

'There's a telegram, sir.'

Miller bent down and picked the small envelope off the ground and handed it to Kit who tore open the envelope. One never simply opens a telegram. By its nature it was urgent. Therefore, one's treatment of it should likewise reflect the need for alacrity. Moments later Miller heard Kit gasp.

'Good lord.'

'Anything wrong?'

'We're leaving again,' said Kit picking up Sam. 'Sorry, old boy, you'll have to stay here.'

Sam barked at Kit, but his heart wasn't in it. As soon as he was set down, he ran over to the sofa and sat near Simpkins who had opened one eye at their arrival before quickly realising his mistake and shutting it again.

Bright was on his feet immediately and asked, 'Can I tag along? Not doing much here. What's happened, anyway?'

'There's been another murder,' answered Kit, looking at both men.

'Another woman?' asked Miller.

'No. Bentham.'

Miller's next thoughts were expressed more passionately than one would expect in a normal master servant relationship. However, the ease with which they associated and the reasons for this had long since rendered these thoughts redundant.

'How could they let him be killed? Are they idiots?' exclaimed Miller after his initial surprise gave way to a more reflective expression of his feelings.

Kit did not believe this. One thought was uppermost in his mind. It had been there since early in the case and now it had risen again, taken flight, and was dominating his field of vision. He felt sure that Jellicoe would be of a like mind.

'Incredible as it may seem, I think one of the people committing these crimes is a policeman.'

30

Chief Inspector Jellicoe invited Kit and Bright to be seated. There was no sign of Wellbeloved. Outside the rain was getting heavier. For a moment the three men listened in collective awe at the low hum of the rain shower.

'He's still at the hotel taking statements,' replied Jellicoe when Kit asked him the whereabouts of his sergeant.

'Bentham is dead?'

'Yes, your lordship. He was killed last night after he was dropped off at the hotel. A single cut to his throat.'

This prompted several questions in Kit's mind but rather than ask them, he let the Chief Inspector tell them all he knew.

'We believe the death took place between eight and midnight last night. The hotel reception was, well it's not the sort of place you would go to, was unmanned so the killer had no problem entering and finding out the location of Bentham. There was no police guard for the simple reason he was not under arrest nor had we any reason to believe his life was at risk. The body was found just inside the door. I would add the door was closed. It would seem he opened the door and the killer struck immediately. There's nothing to suggest the killer entered the room. From this I would conclude Bentham may have recognised the man or woman. It certainly heightens the possibility it was one of the people he described last night. Another possibility suggests itself which I can scarcely credit.'

'That the killer is in the police.'

'Indeed. This means we have two avenues of inquiry. Firstly, we need to find out more about the people that he described to Watts.'

'I'm afraid Doyle could not help us much there.'

Jellicoe nodded but did not seem surprised.

'In addition, we'll need to understand who was in the Scotland Yard building yesterday that might have seen Bentham. There are dozens of people here, of course, but this does not mean they will have seen him or, indeed, have been aware he was here.'

Kit nodded in agreement but was far from hopeful this would yield any result. It wasn't necessary for anyone to have seen him. An overheard conversation might have been enough to condemn him.

Jellicoe noted the look on Kit's face and smiled.

'I agree. I don't hold out much hope either.'

'We need to send the photostats to McDonald and Miss Diamond.'

'Sergeant Wellbeloved did the needful earlier this morning, sir. The picture of Miss Tunstall will be in the evening paper. I hope this generates some leads related to her final days.'

'I'm sure it will, Chief Inspector.'

The meeting had reached its conclusion, so Kit and Bright stood up and went to the door. Bright turned to Jellicoe just as Kit opened the door.

'Thank you again, milord,' said Jellicoe shaking hands. 'Good to see you again Dr Bright.'

Bright had been listening to the conversation between the two men but said little. A thought stuck him, and he turned to the Chief Inspector.

'May I ask a question?'

'By all means, Dr Bright.'

'Was the wound to the throat accomplished via a stabbing motion or a swiping motion.'

Jellicoe seemed surprised by the question initially and then a slight smiled appeared somewhere beneath his beard.

'It was a swiping motion. It's conjecture, of course, but it would have been something like this.'

Jellicoe demonstrated to Bright by sweeping his arm across his throat.

'Why do you ask?'

'Well, it seems rather ghoulish to say, but there are not many blades that can butcher, so to speak, so cleanly. A razor blade might, if you can get close enough, or an attack from behind.'

'Or?'

Bright looked slightly embarrassed at having spoken. Then he smiled and told them the other type of blade that could have slayed Bentham with similarly deadly effect.

Aunt Agatha looked around the room with just enough of a hint of sniffiness to alert the people in her company that she was on the left-hand side of upsettable.

'It's going downhill,' said Agatha.

At that moment a squeal of laughter from another dinner table somewhat cemented the view in Agatha's mind and, perhaps, increased the respect Kit, Mary, Esther and Bright had for her foresight.

Agatha raised her eyebrows as the squeal was greeted with the male equivalent: a louder, stupider sound that began its journey into the open air from deep with the stomach of the emitter but found its freedom, invariably, through the nasal passages.

If there was a look of triumph in Agatha's eyes, it was no less than she deserved. She certainly gave truth to the proposition that you can demonstrate greater forbearance in a difficult situation if you're in the right. From the outset she had held reservations about having dinner at Claridge's but fell in at the insistence of Mary and Esther, itself a sign of the growing easiness in their respective relationships with Kit's aunt.

The Medium Murders

For Mary, the farm-like atmosphere in the dining room was paradoxically as horrifying as it was funny. As each table found new ways to bay their merriment to the wider world, Mary was caught between laughing at the ridiculousness of it all, her dismay at how Aunt Agatha would react and a lurking feeling of guilt at being in such a place when so many others were experiencing such hardship.

Kit never needed any excuse to gaze at Mary. What she was thinking and feeling made its way through the electrical intensity of her eyes and the ever-changing shapes of delight and dismay on her mouth. It made looking at his fiancée as much an intellectual pleasure as aesthetic. Tonight, though, as expert a reader of Mary's mood as he was, he would have been hard pressed to understand the full range of her thoughts. Amusement, certainly. Horror probably, if only to see Aunt Agatha vindicated. Although that would have amused her, too.

'So, with the photostats in circulation, the publication of poor Patty Tunstall's picture in the paper, the police will have many avenues of inquiry now. I think Jellicoe is both happy at the opening of the investigation but utterly despondent about the murder of Bentham. I'm worried that this could rebound on him,' said Kit.

'Really? Why should it?' asked Esther.

'He's the man in charge of the investigation. Mind you, no one could have foreseen Bentham would be a target.'

'You know what that means, don't you?' responded Agatha before drinking some soup that, much to her surprise, met with her approval. Kit gleefully looked at his aunt as she wrestled with her conscience in whether to declare her liking for the soup or maintain her overall negative assessment of Claridge's. Honesty won out, after a fashion.

'The soup is better than I expected from this place.'

Kit doubted the hotel would use this review in future publicity.

'What does it mean, Aunt Agatha?' asked Esther. She was everyone's aunt now.

Agatha fixed her Esther with a gaze.

'It means that the only way the Chief Inspector is likely to escape censure is if he catches the killer and he proves to be a fellow police officer.'

Once again, Kit marvelled at his aunt. She would have made a wonderful detective had she ever followed her obvious inclination and talent. For the second time that evening, Kit was almost right.

The Cavour was an elegant bar with a clientele of a bohemian bent. Artists, aspiring actors, dancers and respectable gentlemen frequented the bar every evening. It was a home for like-minded people with an exceptionally high appreciation of culture. The sky was lit like a Whistler nocturne: dark, thin with hints of light

The Medium Murders

coasting into view behind the black clouds. It was after eleven o'clock; time for Rufus Watts to leave the cheerful company he was in and find somewhere to take supper.

For a change he decided to dine alone. He left the bar which was situated at the corner of Leicester Square. Crossing the Square, he made his way towards Piccadilly Circus. There were any number of restaurants still open for business. As he thought about his options, he was not aware of a group of men who had begun to follow him.

The evening was chilly but, thankfully, the rain had stopped for the moment. All around Watts were young people, couples, and a few others like him: single gentlemen of discernment, no longer in the first flush of youth. Watts marched along, swinging his cane as he went. It was great to be alive, thought Watts. The rain-rinsed air was sweet and energising. At this moment he couldn't have enjoyed more this feeling of independence, the sound of the click of his cane on the street or the admiring looks from women at the certain *je ne sais quoi* of his dress.

He turned off Wardour Street towards Gerrard Street. By now he was aware of the men behind him. They'd done little to hide their presence. The wolf whistles had grown louder as the number of people on the street grew fewer.

Beasts thought Watts. He knew their sort. A lifetime of listening to their comments. The insinuations. The outright insults. The threats: for they would surely come.

Then they would attack.

It had happened before, and he was always ready. They knew it not, but, aware of their aims, he'd led them deliberately onto the quieter, narrower and darker street. The footsteps grew louder behind him as they closed in.

Now he had them.

Watts spun around and said 'Yes?'

This took the three men by surprise. Their leader stopped. He was probably no taller than Watts, which is to say, not very. But he was broad and brutish looking.

'Shouldn't you gentlemen be at home beating your wives, or whatever you do for entertainment.'

The nominal leader of this dismal gang inquired as to who Watts was to ask such a question. At least that was how Watts interpreted the tirade. The man stepped forward. It seemed to Watts the smile on the man's face could have been described as cruel. It certainly did little for his good looks but spoke volumes for the nobility of his intentions.

Watts stood his ground and watched the man approach. A slow smile creased the lips of the diminutive police artist. This might have confused a more intelligent attacker; given pause for thought, even. However, the three men were beyond thought. They saw before them a small, well-dressed man. Easy pickings. Someone different. Someone weaker than them.

The Medium Murders

The leader of the gang was now a few feet away from Watts. At this point the thought did cross his mind – why isn't he moving? A second later he found out.

It happened so quickly that the thug could not comprehend what had happened. His brain shut down and he collapsed on the street. Not unconscious. He'd *fainted*. His two accomplices looked in shock at their friend and then at Watts. The little man was pointing a thin blade at their throats. It moved slowly side to side. The intent was clear, but Watts decided that confirmation would be no bad thing in the circumstances.

'Your next step will be your last.'

The two men looked at the blade, then down at the cane by the side of Watts where once it had been sheathed. Had they been experts in the art of fencing, they would have recognised that the blade circling a foot away from their heads was a foil. Of course, they could not have been expected to know that a man such as Watts was a former champion fencer.

Below them they heard a groan. Blood was pouring from a gash on the lead man's cheek.

'What have you done with him?' asked one of the men.

'I should have thought that obvious, you moron.'

'You've stabbed him.'

'He'll live. Anyway, it's significantly less of an injury than the one you wanted to inflict on me,' pointed out

Watts. 'Now, be good boys and scrape this mess of the pavement and get the hell out of my sight before my good nature gives way to its more barbaric inclinations.'

31

A grey pall hung over Old Paradise Gardens in the middle of Lambeth. The light brush of rain meant it was quieter than normal. There were a few people taking shelter from the elements with their dogs' underneath trees that were shedding their leafy cover. One person sat out in the open.

Lydia Evans looked again at the evening newspaper. She'd picked it up the day before from the pavement. Now, sitting in the park, she was oblivious to the rain. Raindrops ran down her cheeks like tears. She stared at the picture of the young woman.

Patty Tunstall they said her name was.

Patty. It was always just Patty to her. There were no surnames.

A wave of hatred rose in her. Another woman, she thought, killed by men. Why do they hate us? She'd asked this question so often. They're all charm at the beginning. Words of love. The jokes. The suggestive comments. Then…

Then it begins.

The demands. The arguments. The fights. Then the beatings. She thought of her Robert. A husband to be proud of, once. Tall, well made and if he was not good looking then, at least, he had a nice smile. Good teeth, she remembered. Done his bit. When the country had come calling, he'd gone. And he'd survived. Or had he?

Jack Murray

Something had died. He was a different man when he returned. The silences. The angry outbursts. The drinking. He would disappear for a night, sometimes two. Sometimes he'd return home with bruises. A black eye for an old soldier.

When did he start on her?

There'd been signs, of course, before the War. But nothing serious. All men slap their wives, don't they? It was because they cared. He was always sorry. He said so. Insisted, even.

This was for her. For Patty. For all of us, she thought. She rose from the park seat, raised her eyes to the heavens then walked forward purposefully. There was a police station three streets away.

When she arrived, she saw the looks from the policemen. Some thought she just wanted shelter from the rain. Some thought she was a professional. There was no sense that she was welcome. It almost made her want to turn and go. Then she thought of Patty once more. She marched forward to the desk and placed the newspaper in front of the sergeant who was busy trying to ignore her.

He looked up slowly at her. The look that all men gave her. Appraising. Judging. Then his eyes followed hers down to the image in the newspaper. That was all it took.

Half an hour later she was being led up staircase to an office. Inside she saw three men. One looked like the twin brother of King George VI. The second man had a sly, suspicious look about him. She'd have known him to be a copper anywhere. The third looked like he'd stepped from the pages of a romantic novel. He had a gentle, sympathetic smile. If only all men were so…

The sombre man who looked like the King spoke first.

'Thank you, Miss Evans, for joining us. My name is Chief Inspector Jellicoe. And I have with me Sergeant Wellbeloved and Lord Christopher Aston, who is helping us in this matter.

Lydia Evans looked at the three men. It did not take a super sleuth to work out who was the lord. Her nervousness was gradually dissipating. There was a seriousness about the Chief Inspector that she felt drawn to. If diligence was a person, it would look something like this.

'I understand that you have some information related to the recent movements of Miss Tunstall.'

'Yes. I met her a few times at the refuge.'

'Where was this?'

'On Wootton Street. Y'know. Near Waterloo Station.'

Jellicoe glanced at Wellbeloved and asked, 'Have we been to this one?'

Wellbeloved consulted his notebook. He flicked through a few pages and came to the one he wanted. He scanned through it.

'Not yet, sir. I think it's one of the smaller ones. We've been following up on the larger ones.'

Jellicoe nodded but he didn't seem happy. This was not a reflection on Wellbeloved for once. Manpower. There were simply not enough people on the ground.

Lydia Evans glanced towards Kit. There was a look of surprise on his face.

'That's the one where Mary has been going.'

Jellicoe turned to Kit in surprise.

'Lady Mary has been helping out at a refuge.'

'Lady Mary?' asked Lydia. 'You know her?'

Kit coloured a little for reasons who could not explain.

'We're to be married next year.'

For the first time, Lydia smiled. She looked at Kit and said truthfully, 'She's an angel, sir.'

Jellicoe raised his eyebrows and decided to get the meeting back on course.

'Miss Evans, would you be prepared to accompany us to this house so that we can meet the people there and find out more about Patty Tunstall's last days?'

'Of course, sir.'

Lydia Evans felt something new at that moment. It was a feeling that she'd not had in such a long time.

Hope.

The Medium Murders

Hope turned to disbelief on her journey to Wootton Street.

'You've never been in a car like this before,' asked Kit.

'No, sir,' said Lydia Evans, truthfully.

They were in Kit's Rolls Royce. Lydia Evans looked like a child on Christmas Day. Her trips in motor cars had been few enough. None were like this. The leather upholstery felt so soft, so comfortable. She wanted to cry. With happiness. Lord, what a story she would have to tell her friends.

They drove through the morning traffic with a swiftness that was at once terrifying to Lydia Evans as well as depressing. She didn't want this journey to end. For the first time in her life, she was a Princess riding in a carriage with a handsome Prince. It was fantasy of course but while it lasted, she wanted to enjoy every second.

Her face, so fearful before, lit up. Kit smiled at her, but his heart felt heavy. Not only for his passenger who would soon return to the harsh reality of her life but also for Mary. What would she say? What would she think when they burst in upon her?

He wasn't sure what they would find. If Mary was angry, then so be it. There was a wider issue: her safety. He was not at risk. She was. It was that simple. The victims were women. Young women. Many not yet twenty-one, which was significant. Mary was very much a potential target. But still it gnawed at his conscience. Both Kit and Lydia were dreading the end of the journey for entirely different reasons.

'That house over there,' said Lydia Evans pointing to a redbrick terrace. It was a large house and seemed to have been made by joining two terraces together. Miller pulled the car over, directly in front. A police car driven by Wellbeloved drew into the space behind.

'Shall I stay in the car, sir?' asked Miller, clearly aware something was afoot.

'No, Harry. Perhaps you should join us, initially.'

Miller helped Lydia out of the car and the four men followed her to the house. Jellicoe looked at the young woman expectantly and she obliged by knocking the door.

It was answered by an older woman that Kit did not recognise. The woman looked at Lydia Evans.

'Hello Lydia, is everything all right?'

'Yes, Miss Dinsdale. These gentlemen are from the police. Can we come in?'

Miss Dinsdale's eyes widened in alarm, but she immediately stepped back and watched as Lydia Evans and the men entered the house. Lydia was first through the door followed by Kit.

They entered a large room. There were several young women there with children. Kit's mouth dropped open in shock. Mary turned to him. She was standing with Isabelle Rosling and two older women. Mary's eyes narrowed and one eyebrow arched upwards alarmingly. Kit calculated around seventeen questions were contained in this one look.

But that wasn't what shocked him.

'What on earth are you doing here?' The tone was as peremptory as the irritation was familiar.

'Hello, Aunt Agatha,' said Kit in as breezy a manner as he could manage. 'I was just about to ask you the same question.

32

A few hours earlier…

Mary gazed out of the drawing room window which overlooked Grosvenor Square. It was a ghastly morning. The rain was not especially hard but the street, the grass, the trunks of the trees and even the air seemed sodden. Mary sipped at her tea and watched Aunt Agatha and Fish walking together through the park in the middle. Poor Fish thought Mary. Agatha was doing all the talking.

The two septuagenarians had arrived at the exit to the park. They crossed the empty road towards the front of the house. A minute or two later, the door to the drawing room opened and Agatha stepped in.

'Ah, glad I found you, Mary.'

'Awful day.'

'Ghastly. Tell me,' said Agatha, closing off any further discussion of Britain's unfortunate susceptibility to merciless meteorological vicissitudes, 'are you planning to visit the house at Waterloo today with Mrs Rosling.'

'Yes,' replied Mary. 'There's nothing much I can do on the case now.'

'Do you mind if I join you?'

The Medium Murders

Mary grinned at her adopted aunt. Just when you thought you could no longer be surprised by this lady, like any good poker player, a game at which Aunt Agatha was peerless, she always had a card up her sleeve. It took a moment for Mary to remember that this was cheating, but no matter, she always astounded.

'Of course, Aunt Agatha. I'm sure Mrs Rosling would be delighted to meet you.'

To give Agatha her due, the look on her face suggested that she doubted this immensely. She recognised that Mary was exaggerating the truth not to mock her but because she was considerate. She loved this about Mary. Not that she would say. Mary walked the fine line between gentle teasing and esteem with unerring ease. She would miss her when she left to be with Kit. Miss her so much, in fact.

'I'm sure she'll be enchanted.'

Nothing in Agatha's voice suggested she either believed this or, indeed, cared.

Mary broke out into a fit of giggles. This forced Agatha to leave the room, lest she start laughing too, claiming the need to get ready. Just as the old grandfather clock struck eight, Mary and Agatha set off driven by Bernard, Agatha's some time chauffeur.

'We'll be back late afternoon,' said Agatha to Natalie, before she left. 'You should take the day off.'

'Thank you, madame,' replied Natalie hiding her delight. She had intended asking that very thing for today. She closed the door and clapped her hands in delight. She went to the phone and dialled a number.

Downstairs she heard some music begin to play on a gramophone.

Jazz.

'Haymaker' Harris was snoring peacefully in the car as Mary and Agatha walked down the steps of the mansion before stepping into the new Bentley driven by Bernard. He hadn't meant to stay the night. Once Mary had returned to the mansion, he was effectively off duty. However, these days he felt fatigue more. The cold weather wasn't helping either. He'd taken a few nips of brandy from his hip flask to stay warm. Soon he'd fallen asleep.

It was now mid-morning and 'Haymaker' was dreaming that he was in the ring giving Georges Carpentier a good beating. The Frenchman's unquestionably elegant ring craft was proving of little use against 'Haymaker's' speed and power. The fight was just about to reach a devastating conclusion when…

'Haymaker' awoke to the sound of a tap on the passenger side of the car. It was a policeman. The two men regarded one another for a few seconds. In that time both wondered if they'd met before. The policeman quickly assimilated 'Haymaker's' features: the cauliflower ear, the nose, and the slightly hooded eyes. This was not

The Medium Murders

a man who was likely to be an inhabitant of one of the most exclusive locations in London. The policeman tapped the glass once more. No further inquiry was required.

'Hop it,' advised the policeman.

'Haymaker' touched his hat and made ready to oblige. He still felt sleepy though. He rubbed his eyes. As he did this, he turned to the residence he'd been commissioned to watch over by Wag. A young woman was descending the steps. She was wearing a dark coat and one of those cloche hats all the women were wearing these days.

It was difficult to make out her features. Just as 'Haymaker' was able to rub the sleep out of his eyes, the window rapped again.'

'All right, all right, keep your hair on,' said 'Haymaker' turning to the policeman. When he turned back, he was aware of a large car drawing up to the young woman. Moments later she stepped into the car which sped away.

'Haymaker' hurriedly started the car and set off behind the other car. The policeman resumed his leisurely amble around one of the lesser crime hot spots of London, secure in the knowledge that it would remain so thanks to his intelligent intervention.

Jack Murray

He's in a rush, thought 'Haymaker' following closely behind the big car. It was a light-coloured Bentley. It could certainly shift and did so when the road was clear enough. Once or twice 'Haymaker' had to acknowledge a few angry pedestrians who had been foolhardy enough to attempt crossing the road whilst he was trying to keep up.

Thankfully the journey was mercifully short, or perhaps they had been going unmercifully fast. They arrived at a destination just a few minutes' drive away near Sloane Square.

A young man stepped out of the car. He was well-dressed. A 'nob, no question thought 'Haymaker'. Seconds later the young woman emerged from the car. She took the hand of the gentleman and stepped onto the pavement. She looked around at the houses. They were tall, four-story townhouses. Second homes to rich country folk. 'Haymaker' could see two things immediately about her. She seemed impressed by the house. More problematically, she seemed not to be Lady Mary.

'Bloody hell,' said 'Haymaker' or something closely resembling it.

He stayed and watched her enter a big house with the young man. This put 'Haymaker' in a quandary. That he had to return and in double quick time to Grosvenor Square was clear. Equally clear was whether he should admit to Wag about his blunder.

The Medium Murders

An idea suggested itself.

Twenty minutes later 'Haymaker' was, once again, outside the mansion. After a short wait he spotted Bernard the chauffeur walking towards the house. 'Haymaker' leapt out of the car and stopped the chauffeur. The chauffeur glanced at 'Haymaker' suspiciously at first. However, he seemed to be driving a rather expensive car. Such things impressed Bernard.

'Pardon me mate, but I just tried the house. No one is there,' said 'Haymaker'.

'Their ladyships have gone to Wootton Street to a home for women.'

Of course, thought 'Haymaker', he should have thought of that. He thanked Bernard and returned to his car. Bernard looked at the former boxer speed off. He thought nothing more of the encounter.

-

Unless Mary missed her guess, she sensed that Aunt Agatha was a little nervous. This usually manifested itself when she was quiet and not dispensing opinions like confetti at a wedding. She'd noticed this more lately. Something was on her mind. Typically, with Aunt Agatha one got to hear everything that was on her mind except the one thing that was on her mind. Mary supposed all aunts were like this. Perhaps she would become like this, too. A humble chap, if he'd been present, might have pointed out that this was the very definition of being female.

Jack Murray

They soon arrived at the Wootton Street house. Agatha followed Mary into the house. Isabelle Rosling was already there. With her was another woman that it took Mary a few moments to recognise.

'This is Lady Mary, Millicent,' said Mrs Rosling to Millicent Fawcett.

Then Agatha stepped into view.

'And this is?' said Mrs Rosling glancing at Mary. It had taken a few moments for Mary to get over seeing Millicent Fawcett at such close quarters. She nearly fainted a moment later.

'Hello, Millicent,' said Agatha.

'Agatha?' exclaimed Millicent Fawcett. 'Is it really you?'

Mary's eyes widened in perfect synch with her mouth. Mrs Rosling was no less astonished.

'Yes. Older. Not much wiser probably.'

There was a moistness in Agatha's eyes that was the final shock for Mary. Millicent Fawcett stepped forward and took both Agatha's hands. The two women regarded one another for a few moments.

'You left us. What happened?' asked the Suffragist leader.

'I married,' replied Agatha.

'I heard. You loved him?'

'Completely.'

Millicent Fawcett nodded and turned to Mary. For the next few moments Mary chatted with Millicent

The Medium Murders

Fawcett. Her voice shook as she fought to control her emotions. For the rest of her life, she could not remember what she said. Some nonsense, she thought. The excitement was almost too great. The honour too deep.

It was clear, however, that Millicent Fawcett wanted to speak to Aunt Agatha, so, reluctantly, she kept things brief. At least she'd had the sense to do this, she thought afterwards. The two elderly women began to chat in quiet tones. Meanwhile, Mary turned to Isabelle Rosling.

'My aunt only asked me this morning about coming.'

'You had no idea that she knew Millicent. I could see as much on your face.'

'She said she'd met her,' said Mary grinning, 'but I'd no idea it was like this. She's full of surprises my Aunt Agatha. Well, strictly speaking she's not my aunt. She's Kit's aunt. But…'

Mary felt Mrs Rosling take her hand, 'I think I understand. Well, I'm delighted if she's joining us.'

Mary began to chuckle. In fact, it took a little while for her stop. Mrs Rosling joined her laughing although she knew not why. Finally, both women found their composure once more.

'Well, Mary, I think what you're saying, without saying anything, is that I might regret her joining us.'

Mary shook her head, but the smile widened.

'She's certainly unique but I think she'd be an asset. It just won't always seem so. She can be a tad crochety on occasion.'

And that occasion was just moments away as the door burst open. It sometimes seems that doors burst open when policemen, well, any man, arrives at a room. Mary was for, at least third time that morning, shocked as she saw Chief Inspector Jellicoe and then Kit enter the room. There was a woman with them she vaguely recognised.

'What on earth are you doing here?' asked Agatha, who was the first to regain her senses after the initial shock had subsided.

'Hello, Aunt Agatha, I was just about to ask you the same question.' Kit looked from his aunt and then back to Mary. He frowned slightly or was it a grimace? Mary could see he was uncomfortable about their entrance. She wasn't sure if she was incensed, surprised or sympathetic to his plight. She followed her heart.

'Lord Aston. What a pleasant surprise,' said Mary walking forward and kissing him gently on the cheek. 'Are you here to help out?'

In the background she could hear Agatha whispering rather loudly, it must be said, for Millicent Fawcett's hearing was not as acute as it had once been, about the new entrants.

Oddly it was Miss Dinsdale who saved the day.

'Shall I get the gentlemen some tea?'

The Medium Murders

This eminently sensible suggestion was greeted with acclaim and allowed calm, rational explanation, and an exchange of information to flourish. Chief Inspector Jellicoe and Sergeant Wellbeloved stepped forward and explained their presence. Over the next few minutes, while Lydia Evans and Mrs Rosling filled in the pieces of the jigsaw related to the last movements of Patty Tunstall, Kit took Mary aside.

'My darling, I would have given anything not to intrude. I'd no idea this was the same place you were working until Miss Evans mentioned it.'

Mary took Kit's hand and gazed up at him.

'I know. I understand, I could see it on your face. I think you're not quite so sure about Mrs Rosling. I wish you would see her as I see her. She's a remarkable woman. I admire her tremendously.'

Kit smiled then kissed Mary on the top of her head.

'I'm so sorry. I've been a bit of a fool. A jealous fool. If there's anything I can do to support what you're doing here, I will. I want to help.'

Kit grinned as he made this last point. Mary's eyes narrowed.

'Well, ignoring the implicit paradox of that statement for a moment, as you're such a changed man...' Mary was tempted to add that she was also a changed woman because of him but opted instead for a more romantic method of conveying both forgiveness and confirmation of their future. This lasted for a minute or two in the entrance corridor of the refuge. It was ended by a polite clearing of a throat.

Aunt Agatha and Millicent Fawcett were standing looking at the couple.

'This is my nephew, as I was saying, Millicent. Mary and he will be married next year. Although if they continue to conduct themselves like two animals in a field, we may have to consider moving the wedding forward.'

The Suffragist burst out into a fit of giggles at Agatha's stern rebuke to her nephew.

'You haven't changed, Agatha.'

When 'Haymaker' arrived at Wootton Street, his heart sank. Outside the house was a police car. Then he noticed a familiar Rolls Royce. Relief flooded through his body like a tidal wave on a canal. He settled down and waited. Thankfully, he did not have to wait too long as the sounds coming from his stomach reminded him, he'd had nothing to eat all morning.

Kit Aston emerged from the house accompanied by Lady Mary and that cranky old aunt of his. Mary was smiling, walking hand in hand with Kit. Lucky, lucky man thought 'Haymaker'. There was no envy. He liked his lordship. And he was paying exceptionally good money for 'Haymaker's' services. A real gent. Of course,

Wag got his cut, but why not? He looked after him, did Wag. Another gent.

The two ladies stepped into the Rolls. Meanwhile Kit paused for a moment and looked around. Then he spied 'Haymaker'. He tipped his hat to the former boxer causing 'Haymaker' there and then to commit his life or, at least, his fists to the protection of the young lady.

'Who were you tipping your hat to?' asked Mary.

Kit slipped into the car and raised his eyebrows in what he took to be a show of innocence. Mary was having none of it. Her eyes narrowed and she pressed him again.

'Out with it.'

Kit reddened slightly, temporarily lost for words or even a decent defence. They drove past 'Haymaker'. Mary caught the former boxer's eye and smiled to him. The boxer waved back before realising he was meant to be incognito.

'Ahh,' said Mary turning back to Kit with laughing eyes. 'Your pugilist friend.'

Kit shrugged and had the decency to look ashamed. Mary wasn't exactly angry, especially as it was a gilt-edged opportunity to practice putting her future husband onto the back foot. She was enough of a woman to clasp the opportunity to her bosom; she was lovestruck enough to feel a pang of guilt in doing so. It was difficult to go against the nature of her gender. The womb decides all.

'My guardian angel?'

'Yes,' admitted Kit. 'We live in a dangerous world.'

'We do.'

'Are you angry?'

Mary gave a sharp kick to his leg.

'Wrong leg,' said Kit smiling at the wooden thud made by her foot.

'I know,' said Mary with a smile. 'It was a shot across the bows.'

Agatha, if she heard any of this, made no comment. She was once more lost in another world, her gaze fixed outside the car window. This was noted by both Kit and Mary as their skirmish petered out. Mary shot Kit a look and then one towards Agatha. Kit shrugged. He'd noticed it too but had no more idea than Mary as to its cause. Perhaps they could speak to her when the case was finished. If it ever finished. Kit shut this thought down as quickly as it entered his head.

They would find the killer.

33

Supper in the Grosvenor Square mansion was a muted affair. Agatha's mind was elsewhere; Mary and Esther were talking weddings. Kit and Bright had nothing to offer on this topic. Their job was to be there on the day, ideally sober, ready to commit the rest of their lives to the Cavendish girls. Not the worst prospect, acknowledged Bright.

They were all worried about Agatha but something else was now becoming an issue.

'Did Natalie say where she was going?' asked Esther.

'No, I didn't ask her,' admitted Agatha. 'I just gave her the day off and, well, off she must have gone.'

'Fish or Bernard have no idea where she went?' pressed Mary.

'Naturally I inquired,' responded Agatha, a hint of her spirit returning signalled by the dismissiveness in her tone. 'And before you ask, I did speak to Hemmings in the kitchen before she left. Natalie said nothing about her plans for the day. So, there's no point in asking me anything more on the subject.'

'Has she done this before?' asked Kit, quite literally taking his life in his hands. Agatha was holding a butter knife; it must be added. Who knows what thoughts crossed her mind? They may have been not too dissimilar to Kit's, as he glanced down at the silver cutlery glinting dangerously in the light.

'No. She has not.'

Kit was clearly troubled. If he was troubled, it was less than a second or two before his mood spread throughout the room.

'What should we do, Kit?' asked Mary.

Kit wiped the side of his mouth. I don't like this. We'll go to Scotland Yard. I think they should know. Just to be safe.'

'I'll come with you, Kit,' said Bright. 'If something's wrong, I'd feel better doing something about it.'

'Will there be anyone there at this time, Kit? It's quite late.' asked Esther.

'Sergeant Wellbeloved', said Kit, 'I was hoping I'd find you still here. Detective Inspector Bulstrode, a pleasure.'

Wellbeloved and Bulstrode were sitting together outside Jellicoe's office. Both were eating sandwiches and drinking beer. They looked somewhat embarrassed to be caught drinking on duty.

'Can I introduce my friend Dr Richard Bright?'

There was a round of handshakes and then the visitors pulled over two nearby seats.

The Medium Murders

'Please don't let us interrupt you,' said Kit, although it was plain that each man had lost something of his appetite and thirst. 'Did you make any further progress on establishing Miss Tunstall's last movements?'

'It's incomplete, sir, but we now have a few additional lines of inquiry which will be followed up tomorrow.'

'I'm glad to hear it,' said Kit. He looked at Bulstrode. 'Will you be re-joining the case at any point?'

This was greeted with a snort, or at least it would have been, had Bulstrode not stopped himself in time.

'No, sir. We're down several men who've been diverted onto this case. I'm picking up what's left.'

'I see,' said Kit, and he did. Oddly, he was reassured to see the two men working so late. Thuggish they may be, but there was no faulting their commitment to the cause.

'May I ask what brings you here at this time of night, sir?' asked Bulstrode. The four men glanced up at the clock on the wall. It was after half past eight.

'It may not be a problem, and we certainly hope it isn't, but Natalie, my aunt's young maid, has not returned from her day off. It's not happened before, and we can think of no reason why she should not have returned. Given the events surrounding the death of Bentham…'

Kit left the next thought hanging in the air. It was clear, looking into the eyes of both men, that they knew what he meant. The two policemen exchanged glances.

'Best not to take any chances,' said Bulstrode.

'I agree,' replied Kit.

If Rufus Watts was dismayed at seeing the arrival of Wellbeloved into his office, he was damn sure he was going to let the detective know it. Then he saw the arrival of Kit. This was a surprise and not an unpleasant one. He recognised Kit. He was becoming a regular fixture at Scotland Yard. As well as this, he'd seen the nobleman at the Royal Opera House and the National Gallery. He was a man of culture, like himself.

'Evening, Mr Watts,' said Wellbeloved, 'you remember his lordship.'

'Lord Aston, it's a pleasure to meet you again. Is this a social call or business?'

Kit smiled ruefully.

'Business, alas. I hope I'm not keeping you back from an engagement. It's terribly urgent.'

The little artist smiled and held his arms out expansively.

'I keep strange hours. What would you like me to do?' Watts turned to Wellbeloved and said, 'And you'd better check if Shepherd is still here or telephone him to come in. Half an hour to an hour should do it.'

'Will do, sir.'

The Medium Murders

The portrait emerged over the next forty minutes like a ship appearing through fog. The shape became distinct first, then the features, then the shadow and finally, much to Kit's astonishment, a hint of the person.

'You've missed your calling, Mr Watts.'

Watts did not contradict him, which amused Kit greatly. He nodded in approval at the finished image of Natalie.

Rufus Watts smiled. It was always this way. For someone of his talent, this was a mere trifle, yet critical acclaim was always forthcoming, and he enjoyed every second of it. Normally his audience comprised people without discernment or taste. However, the reaction of someone of Kit's rank was especially gratifying.

Despite Kit's effusiveness, the artist could sense the anxiety. And he was right. Kit was worried. His senses were tingling again. If something happened to Natalie, he doubted he could forgive himself for even indirectly endangering her. He didn't want to think about what could happen, but images of the young, murdered women entered his mind.

'We need to get this down to Shepherd,' said Watts.

'Lead on,' replied Kit.

As he said this, he spied Watts' walking stick lying propped against the wall. The handle was made of silver and depicted a serpent. Watts noticed the direction of Kit's gaze. He stood up and took the walking stick over, removing the sword contained within.

Kit smiled and said, 'D'you know I was wondering about that. I have an associate who has something similar.' Thoughts of Smith-Cumming sprang into his mind.

The tip of the blade was a foot away from Kit's face. Then Watts lowered it and handed the sword, hilt first to Kit. Rising from his seat Kit made some swipes and thrusts with the sword.

'You fence, I see, your lordship.'

'Used to.'

'Why did you stop?'

Kit laughed, 'My fiancée was beating me too handily for my liking.' He handed the foil back to Watts who began to make some fencing moves himself. It was clear that he knew what he was about.

'What did you make of what happened to poor Bentham?' asked Kit, looking at the artist lunge, feint, beat and riposte an imaginary opponent.

'I was shocked, of course. How could anyone know he was working with us?'

'How do you think?' pressed Kit.

Watts stopped for a moment and looked at Kit. His eyebrow was raised, and he said after a few moments, 'The answer to that would be concerning.'

Kit rose from his seat and adopted a fencing stance. His walking stick became his sword.

'On guard.'

The Medium Murders

The two men were stood thus when Wellbeloved entered the office. They stopped immediately like two naughty schoolboys caught smoking in the lavatory.

'I will take it from this that the drawing is ready, Mr Watts.'

'It is Sergeant dear. Let's go down to Shepherd and get him to make the photostats. Did you mention to him we were coming?'

'It's not necessary for you to come down, Mr Watts,' pointed out Wellbeloved.

'It is. He still has the original five drawings I made with Bentham.' Turning to Kit he explained, 'I like to keep the originals.'

Kit looked at the little artist oddly. Five drawings? The three men walked to the office of Shepherd who, like Watts, tended to work late into the night. He was still there and was expecting them. The photographer was in his sixties, guessed Kit. He'd probably been using a camera all his life if some of the pictures on his walls were anything to go by.

'Are they yours?' asked Kit looking at the gallery. They showed, for the most part, a woman at various stages of her life.

'Yes,' replied Shepherd. 'I started this thirty years ago. Never thought it would be my job.'

'When can we have the photostats?' asked Wellbeloved. He was not a man for small talk. For once

Kit didn't mind a sense of urgency and he was glad the sergeant's tone conveyed this.

'Tomorrow morning,' replied Shepherd. Then he picked up the new drawing and looked at Natalie.

'Beautiful girl. Another victim?' There was more than a trace of sadness in his voice. Kit felt his heart lurch.

'We hope not,' said Wellbeloved, quickly. 'First thing?'

'First thing,' confirmed Shepherd. He turned to Watts, 'You want the originals back, Rufus?'

Watts nodded, 'Yes. You know me, darling.'

Shepherd smiled and reached into a drawer and took out an envelope. He lifted a letter opener and, with a swift cut, opened an envelope from which he extracted the drawings.

'There you are Rufus.'

Kit looked at the letter opener in surprise. It looked like none he'd ever seen before. In fact, it looked more like a…

'Scalpel,' said Shepherd, smiling at Kit. Dr French gave it to me when I complained about losing my letter opener. Or maybe it was stolen. You can't trust anyone in this building.'

The three men left the photographer's office and returned upstairs from the bowels of the building to the main entrance.

'I must hand it to you chaps,' said Kit. 'You work long hours.'

The Medium Murders

'It helps not being married,' said Watts gaily.

Kit looked at the artist but did not press further on the subject, but a thought struck him about the photographer.

'I noticed a lot of photographs of a woman in Mr Shepherd's office. The same lady.'

'His wife, sir,' said Wellbeloved. 'Spanish flu got her. He's a widower.'

Watts' next comment stopped Kit in his tracks.

'Yes, poor chap,' said Watts. 'I gather he's taken to attending séances. Very strange if you ask me.'

'Do many policemen attend séances to your knowledge?' asked Kit. They were standing at the entrance lobby to the Scotland Yard building.

Watts laughed at this.

'I really have no idea. He just mentioned it to me in passing. I was tempted to tell him it's a lot of nonsense, but it seemed to be a comfort. Who am I to criticise? In fact,' said Watts, looking through the drawings, 'If you look at this one you might think I attended these ridiculous things as well.'

He handed Kit the face that Bentham had described. There was a resemblance to Watts.

Kit smiled and said, 'Yes, I see what you mean.'

Watts took the drawing back, but he seemed puzzled.

'What's wrong?' asked Kit.

'One of the drawings is missing,' said Watts. 'Never mind. I'll see him tomorrow, I'm sure.'

Watts turned and headed in the direction of the stairs. The missing drawing seemed too much of a coincidence. He would mention it to Jellicoe the next day.

34

The ticking of the clock was the loudest noise at breakfast the next morning in Grosvenor Square. There was no question on anyone's mind that Natalie was missing and, most likely, for reasons to do with the case. When Kit arrived to join them, they agreed that a search of Natalie's room was unavoidable. Until this point, they'd held out hope that she might return. Now time was of the essence.

'You and Mary search the room, Christopher,' suggested Agatha. 'I'll join you in a moment.' She headed down the corridor to Fish's room. After giving the door a quick knock, she entered the room.

Kit and Mary looked at one another.

'Are you going to ask what's going on?' asked Mary, entering Natalie's room.

Kit shrugged away any responsibility for asking such a question.

'Coward,' said Mary accurately of the war hero.

The first thing that confronted them was a large bouquet of flowers.

'Good lord,' said Kit.

'Don't be too excited,' said Mary. 'These flowers were meant for Esther. We diverted them away to avoid any unpleasantness.'

'Booby Andrews?'

Mary shot Kit and look then grinned.

'You mean Bobby, I think. No, Xander Lewis. I think Aunt Agatha would describe him as a fathead. Accurately, it must be said.'

The search of the room revealed no sign of any sweetheart. There were a handful of photographs of family and some letters to a cousin in France. Nothing that seemed to provide the least clue as to her whereabouts.

They gave up after half an hour and re-joined Agatha and Esther upstairs. The mood was decidedly downbeat.

'Where's Richard by the way?' asked Kit to Esther. 'He wasn't around this morning.'

Mary answered, 'I asked him to visit the refuge. He'd said he was somewhat unoccupied at the moment.'

Esther smiled proudly. She was worried, however. They would begin married life soon and things would be better if her husband had a job. Money was not the issue. His pride required that he work but he wanted to earn an income whilst doing something socially beneficial. Finding a role that combined these objectives was proving more difficult than he'd anticipated.

The arrival of Betty Simpson an hour later lifted everyone's mood. She whooshed into the room like a runaway train racing down a steep hill.

'I'm here.'

'We'd noticed. How did you get in?'

'Front door was open.'

The Medium Murders

Agatha gave Kit a stern look which caused a wide smile to appear on Mary's face. Then she remembered what day it was.

'I'd forgotten,' said Mary to Aunt Agatha, 'You have your séances today.'

'Indeed. I hope Doyle has come up with something better than the last ones.'

'Are you going like that?' asked Betty who caused the second stern look in as many seconds from Agatha.

By late afternoon, the only thing sinking faster than the sun were the spirits of Agatha and Betty. Two separate séances had demonstrated what the two ladies firmly believed: misfortune favours the fool. Betty was particularly angry as she climbed into the car.

'Utter waste of time. I doubt any of those people could dress themselves without assistance. We should set up shop as mediums, Agatha. We'd clean up.'

'Dispiriting.'

'Very good, dear,' replied Betty.

It occurred to Agatha a few moments later that she'd made an unintended pun. She was too anxious to laugh. The car took off and they were on the road towards the last address of the day. Near Sloane Square.

'I hope the police have made progress with finding Natalie,' said Agatha. They passed a newspaper seller on the street. Betty did not have to ask. She pulled over immediately and allowed Agatha a chance to hop out and buy the early evening edition. As they set off again, Agatha leafed through the paper.

'Yes, it's here. Good likeness of Natalie. Whoever did this, certainly knows what they're about.'

'Show me.'

'Keep your eyes on the road dear.'

Both had long since given up on the idea that this avenue of inquiry would yield anything other than exposure to the most credulous in high society. As they were early, the ladies decided that it would be prudent to stop over for a little bit of replenishment to carry them through the ordeal ahead.

'Two large brandies please,' said Betty to the waitress in the Royal Court Hotel.

Agatha gazed out at Sloane Square. It was early evening, and the sky was darkening ominously. The blackness of the clouds was like a pall thrown over a coffin.

'I don't like the look of that sky,' said Agatha.

'This brandy is tip top, I must find out what it is,' replied Betty.

'I wouldn't be surprised if that's a storm coming.'

'Hurry up and finish that one, dear,' said Betty. 'We should have time for another.'

Twenty minutes later the ladies were sufficiently revitalised to venture out into the light rain which was now falling. The air was thick and oppressive as they walked around the corner towards the location of the final séance. It was a five-minute stroll to the house. They arrived at the front door of the large townhouse just before the heavens opened.

The host was a middle-aged man with a grey and black beard and a smile that seemed just a little too eager to please. He introduced himself but the ladies promptly forgot his name. They followed him into a room with half a dozen men and women standing having a drink. The usual crowd: widows, widowers, parents wanting to contact the sons they had lost. Agatha's emotions were a lethal mix of anger, alcohol, and sadness. She had long since realised that spiritualism was a business like any other. It preyed on the gullible and profited from grief.

The candle-lit room resembled many of the others they'd seen. Black curtains fell from the ceiling to the floor, a religious scene over the mantelpiece showed the Temptation of Christ. After a few moments, the host came over to join Agatha and Betty.

'Good evening, ladies. This is your first time here, if I'm not mistaken.'

You're not mistaken,' said Agatha a little coldly prompting Betty to nudge her in the ribs.

'Beautiful house,' said Betty with a smile. 'Is it yours?'

'No, not mine,' said the host somewhat evasively. 'May I ask what your interest is in coming this evening?'

They each had their story prepared. Both had lost their husbands. Both wished to communicate with them again. They had not had much luck elsewhere, but they remained optimistic.

Did the smile on the host dim a little? He seemed like a salesman working on gaining a commission. The question, of course, was what was he selling? Agatha probed a bit further.

'We've always been interested in more esoteric philosophy. Currently, such ideas can be frowned upon by less enlightened people. It's a great pity that so much ancient knowledge has been denied us by religious institutions who demonise such thinking.'

Agatha raised her eyebrows at the end hoping to prompt a response. The host's eyes lit up again. He nodded his head vigorously. This prompted Agatha to continue.

'I was only saying to my young granddaughter the other day how badly the occult is perceived today.'

'It seems an unusual subject for a young girl to be interested in,' laughed the host.

'Well not so young. She's twenty-one soon. I'm trying to persuade her to move away from life modelling for artists and find a more cerebral interest,' said Agatha, pausing to gauge the reaction to this piece of news.

It was clear she'd judged her audience perfectly. The host was positively panting at this point. Betty was somewhat breathless herself, fearful that her friend was laying it on a bit thick. A life-modelling twenty-year-old girl? Thankfully this proved not to be the case.

The Medium Murders

'Perhaps when our meeting is finished, we could talk privately about this?'

Just as he said this, the grandfather clock struck six. Outside there was a roll of thunder. Agatha glanced at Betty with a raised eyebrow. If this was some sort of theatre created for their benefit, then it was surprisingly effective. There *was* an atmosphere about the house. Agatha turned to their host as the clock chimed.

'Would I have time to pay a visit to the bathroom?'

'Of course, top of the stairs and second on the right.'

Agatha nodded to Betty and left the room. There was no one in the entrance hallway. Rather than check downstairs, she immediately made her way to the next floor. She noticed another flight of stairs ahead. The lights flickered for a moment, causing Agatha to glance upwards.

From nowhere, a woman appeared. This took Agatha by surprise, and she stepped backwards almost falling down the stairs.

'Where are you going?'

'The bathroom,' said Agatha, attempting a smile to cover her surprise.

The woman looked at her and did not try to hide her disbelief. She was around forty years old with dark hair and grey streaks at her side of her hair. The eyes were dark pools conveying a force that Agatha found undeniable. Undeniably chilling, that is.

If this was a medium then, without question, she looked the part.

'Thank you,' said Agatha and went to the bathroom.

When she came out a few minutes later, the woman was still there. This was odd, to say the least. She motioned with her arm for Agatha to come down the stairs with her. Nothing was said. Outside the rain was a percussive rattle against the windows as the thunder gave a low growl.

The woman opened the door for Agatha and they both stepped into the room. Agatha gave Betty a shake of the head to indicate she'd not been able to accomplish her mission. A quick glance towards the woman indicated why. The host gave a light cough and the room immediately silenced and looked expectantly at the woman.

The drumming of rain against the window caused Agatha to shiver; the room seemed colder than before. Betty attempted to button up her tweed jacket with limited success. The host took his seat.

'Please be seated.'

The host removed a tablecloth. Agatha and Betty froze when they saw the design on the table. It was a pentacle. At its centre was the outline of a goat's head. The woman Agatha had just met was the last to sit down. She glanced towards the host. He exhaled slowly. The room was so cold now it caused a vapour to appear. Silence. The only sound was that of breathing.

The Medium Murders

Agatha felt a cold draught lick her face. It felt malign, like an icy spray. A queer sickening thrill ran through her body. For the first time in as long as she could remember, she experienced fear. This séance was of a wholly different order to what they'd undergone before. There was an invisible, overwhelming presence here. She could feel it on her skin. Touch it almost.

A clap of thunder made everyone jump.

Nervous laughter immediately ceased when they looked at the medium. Outside the room in the entrance hall, the door opened with a creak. Agatha could hear footsteps falling quietly on the floor. Lots of footsteps. A glance towards Betty told her she'd heard them, too.

'Thank you for joining,' said the host, oblivious to the muffled sounds outside the room. 'We have with us today, for the first time, a medium of great repute.'

All eyes turned to the medium.

'May I present Miss Eva Kerr.'

35

One of the things that Wag McDonald liked most about 'Haymaker' Harris was that he could trust him. He'd hired him not for his capability as a fighter or bodyguard. Rather it was his integrity. There was not a dishonest bone in his body. In over fifty professional fights he'd never taken a dive. The reason for this went beyond the robustness of his jaw.

He'd not mentioned anything about the events the other morning when he'd slept on the job. It preyed on his mind, though. After a sleepless night he came in to work the next morning with one clear idea. In fact, 'Haymaker's' mind rarely held even one thought at any given time. He was one of nature's doers.

Arriving at the pub, he quickly mounted the stairs and knocked on McDonald's door. A voice from inside shouted to come in. Inside were the McDonald brothers and Alice Diamond. They were obviously in a meeting. The sort of meeting that 'Haymaker' was never invited to. He looked at them. They looked back at him. As much as McDonald liked 'Haymaker', it was best not to test his patience levels.

The Medium Murders

'Yes?' said McDonald in a voice that prompted 'Haymaker' to get on with it.

'Sorry, boss, maybe I should come back.'

'No, just make it quick.'

'Haymaker' took off his hat and gripped it in his hands.

'It's about yesterday morning. I fell asleep on the job. And when I woke, I followed the wrong woman. I'm sorry boss. I wanted to mention it.'

McDonald's face suggested he could think of nothing he was less interested in at that moment. Thankfully, 'Haymaker' was unlikely to pick up on the signs. However, he stood there waiting for an instruction, or forgiveness, ideally both.

'No harm done,' said McDonald, looking back to the others. A thought struck him, and he looked back up at the boxer.

'Look why don't you take the day off. You've had a lot of late shifts nursemaiding the flap.'

'Thanks, boss,' said 'Haymaker' and scurried from the office like a schoolboy mitching school. He hurried downstairs out into the open air. As he walked towards the bus stop, he failed to see a Rolls Royce fly past him, but 'Haymaker' was miles away. His mind, unburdened by his confession to Wag McDonald, was thinking about what he could do now.

It must be said that the annals of crime literature are not filled with tales about what criminals do on their day off. This is for the very good reason that their job tends to be more exciting than the activities they are likely to get up to when not breaking the law. 'Haymaker' scratched his head, quite literally, as he strolled along the south bank. What to do? Then inspiration hit him. Even hardened criminals have family responsibilities; he would visit his mother.

'Daniel? Is that you?' said Mrs Dixie Harris from the sitting room of her small, terraced house in Lambeth. One of thousands of two-up, two-down red brick houses in the area.

'Yes, ma,' said 'Haymaker' closing the front door.

Seconds later 'Haymaker' was confronted by one of the most terrifying sights known to humankind: an outraged mother on the warpath. Mrs Harris was on her feet and across to the entrance hall with a speed of movement that, sadly, had not been passed on to her son.

'Have you lost your job with that nice Mr McDonald?' yelled the five-foot titan. 'Haymaker', realising he was seconds away from a clip round the ear, immediately fell into his boxing stance and began to bob and weave. In fact, Mrs Harris' first blow was a well delivered slap, executed with a speed that even a master ring technician such as Jack Johnson might have done

The Medium Murders

well to evade never mind 'Haymaker'. Defence had never been his strongest asset.

'That hurt,' complained 'Haymaker' who felt, not unreasonably, he was at the receiving end of rather unjust punishment. In addition, he wasn't sure the word 'nice' was quite how he would have characterised Wag McDonald, as much as he liked his boss.

'Have you eaten?'

The ability of a mother to move seamlessly from violence to nutrition had never ceased to amaze 'Haymaker'. Thankfully, he loved his mother's cooking.

'Is that steak and kidney pie, I smell?'

A few minutes later he was in the sitting room tucking into one of his favourite meals. By now, he'd just about managed to convince his mother that his employment with the Elephant Boys was in no way threatened by having a day off. All around the room were photographs of him from his prize fighting days. However, pride of place on the mantelpiece was a picture of him with Wag McDonald wearing army uniforms. He'd stuck with his boss for four years in Flanders.

Around five in the afternoon, 'Haymaker' announced that it was probably time to go. His mother reached into her pocket and gave him a shilling.

'Run and get me the evening paper, Daniel.'

'Haymaker' rolled his eyes and complied. Physical or verbal violence aside, the other special talent of mothers the world over is to make their sons feel like they are still six years old. His mother refused to accept the money back and insisted she pay for the paper.

A few minutes later 'Haymaker' returned with the paper and was made to promise that he would not leave it so long again before he visited his old mum. He calculated his previous visit was four days ago.

A short walk took him to the bus stop and then back into town. He didn't see the big black car racing past the bus, headed for Lambeth.

Mrs Harris was disturbed ten minutes after her son had left by banging on the door. She didn't like the tone of the knocking and was up, on her feet ready to give the caller what for.

When she opened the door, her mouth fell to the floor. She'd met him a few times with her boy. In this part of town, he was a legend.

'Mr McDonald, what are you doing here?'

'Mrs Harris,' said Wag McDonald, 'We're trying to find Daniel. Is he here?'

Twenty minutes later 'Haymaker' arrived back at the offices of the Elephant Boys. He nodded to the barman as he entered but ignored the downstairs bar and headed immediately upstairs. The upper floor was surprisingly quiet. There was no one around which was unusual. It felt like they'd left in a hurry because there were a few newspapers lying around, half read. As there was

The Medium Murders

nothing better to do at that moment, 'Haymaker', settled down to read the paper himself.

He always started from the back where there was sporting news. Then he would work his way to the front methodically. He was a slow reader but discriminating. Business, politics, and court news he skipped. Crime he read.

Then he reached the inside front page. There was a drawing of a woman. He studied the picture closely then looked at the name. It was her. The woman he'd mistaken for 'the flap'. His brain froze in that moment. For one of the few times in his life two thoughts entered his head simultaneously. He knew where she was, and she was in trouble.

His chest felt constricted. 'Haymaker', for the first time in as long as he could remember had to make a decision that had not been made, earlier, by someone else on his behalf. He looked around the upstairs bar. It was empty. There was nothing, no one to guide him on what to do. He felt a sense of panic. So much panic that, in truth, he felt like crying.

There was only one thing to do. Actually, two.

A few moments later he was outside the pub and hailing a taxi.

'Sloane Gardens,' said 'Haymaker' to the driver. The driver glanced at the former boxer and wondered what on earth he would be doing there. A fare was a fare though. They set off.

'Can you go any faster?'

The driver looked at the passenger. There was no question this was a man who'd been in the ring. The nose was a boneless ripple, his eyes were sunk behind pads of scar tissue and his ears were like pincushions.

He pressed his foot down on the accelerator.

They arrived less than ten minutes later. Much to the cabbie's surprise, he was rewarded with a tip or, more likely, the man was in a rush. No matter, a journey had been made. A fare was earned.

'Haymaker' stared across the road at the large house. The street was empty, and night was falling. This was an unusual situation for him on several levels. Devising a plan had never been his forte. He needed one now. Rescuing damsels in distress was a new one for him. He thought for a second about the moving picture heroes he loved to watch. What would Tom Mix do?

As he was pondering how evading a posse or rounding up rustlers might help him in his quest, he noticed that the street had become busier. Cars were beginning to pull up outside the house. Men and women were climbing the steps to go in. Others were arriving on foot. 'Haymaker' didn't stop to ponder his next move. He was crossing the street before he knew what he was doing. He was sure he'd seen Tom Mix do this. He followed the men and women into the house.

As he entered through the door, a man turned to him and said, 'I don't think I've seen you before.' The voice, the suit, the condescending look all said one thing to 'Haymaker': this man was a 'nob.

The boxer removed his hat, smiled, and said in a voice that would have been as unrecognisable to Wag McDonald and highly amusing to Kit.

'I'm new.'

36

Mary stalked the perimeter of the drawing room like a caged animal. Following the departure of Agatha and Betty, Kit had spoken to Jellicoe but there was nothing he or Mary could add to the police effort being conducted already.

'There must be something we can do,' said Mary, her face unable to hide the concern she felt.

'Perhaps,' said Kit.

Mary looked at him quizzically, but Kit was already on his feet. He went back to the hallway and called Miller. Soon they were in the Rolls travelling down to Elephant and Castle.

'Chance to renew your acquaintance with Miss Hill, Harry,' said Kit.

'I can hardly wait, sir.'

Mary looked less than impressed by the two men and kept a dignified silence as the pair of men joked about the unrequited love of Maggie Hill. Finally, she could take no more.

'I fail to see what's so funny. This poor girl has been brought up in a poverty which is unimaginable to us. Now she seems to have fallen for a man who not only does not love her but seems to think it amusing that she has feelings towards him.'

Kit and Miller, duly admonished, immediately silenced their music hall repartee. Mary was, of course, quite right, as ladies often are when it comes to matters of the heart and almost every other subject save, perhaps, cricket. Apologies were given. Apologies were accepted and they were soon driving along Waterloo Road.

'Isn't that my guardian angel?' said Mary, pointing to a lone figure walking along the pavement.

'Yes, certainly looks like 'Haymaker'. I wonder where he's going?'

They soon arrived at the Duke of Wellington. Kit asked Miller to wait for them while he and Mary went into the pub and upstairs to McDonald's office. They passed a few men who seemed somewhat surprised to see Mary. She smiled at them. Hats immediately came off heads. Kit glanced wryly at his fiancée who merely shrugged at the stir she was creating.

Wag McDonald rose immediately when he saw Kit and Mary enter his office. Alice Diamond remained seated eyeing Mary.

'This is a surprise,' said McDonald.

'I'm afraid it's not good news, Mr McDonald,' said Kit.

'Another murder?'

Kit felt his heart crash. He didn't want to consider such a possibility.

'Natalie, my aunt's maid has gone missing. We think she may have been abducted.'

'I'm not so sure,' replied McDonald.

Kit and Mary looked askance at the leader of the Elephant Boys.

'What do you mean?' asked Mary.

McDonald related what 'Haymaker' had told him earlier. This was not what Kit and Mary were expecting to hear.

'Unfortunately, I gave 'Haymaker' the day off so I can't tell you where the car took her.'

'We saw 'Haymaker' walking down Waterloo Road on our way here. Look, we think this may be more of an issue than you think. Tonight's evening paper will carry an artist's impression of Natalie. We can't take chances with this monster.'

'Wag, it may be something,' said Alice Diamond.

McDonald glanced at Alice Diamond who nodded to him. In a moment he was on his feet again. It was clear from both the tone of their voices and the look on their faces that they were worried.

'Can you show me where you saw him?'

There was no sign along Waterloo Road as Miller drove McDonald, Kit, and Mary. Alice Diamond, Wal

The Medium Murders

McDonald, Wag's brother, and their associates followed in a car behind. It was only the presence of Mary that prevented the two men giving more vocal expression to the frustration they were feeling.

Then Mary had a breakthrough.

'Could he have taken a bus?'

The two men looked at one another. McDonald's second thought about Mary was that Kit was a very lucky man.

'The 381 goes to his flat in Southwark. He'd have caught it back there,' said McDonald pointing to a stop they passed a minute previously.

Miller was already turning the car left as McDonald gave the address. The car behind followed suit. Soon they were heading along Stamford Street, and a few minutes later arrived outside 'Haymaker's' flat. Kit and Mary stayed in the car and waited for McDonald to get hold of the boxer. The building was as ugly as it was unwelcoming. Kit and Mary glanced at one another, a reminder of their good fortune.

The look on McDonald's face told its own story as he returned from the building. He climbed into the car and sat down glumly. He didn't have to say anything and neither Kit nor Mary asked. A few moments later, Alice Diamond and Wal McDonald appeared at the passenger window.

'I'll take it the news was not good. Where to now?' asked Wal McDonald.

'Do we know any places he is likely to visit. A pub? Family? Friends?' asked Kit.

'I'm not sure he has many friends outside of us. If he has a drink, it's likely to be at the duke,' replied Wag McDonald. He looked at his brother then he clapped his hands.

'The Ring.'

'Of course,' said Wal.

'His boxing club. He still goes to train a few times a week,' explained Wag McDonald as he saw his fellow passengers look at him quizzically.

Half an hour later and they were no further forward in locating 'Haymaker'. The mood in the car was despondent.

'Did you say he has family?' asked Kit

'His mum, Dixie, lives somewhere in Camberwell. I don't know the address,' said McDonald, sadly.

'I'm sure Jellicoe could find out.'

McDonald nodded and then looked out of the window. He spotted a café called 'Mario's' further up the street.

'Harry, can you pull over there? We'll have a cup of tea and perhaps you can call 'old Bill', your lordship.'

When Mario Marino saw the McDonald brothers and Alice Diamond walk through the door of his café, he wasn't sure whether to run for the hills, open the till or feel honoured by the presence of gangland royalty. Short and rather stocky, Mario was a Sicilian by birth and knew all about *Mafiosi*. He'd left the island thirty years ago with his bride to start a new life away from such people. He soon comprehended there was no escape. Racketeering existed the world over. It was for this reason he was a little surprised when he saw the last two people to enter the café. They were, by dress and demeanour, distinctly at odds with the more rough-hewn McDonald brothers.

'Buongiorno, Mario,' called Wal McDonald with a cheery wave. 'A few teas and buns over here, please.'

Mario Marino nearly sobbed with relief. He was a man highly disposed to crying. Happiness, sadness, or anger. It was all the same to him and usually ended, quite literally, in tears.

'Prego, Mr McDonald. Teas coming up.' Mario set to work. As he did so, the associate of the McDonald's came over towards him. Mario wondered if he was their lawyer.

'It's Mario, is it?'

'Yes, sir. Mario Marino.'

'Pleased to meet you, Mr Marino. My name is Aston. Do you have a telephone I could use for a few moments?'

Mario lifted the counter and allowed Kit to come through to the back. He called through to Anna to let her know that a man was coming to use the telephone. This was met with a burst of Sicilian dialect that Kit needed no translator to understand. Anna Marino was less than happy at a customer coming into the back of the cafe. Anna Marino's irritation immediately turned to something more welcoming when she saw Kit walk through. The fact that he was six feet tall, well made, with fair-hair and blue eyes that a moderately-talented romantic novelist might have described as piercing, played no part in this at all, of course.

'Mrs Marino, may I use your phone?'

Kit called Scotland Yard and spoke briefly to alert Jellicoe and Wellbeloved of the potential lead.

'We can't find 'Haymaker' anywhere,' admitted Kit. 'Do you have an address for a Mrs Dixie Harris? He may have gone to see his mother. She lives in Camberwell; I gather but the McDonald's can't remember where exactly.'

Kit listened as Jellicoe spoke. As he did so he called Anna Marino over. This required no second invitation, and she was over like a greyhound after a hare. By gesticulation, Kit asked for the café's phone number. He handed her a pen, and she wrote it down. A minute later, Kit re-joined the others.

'He'll call us as soon as he knows.'

'Has my boy been up to no good, Mr McDonald? If he has, he'll get the back of my hand,' said Dixie Harris.

Wag McDonald did not doubt for a moment that the old woman in front of him was well-nigh capable of meting out plenty of trouble for her son should he ever err. It was an insight into why he knew he could trust 'Haymaker'. The values he associated with him, decency, uprightness, and honour had probably been whacked into him by his formidable mother.

'Daniel has done nothing wrong, Mrs Harris. We need to get hold of him urgently, that's all. He's a good boy, believe me, Mrs Harris. The best.'

Dixie Harris' eyes grew moist. Her Daniel. Her boy. A man among these men. She felt a surge of pride. Then she recognised the look of urgency in Wag McDonald's eyes.

'Oh, Mr McDonald, you've just missed him. He left ten minutes ago.'

'Did he say where he might go?'

'No. He didn't, Mr McDonald. He said nothing about where he was going.'

Wag McDonald trooped back to the car dejectedly. The convoy set off in the direction of 'Haymaker's' flat and then the Duke of Wellington. It was after six by the time they returned. Kit and Mary joined the others in walking upstairs to McDonald's office.

'I'm sorry, your lordship. We tried.'

'Yes, I know, Mr McDonald,' responded Kit. His heart felt heavy. Mary looked crestfallen. The worry on her face was all too clear. They entered McDonald's office.

'I'll get some drinks sent up,' said Alice Diamond. 'I don't know about you…'

Everyone nodded absently; no one was really listening. Kit took Mary's hand and they sat down across the table from Wag McDonald. Sitting on the table was the evening newspaper. It was open at the page featuring the artist's impression of Natalie.

All at once everyone was staring at the picture. Slowly McDonald picked it up. Then a smile slowly creased his face. He showed the page to Kit and Mary. Written on top of the picture was a message:

I KNOW WHERE SHE IS. I WILL GO THERE NOW – DAN.

Underneath was written the address.

'Good lord,' said Mary, 'That's where Aunt Agatha's séance is.'

The door burst open at this point and Alice Diamond raced in with Maggie Hill. Her eyes were excited. Maggie's eyes were as dead as ever.

'We missed Dan. He was here twenty minutes ago, 'said Alice Diamond breathlessly but the others were already on their feet. McDonald waved the paper at Alice Diamond.

'We know where he's gone,' said McDonald, 'Let's go.'

37

Neither Betty nor Agatha dared look at one another when Eva Kerr's name was announced. They could see that no one else was shocked, or perhaps in awe. It took a few moments for the two ladies to recover. Oddly, something on the face of Eva Kerr suggested she was surprised, too.

Silence hung heavy in the room until there was a low rumble outside.

'Please join hands.'

Eva Kerr's voice was like a stone thrown into a pool at dawn. Betty flinched slightly. She flinched even more when Agatha deliberately squeezed her hand a bit harder. Betty, of course, retaliated. A tacit armistice was quickly agreed between the two ladies lest things got further out of hand.

'Clear your minds,' ordered the medium. 'Listen only to the sound of your breathing. Only your breathing. Breathe deeply.'

Her voice was liquidly hypnotic. Agatha wondered if this was part of the trick.

'Close your eyes,' continued the medium. Everyone did so.

Except Agatha.

She kept her eyes firmly on the medium. Eva Kerr did likewise with her.

'I call to the spirits of the dead. I call to those who would speak for them. Please. Speak.'

Then out of the silence there was three knocks. Moments later three double knocks were followed. Then three knocks again.

Eva Kerr's eyes remained glued to Agatha's, but her eyebrow was raised. It was clear the medium was well versed in Morse code.

A crash of thunder caused several of the people in the room to jump out of their seats again.

'Let us try again,' said Eva Kerr. 'Everyone, close your eyes.' She watched everyone except Agatha do so. She nodded imperceptibly to Agatha. Then she gave along blink. Agatha nodded then closed her eyes.

Outside the thunder rumbled ominously and the beat of the rain intensified.

'Listen to the rain. Think of nothing else except that sound.' The last three words were enunciated with emphasis on the hard consonants.

'Breathe slowly,' she whispered. 'Clear your mind. Breathe. I call to the spirits of the dead. I call to those who would speak for them. Please. Speak.'

For the next minute there was no noise in the room save the hushed breathing of the séance. Agatha shivered involuntarily but now suspected this was more to do with poorly fitted windows than any evil manifestation in the room.

Eva Kerr's breathing became heavier and sonorous as if she was being strangled. Agatha wanted to open her eyes but could not. It was as if some mysterious force was compelling them to stay closed.

Then Eva Kerr screamed.

Everyone immediately opened their eyes. Then the two other women screamed. Eva Kerr's head was twisted at an inhuman angle. Agatha and Betty rose immediately to see what was wrong.

Then suddenly Eva Kerr's body jerked upright. The irises of her eyes had disappeared. It was an ungodly blue, white. Her head began to twist spasmodically from side to side like she was part of a spirit tug of war. Her face was damp with perspiration. Then as suddenly as her movement had started, it stopped.

All was still in the room. Everyone was on their feet. The men were comforting the women. The host was standing open-mouthed, noted Agatha. Looks like you've seen nothing like this before, she thought.

Eva Kerr began to moan.

Softly at first and then gradually louder. And louder. Now it was an anguished cry like a wounded animal. It was unearthly. Deep, viscous, and pained.

Betty looked at Agatha. She was not a woman given to idle fancies, fainting or fear but this was all a bit much.

She wondered if Eva Kerr was foreign. This medium business did not strike her as being particularly British.

Agatha was still unsure if this was really some sort of manifestation or just a very well-rehearsed routine.

Eva Kerr's body jerked again. Then she stood up, put her legs wide apart and crouched. Her two hands gripped her skirt. For one horrible second Betty Simpson feared the worst.

But the gripping of the skirt and the pose only emphasised what happened next. She howled like a wolf. Amidst the howl Agatha could hear two words. Indistinct but she knew what she'd heard.

'Help me.'

Eva Kerr collapsed to the ground unconscious just as the next crash of thunder rocked the room.

Agatha looked around her. A few were whimpering in fear, and that was just the men. The two other women were sobbing. Agatha and Betty moved at the same time towards the fallen woman.

'Fetch her some water, dear,' said Agatha but noted Betty had already had the foresight to grab a glass of brandy. She noted unkindly it was Agatha's brandy rather than her own.

Betty knelt and put it to Eva Kerr's lips. There was no response.

'Betty, take her arms, I'll take her legs.'

'Where are we taking her?' asked Betty, somewhat astonished.

The Medium Murders

There was an imperceptible shake of the head. Betty didn't need to be told twice and seconds later she had picked up Eva Kerr as if she were a child and thrown her over her shoulder fireman style. Agatha was as astonished as she was impressed.

'Not quite what I was expecting, but effective nonetheless.'

Betty followed Agatha out of the room. At this point the host recovered his senses.

'I say, where are you taking her?'

But Agatha and Betty were out of the room with the stricken medium. Agatha shut the door and, noticing there was a key, locked it.

'Put her down, Betty, dear.'

Betty Simpson laid Eva Kerr gently onto the floor.

'Miss Kerr, the room is locked,' said Agatha in a low voice.

A moment later, Eva Kerr's eyes opened.

-

'Haymaker' Harris followed the dozen men and women up the stairs, keeping his head down like Tom Mix had done in 'The Cyclone'. No one else spoke to him. In fact, there was a rather eerie silence as they ascended the stairs. At the top of the stairs, they all entered bedrooms leaving him standing in the corridor alone. This was a problem. A rather big problem. Unless he did something, he would soon be exposed.

He looked around him.

The house was empty. Outside the noise of thunder was growing. His sense of panic was growing. If only Wag were here to tell him to hit someone.

Of course. Hit someone.

'Haymaker' chose a room that he remembered a man entering on his own. He walked to the door and opened it just as the thunder crashed.

The man inside was no longer dressed in a dark suit. He was wearing what looked like a nightdress. A white nightdress. There was a star on the front like the one Wag had mentioned. The man looked up in some confusion at the new arrival. Amid his confusion was no small degree of alarm. 'Haymaker's' features hardly suggested a member of society's upper echelons.

'I say, who do you think you are?'

At this point Daniel 'Haymaker' Harris demonstrated how he'd earned his soubriquet. The punch which despatched the man was a short-left jab which benefitted from its unexpectedness. The man was laid out flat on the bed. At this point, 'Haymaker', could have sworn he heard screams. He ran to the door. There was a commotion from somewhere. Even more reason to get a move on. He ran back to the prone man and started to take off his shift.

Much to the boxer's disgust, the man was unclothed underneath his nightdress. This led to 'Haymaker' making a few unchristian comments that were entirely in keeping with the character of the house they were in. He

The Medium Murders

certainly wasn't about to do what this man was doing. He slipped the white shift over his shirt, and he kept a pair of British trousers on. He considered rolling the trousers up but, serendipitously, the man had been so tall, and 'Haymaker' so short, that it went all the way down to his feet. This meant he could keep his socks on, which was a great result in anyone's book.

He could hear a commotion outside in the corridor. Leaping forward he opened the door enough to spy outside. The others were emerging from the bedrooms. All were dressed as he was. Some wore hoods. He reached behind his neck and pulled the hood up. Like a monk.

They started to ascend the second set of stairs. 'Haymaker' waited until the last had gone before joining the tail. Again, no one spoke. Outside the thunder boomed thunderously. He went up the next flight which led to double doors at the top. He walked inside and found himself in a dimly lit chapel.

'Haymaker' was not exactly a Christian. He'd been brought up as a Catholic but, over the years, he'd found himself less interested in organised religion. If pressed he would have professed a faith of sorts. And he'd prayed to God on many a cold night at the front in Flanders. However, when he stepped into this temple, he knew with absolute certainty he was in a place of evil. For the first time since the war, he felt fear. The chill prickling his skin was not just a consequence of the cold inside this strange temple.

It was a large room which took up the whole of the top floor. The ceiling was a sloped skylight, but a few candles aside, it had no light. In the middle of the room was a stone altar. It was at the centre of a pentacle. A candelabra stood at each point of the star. Behind the altar, at the back of the room, was a large black wood carving. It was half man, half goat. 'Haymaker' required no one to tell him what it depicted. To the right of the carving, high up on the wall, was a large crucifix. It was upside down. Just below it was a cabinet. The painting on the front was of Adam and Eve. A serpent was encircling Eve in a manner he'd not seen in any church painting lately.

The congregation was kneeling in front of the altar. They emitted a low murmur which battled, unsuccessfully, against the rumble of thunder outside. 'Haymaker' stood at the door, rooted to the spot. Even if he'd wanted to, he doubted he would be able to move. His breathing became shallower and shallower as if the evil in the space was attacking him, strangling the life from him.

There was strange smell in the room. It was a little like the incense he remembered from when his mother had dragged him along to the Sacred Heart Church. For the first time he became aware of music. Or something supposed to be music. The volume was very low, the melody discordant. 'Haymaker' stepped back behind the pillar near the door which rose to the skylight. There was no sign of the girl.

Then two men emerged from another door to the side of the altar. One was a young man in his twenties. He was carrying a large leather-bound book. The other man was much older with grey hair and ridiculous facial hair. Then two more men appeared from the same door and then two more after that. The new arrivals were wearing heavier white robes. The last two were carrying something wrapped in black silk. 'Haymaker' had seen enough bodies wrapped thus to know what was contained in the sheet. They laid the body carefully on the altar and with infinite care and a theatrical suspense, they unwrapped the sheet.

'Haymaker' knew what was coming but still gasped involuntarily as the body of Natalie was revealed. Thankfully, the sound of thunder drowned out his reaction. There were no marks, as far as 'Haymaker' could see, on her body. He suspected she had been drugged.

Then he saw one of the robed figures open the cabinet. From inside he took out something that glinted in the candlelight.

A plan unformulated in 'Haymaker's' head.

The knife, when he saw it, was the final confirmation that 'Haymaker' had no prospect of success. He was unarmed. A knockout punch and an endless reserve of courage was unlikely to prevail against these numbers and someone carrying a knife.

It was hopeless. All was lost.

For the second time that day, 'Haymaker' felt like crying.

-

There were two surprises awaiting Kit and Mary as their Rolls pulled up outside the house identified by 'Haymaker'. The first was the presence of Sergeant Wellbeloved. He spied the convoy, which now comprised two other cars aside from Kit's and waved. Overhead there was a crash of thunder.

McDonald was first out of the car followed by Kit. As Mary went to join them, Kit turned around to her and raised an eyebrow. Mary stopped for a second and was about to argue when she saw some of McDonald's men stepping out the cars carrying iron bars. Alice Diamond and Maggie Hill appeared in view. Maggie had a faraway look in her eyes that certainly suggested someone's night was not going to end well. For once Mary's discretion was the better part of valour.

'Perhaps I'll wait.'

Kit smiled and nodded. Harry Miller appeared alongside him. He handed Kit a Webley revolver. Mary felt her chest constrict. She looked at her fiancé fearfully. Then she remembered he'd probably been through more dangerous moments in his life. So, had she. Their eyes met and they nodded to one another.

The Medium Murders

'What are you doing here?' asked McDonald to Wellbeloved. He didn't sound welcoming. 'Are the rozzers coming?'

'Not yet,' admitted Wellbeloved just as their faces lit up by lightning overhead.

'Good,' replied McDonald. His eyes were fixed on the house. 'Haymaker's in there already. He thinks the girl's there, too.'

This was clearly news to Wellbeloved. He turned to acknowledge Kit who had joined them.

'Shall we, gentlemen?' said Kit.

The two men nodded. Then Wellbeloved added, 'You have ten minutes Wag. No killing. Understand?'

'Understood' said McDonald who was already crossing the road with Wal McDonald. Six men and two women crossed the road. All were carrying weapons although only Kit had a gun.

It was when they reached the door that Kit had his second surprise.

38

Eva Kerr looked up at the two women. All three were silent for a moment. Behind them they could hear banging on the door from the room they'd just left.

'Agatha?' asked Eva Kerr.

'Bloody hell,' said Betty Simpson in an awestruck voice, 'She really *is* good.'

Agatha rolled her eyes and looked at Betty.

'She's with the police, dear.'

But something in the medium's tone had posed a question to Agatha with an answer that was impossible. She looked at Eva Kerr again. There was something in her eyes which, thankfully, once more had their irises, that suggested she wasn't asking a question. Its tone was of someone you'd met before. But this was impossible, wasn't it?

Eva Kerr's attention switched to the door and then back to Agatha. She seemed confused and then Agatha showed her the room key.

The medium nodded and said, 'Good thinking.'

The two ladies helped Eva Kerr to her feet. She immediately went for the front door.

The Medium Murders

'We need to get help. I think they're holding the girl here. I didn't have time to find out where. There's a temple upstairs.'

Agatha and Betty followed her to the door. Eva Kerr pulled the door open. Standing on the doorstep was Kit along with the McDonald brothers and Sergeant Wellbeloved. Everyone stood still for a moment.

'Ah you're here,' said Agatha who, inevitably, was the first to collect herself. 'Well don't just stand there.'

They didn't. All of McDonald's men and the two women piled into the house followed by Kit and Miller.

'Aunt Agatha,' said Kit, 'Glad to see you're all right.'

'Why wouldn't I be?' responded Agatha irritably. Then she indicated the room they'd left. 'We've locked some of them in there. The man with black and grey beard is part of this. The rest are blithering idiots.'

In the background, Kit could hear Eva Kerr giving Wellbeloved and the Elephant Boys instructions on where they should be going. All at once they began to mount the stairs. Agatha seemed on the point of joining them when she felt an arm restrain her. To her surprise it wasn't Kit.

'You need to go home.'

It was Eva Kerr.

'I'll be…'

Agatha did not get a chance to expand on this thought as she looked into the eyes of the medium. They were colour of night. Yet light seemed to shine from them. Something deep inside Agatha's mind was shouting. A voice. A face. But it remained tantalisingly out of reach, like a memory lost. Or buried.

'You have to go home now. He needs you.'

An image flashed in Agatha's mind. It was almost as if this woman had placed it there.

'What's wrong, dear?' asked Betty.

'We have to go,' said Agatha. She looked at Kit and Harry Miller and snapped her fingers. 'Keys.'

Miller looked reluctant. Kit no less so. Then a look came into Agatha's eyes that could only be described as murder of the blue kind. A nod from Kit to Miller and Agatha had the keys to the Rolls. Kit, meanwhile, followed Miller up the stairs.

The two women went out into the wet night. They spied Kit's Rolls parked across the road. Inside they could see Mary waiting. There was a shocked expression on her face when she saw who was coming.

'Let me drive,' said Betty.

'Nonsense,' retorted Agatha, 'You're five sheets to the wind.'

'Well, really,' said an affronted Betty Simpson. She glared at her friend and sparring partner all the way to the car. The two ladies quickly climbed inside the car to escape the rain.

'What's going on?' asked Mary.

The Medium Murders

Agatha started the car prompting Betty to say tartly for Mary's benefit and her friend's ears, 'Apparently no time to explain.'

In desolation there is submission. But there is also anger. And 'Haymaker's' tears of sadness, which he shed freely, slowly transformed into rage. They became a free-flowing hatred for the people who would end the life of a young woman with so much to live for. Whatever happened, he would make them pay.

He looked around him for a weapon. He saw a walking stick propped up against the wall. Not much. More likely to sting than damage but, it might get him into the fight. If he could just get to the man with the knife. He looked at the older man and a wave of revulsion coursed through his body. A middle-aged man. No, an old man. His life lived. What right had he to decide this young woman's fate? He stared at him. This would be his target.

Slowly he made his way towards the group. All were standing, intoning some chant that made absolutely no sense to the boxer. They seemed drunk. Some were swaying, others were bent double. The sound they made was unworldly. Low, slow and in a language that was certainly like nothing he'd heard at the Duke of Wellington, even at closing time.

Bit by bit he edged around the outside of the group. No one appeared to pay him the least bit of attention. Soon he'd worked his way to the front. The door from which the men had come was at the other side of the room. 'Haymaker' guessed this led to a staircase which might mean a way out. He didn't want to think of the odds of succeeding.

Around him the pitch of the chanting seemed to be changing. It was a beat quicker. The men arrayed in a semi-circle around the young woman on the altar. The congregation, all completely enclosed within the pentacle, were in front. Suddenly, the older man raised his arm in the air.

Silence.

The young man opened the leather volume and began to read. It seemed a shorter reading than what he remembered from mass. 'Haymaker' was almost grateful. His nerves were shot enough as it was.

Then the chanting began again.

The older man stepped forward with the knife. This was it. Now or never. 'Haymaker' tensed himself and exploded from the congregation towards the man with the knife. Two of the other priests were battered out of the way as 'Haymaker' charged. He caught the older man in the middle of his stomach. He heard a satisfying grunt. The knife fell free. The temple erupted into screams and shouts.

And then all went black for 'Haymaker'.

The Medium Murders

The McDonald brothers burst through the door just in time to see 'Haymaker' rugby tackle the man with the knife. On the altar they saw Natalie. There wasn't any time to stand and survey the scene. The arrival of the other gang members forced the McDonald brothers forward. Kit and Miller followed on.

Kit saw a young man with a heavy book club 'Haymaker' unconscious. The older man was on his feet and Kit cursed himself that he could not see the face, distracted as he was by the assault on the boxer.

This attack was as nothing to the punishment being meted out by the Elephant Boys and Sergeant Wellbeloved. Kit winced as one male neophyte took a swing at the diminutive Maggie Hill. She easily evaded the punch. Where she put her iron, bar gave more than just the man tears in his eyes. Kit could almost feel his pain. Alice Diamond had chosen to forgo any weapon. With good reason, as far as Kit could see. Her fists had already clubbed one male attacker senseless, and she was laying into another with gleeful abandon.

Kit hobbled forward and could see the older man escaping out of a door. His young associate was following him when Wag McDonald executed a startling dive that clipped his feet. The young man was on the floor. Seconds later Wal McDonald was on him and that was its own introduction to hell for the young man.

Jack Murray

The battle, if the one-sided carnage could be so described, was short, brutal, and bloody. Viewing the scene from the door was Eva Kerr. She turned away and calmly walked down the stairs. When she reached the bottom, she went to the phone and picked it up.

'Whitehall 1212. Yes. Put me through to Chief Inspector Jellicoe immediately. I'll wait.'

A short wait then she heard a voice on the line.

'Chief Inspector, this is Eva Kerr. I'm with Sergeant Wellbeloved. We have the Satanists.'

She gave the address before putting the phone down. Then with an unsympathetic glance at the room where the prisoners were still making a commotion, she moved towards the front door. Beside the door was a coat rack and a selection of umbrellas. She picked out a black overcoat but ignored the umbrellas. Then she walked out into the rain and disappeared into the night.

Kit's movements down the stairs were never going to match the other two men. Wag McDonald was giving chase to the other man. Kit felt the prosthetic leg chafing against his skin. Every step was becoming increasingly sore. He looked down at the two figures on the flights below him. Frustratingly he could not see the face of their quarry.

Then he heard a door slam.

The Medium Murders

The fugitive had escaped, and Wag McDonald was banging the door in anger.

'Bugger's escaped,' exclaimed McDonald as he saw Kit arrive.

Kit took out his revolver.

'Step back.'

He fired two shots and the door was open. The two men found themselves at the side of the house. An alleyway led to the main street. McDonald raced to the street and Kit could see him looking desperately in both directions. The rain poured down on them both. Finally, he looked up to the heavens. His face lit by lamplight, and he screamed in frustration. Kit knew how he felt. Then a thought struck him.

Perhaps it wasn't over yet. There was still a way.

He went to McDonald as the sound of bells on police cars grew louder.

'Best to get your men out of there now. Wellbeloved and the police can handle this,' said Kit.

McDonald nodded and the two men went back inside. Soon they were back in the chapel. Harry Miller and the Elephant Boys had the Satanist neophytes lined against a wall. Miller had a gun trained on them but, in truth, no one was moving a muscle. Maggie Hill was patrolling a foot in front of them dispensing occasional slaps to remind them that the outlook was not good.

Alice Diamond was with 'Haymaker'. From where he was standing, it was difficult to tell how badly injured he was. Kit went to the altar and checked Natalie's pulse. Thankfully it was strong. In the background, he could hear McDonald giving orders to his men to make ready to leave.

Kit went to Miller and Wellbeloved as the Elephant Boys evacuated the scene using the back stairs. Kit nodded to Wag McDonald as he exited. Outside on the stairs, Kit could hear a commotion. Moments later Chief Inspector Jellicoe entered. He stopped and surveyed the extraordinary scene before him. Then he took off his hat and shook his head.

'You have everyone?'

Wellbeloved answered, 'No. We think their leader escaped.'

Jellicoe nodded, still too astonished to be angry. He walked along the line of rather injured, it must be said, worshippers. There were three women, not young but not elderly, whimpering. A few of the men were whimpering, too. One man wasn't. The young man who'd assaulted 'Haymaker' looked at Jellicoe with burning eyes.

Jellicoe smiled at him. The young man was startled by this, but the click of Miller's revolver stopped him. Then Jellicoe turned to Kit.

'One of these people will talk. We'll find him. Anyway,' said Jellicoe, turning back to the young man, 'we may have a lead on him. He won't get far.'

He turned to the young man and stared at him again.

The Medium Murders

'And who might you be?' asked Jellicoe.

A look of contempt crossed the man's face. Kit left Natalie and went over to the Chief Inspector.

'Meet Xander Lewis, Chief Inspector. He's the son of Lord Lewis. He of the conglomerate, Lewis & Wolf.'

Lewis snarled a reply that was more Anglo Saxon than Satanic-Latin.

Kit ignored Lewis and turned back to Jellicoe, 'We'll need an ambulance for Mr Harris. He's a hero. His actions unquestionably saved Natalie's life.'

Jellicoe nodded then turned to a uniformed sergeant, 'Take them away.'

39

Esther Cavendish and Richard Bright knocked on the door of Agatha's Grosvenor Square mansion. No answer. Esther knocked again. Again, there was nothing.

'Do you have a key, darling?'

Esther shook her head.

'I went out without it. Sorry.'

Bright looked at his watch. The time read quarter after ten. He shrugged to Esther and decided to give the door frame a more robust test than the genteel rap recorded by his fiancée. It was cold and wet. He wanted to be indoors.

Finally, after another firm rap, they could hear the door opening. It was Mary. There were tears in her eyes.

'Richard,' she exclaimed, 'I'm so glad you're here. Come quickly.'

The three young people hurried downstairs to the servant's quarters. Mary was too upset to say anything more. They arrived at the bottom of the stairs and made straight for the Fish's bedroom. For once there was no music.

'What about Natalie?' asked Esther.

The Medium Murders

'They found her. Kit rang me an hour ago. She's safe,' replied Mary quickly before knocking on the door of the elderly butler and walking straight in.

Agatha and Betty were both sitting on his bed. Fish lay motionless. Asleep. Agatha was holding his hand. There were tears in her eyes. Esther put her hand to her mouth and gasped. Bright immediately went over and searched for a pulse. There was none. He seemed at peace.

Agatha looked up at the new arrivals. Her voice cracking with sadness.

'He didn't tell me he was ill until last week. His heart, apparently. If only he'd said something.'

'Poor Fish,' said Esther, putting her arms around Mary.

Esther and Bright looked around the room at the visible mementoes. There were photographs, books, a telescope, the new gramophone player with a handful of 78's and, if Bright wasn't mistaken, what looked like a knuckleduster. He raised his eyebrows as Esther picked it up and held it in her hand. She looked questioningly at Bright who, in turn, raised his eyebrows to Aunt Agatha.

Then Esther spotted a photograph of a young Judson Fish with his master, Lord Eustace 'Useless' Frost and an attractive young woman.

'Who's that?' asked Esther.

'Gabrielle,' replied Betty. Her eyes were moist, but the sadness was as much for her friend as for Fish. She could feel the pain in Agatha, the guilt, too. And something else. As one aged, one became more aware that life is as much about endings as the next new beginning. Esther looked at the photograph of the woman again. Fish had his hand on her arm.

'Fish was married?' asked Esther, genuinely shocked, although she wouldn't have been able to explain why.

Agatha nodded slowly. A tear dropped onto Fish's hand.

'What happened?' asked Esther, unable to resist the urge to know.

'She was murdered. Fifteen years ago,' replied Agatha slowly. 'It was my last case.'

40

Early the next morning a rather dishevelled looking Kit and Chief Inspector Jellicoe arrived at Grosvenor Square. It was clear that neither had slept the previous night. Mary broke the sad news about Fish to Kit as she led him and the Chief Inspector into the drawing room. Then she went to fetch Aunt Agatha and Esther.

Kit couldn't remember the last time he'd hugged his aunt. Before she could object, he did so as soon as she entered. He looked at her. The sadness on her face was plain as the lack of spark behind her eyes. He held her hand as they sat down.

'How is Natalie?'

'She's very unwell,' replied Kit. 'They gave her a powerful drug to knock her out. She's still feeling the effects of that and will have to stay in hospital today but should be released tomorrow. She was worried about you, Aunt Agatha, and Fish. I understand why now.'

Agatha nodded absently. She felt Mary take her other hand and did not, for once, object to the attention being paid to her.

'The news, I'm afraid is mixed on last night,' admitted Kit. 'We rounded up everyone except their leader. He escaped and we have no idea who he is. We're hoping that 'Haymaker' will be able to help us when he comes around. He got a frightful whack.'

'Do we know who these people are?'

Kit looked at Mary and there was a ghost of a smile.

'Yes, we do.'

'Bobby Andrews?' asked Mary.

'No. He wasn't there. I must admit I was wondering about him. No, it was his friend Xander Williams.'

Mary and Esther's eyes widened. They looked at one another, each with the same thought. Kit spoke again giving voice to what they were thinking. There was a hint of anger in his voice. And relief.

'Yes Xander Lewis, the buffoon. Not such a fool now. It might have been one of you last night.'

Mary and Esther could say nothing in their defence and remained silent. The Chief Inspector gave the names of the other people in custody. All were from wealthy families and in a few cases, titled. But Esther and Mary were still in shock about the news regarding Xander Lewis.

'It was staring at us in our face all this time,' said Mary. 'The flowers.'

'I know,' said Kit. 'I must speak to Peter Wolf. Xander Lewis is the son of his business partner.'

'Why would they do these horrible things?' asked Esther.

The Medium Murders

Jellicoe thought for a moment but could think of nothing to say. After decades of investigating murder, he'd never dealt with something like this. It went to the very nature of man. The proximity to such barbarism was something that appalled him. Kit, too, felt shame. Each shook their heads, but no words came.

Finally, with all the news communicated, the two men rose.

'I need a bath and a nap,' said Kit. He looked at Jellicoe.

'I shall have to go back in, but I'll return to Mrs Jellicoe and let her know all is well.'

As they walked through the entrance hallway, the telephone rang. Mary answered it.

'Hello, Isabelle. Yes, I'm well.'

A minute later, she nodded and then replaced the handset. She turned to Kit.

'Could you ask Richard if he can come to the refuge today? Apparently, Dr French didn't come in today.'

Kit looked at the Chief Inspector. Jellicoe looked non plussed by this. However, he saw Kit was disturbed by this news.

'Didn't you say the artist chap, Watts, came to you yesterday about a missing drawing? One that turned out to resemble French?'

'He did, but he thought it was funny. I don't think for one moment he was accusing French of anything,' pointed out Jellicoe. 'He told me that he gave the drawings to the Commissioner, anyway, not French.'

'But I'm right in thinking that French's office and the mortuary are both located in the basement, just down the corridor from the photographer?'

Jellicoe shook his head, unable or unwilling to follow Kit's train of thought.

'Commissioner Horwood could have been going to see Dr French,' acknowledged Jellicoe. 'But this is extraordinary. Dr French has been a Medical Examiner with the police for as long as I can remember. He could have been Crown Coroner if he'd so chosen. You can't seriously be saying that he's the perpetrator of these vile acts.'

Kit had a look in his eyes that Mary knew all too well. His mind had already moved on.

'Do we have anyone guarding 'Haymaker' and Natalie? They can identify him. Chief Inspector I think we need to go to the hospital. Immediately. If it is him, then he'll have no problem gaining access to their rooms.'

St Thomas' Hospital is situated across the river from the Houses of Parliament in Lambeth. It was here that 'Haymaker' Harris, not for the first time in his life, lay out for the count. A combination of the youthful vigour of Xander Lewis and the fact that the book with which he'd been struck was embossed with a metal pentacle meant he'd received quite a blow to the head. He'd come to during the middle of the night but soon fell into a deep sleep.

Kit had organised for him to have his own room in the hospital. A few rooms down lay Natalie. She, too, slept. Between the two rooms was a sole policeman, Constable Ron Wardell. He'd been in the police force for nigh on thirty-seven years. Retirement could not come soon enough. Thirty-seven years of public service. He was tired of it all. Policing was a young man's game.

As he slept, nurses, doctors and hospital visitors passed by quietly, making sure not to wake him. Even the sound of his own, very loud snores, was not enough to penetrate the deep slumber that Wardell was enjoying.

The corridor was quiet when a man appeared and stood over the resting rozzer. He glanced, first, into the room of Natalie. A nurse and a doctor were there taking her blood pressure. He moved down towards the room with 'Haymaker'. A woman was in there with her back to the door.

The man looked one way down the corridor and then the other. It was empty save for the prone policeman. He reached inside his pocket and took out a handkerchief. He poured some liquid onto it. Heart beating fast, he moved towards the door of 'Haymaker's' room. His movements felt strained. Almost certainly the big lug had inflicted a broken rib on him. The pain, however, acted to distract him from the nervousness that he felt.

The door was ajar. He pushed it open quietly but not quietly enough. The seated woman turned around. He was expecting her to scream. But why should she? She was a common sort of woman. Reddish hair. Small. Very small, in fact. She would see a distinguished middle-aged man enter. A doctor perhaps. She could have no suspicions.

The man smiled and walked forward. His left hand concealed the handkerchief, his right hand, a surgeon's scalpel. One or other would be necessary. At this point he no longer cared which.

'Hello Miss?'

'Hill,' replied the woman, 'Maggie Hill.'

Riding in a police car going full pelt with the bells ringing was certainly one way to negotiate the growing congestion in the capital. And yet for all the haste they were making, it was not fast enough for Kit. His senses were tingling. Something was going to happen if it had not already done so. Both 'Haymaker' and Natalie had been well-guarded for most of the night but with St Thomas' returning to normality in the early morning, Kit was less sure this would be the case now. Visitors, of course, would not be allowed. But a doctor?

The Medium Murders

Even Jellicoe seemed on edge, sitting with Kit in the back. Or perhaps it was the lack of sleep. His finger kept drumming against the window. They pulled up outside the hospital less than ten minutes later.

'Come with us,' ordered Jellicoe to the police driver. The more men the better. It was impossible to know if Dr French, if it was him, would be acting alone or if there were others.

They burst onto the corridor a minute or two later and Kit's heart sank. Outside 'Haymaker's' room there were a few doctors and nurses. Jellicoe took out his badge and they made their way through to the room.

It was quite a sight.

'Haymaker' lay in bed blissfully unaware of the commotion around him. Maggie Hill was sitting on the bed, holding his hand. Dr French, meanwhile, was being attended to by a nurse. There were several nasty cuts on his face and, if his foetal position and whimpering were any indication, probably serious damage in the vicinity of his groin.

'Well, I see you've matters in hand, Miss Hill,' said Kit when he'd regained his composure.

Maggie Hill nodded and said simply, 'He had a knife'

Much good it did him, thought Kit then he looked at Jellicoe. The Chief Inspector raised one eyebrow then the two men turned to Maggie Hill. There was a glint in her eye that might have been fear, relief, or something else.

'Well, Miss Hill,' said Kit, finally. 'You seem to have caught our killer.'

Epilogue

Dixie Harris looked on with a mixture of pride and no little shock as three young women of quite exceptional beauty walked into the hospital room of her son. 'Haymaker' was awake and none the worse for the injury sustained in the rescue.

By now Mrs Harris was aware of the exceptional bravery exhibited by her son. But this was not news to her. This was the boy she'd brought up. These were the values he'd learned. Notwithstanding a mother's certainty on such matters, she could not prevent a tear trickling down her cheek as each of these ladies took it in turns to give her son a delicate kiss on the cheek.

'Haymaker' of course, cried like a baby.

Then the tall gentleman she remembered calling the other day came over to her. He started speaking to her and she could barely take in what was being said. She recognised it was English, but it was spoken in a way she'd not heard before. Kit kissed her on the cheek and thanked her for having such a wonderfully brave son.

A few minutes later, Wag McDonald walked in accompanied by his brother Wal, Alice Diamond, and Maggie Hill. She'd never been too sure of the Hill girl before, but her reaction was instinctive. Dixie Harris was over and embracing her before Maggie Hill could execute the right cross she would normally perform in such circumstances.

A few days later…

Mansfield Smith-Cumming walked in the park past a group of mothers and their children, a park keeper and a man clearing leaves into a large pile. He stopped to look at the man and then walked towards him.

'I say, what are you planning to do with those leaves?'

The man seemed surprised to be addressed by Smith-Cumming. He looked at the retired naval officer and, unbeknownst to him, the head of British Intelligence.

'Burn them, sir,' replied the man after a few moments.

Smith-Cumming nodded and went on his way. Up ahead he saw Vernon Kell arriving from a different park entrance. Neither waved to the other. Their greeting was business-like but cool. Kell glanced down at the large file being held by Smith-Cumming. He showed Smith-Cumming a similar file he was carrying.

'You've come prepared, I see,' said the head of MI5.

Smith-Cumming smiled and replied 'Indeed.'

'When are we expecting Aston?'

The Medium Murders

'He should be here in half an hour. In the meantime, I rather thought we would avail ourselves of that gentleman's help, over there.'

Smith-Cumming pointed to the man he'd spoken to earlier. Kell looked at the man with no little confusion. Then he saw the man crouch over the leaves. Moments later he lifted them up and deposited them in a large metal fire basket. Flames were already licking the side.

'Good idea,' acknowledged Kell. He started to walk alongside Smith-Cumming in the direction of the small fire. The keeper looked at the two men.

'Do you mind if we use this, too?' asked Smith-Cumming.

The keeper looked at Smith-Cumming and shrugged his shoulders. This seemed to be permission enough. The two men carefully placed their files into the fire basket. The heat intensified. From a distance it was quite pleasant in an otherwise cold October day.

'What will you say to Aston?'

'It's for the best. He won't like it but he's a rational enough to know that we're right. No one can know what happened. No one. It must stop with us. With him.'

'Will he really go along?'

'Hard to see what choice he has. The traces are being kicked over as we speak. Commissioner Horwood is ex-army. He takes orders. He'll no more want it revealed that a police doctor was responsible for the deaths of so many women than we do. Your sergeant has hopefully mopped up any other paperwork.'

'Trial?'

Smith-Cumming laughed at this and shook his head.

'French was moved to an insane asylum. We won't hear from him again.'

'Glad to hear due process was followed.'

Smith-Cumming seemed remarkably unconcerned by this and, anyway, Kell's tone hardly suggested a soul deeply troubled by the prospects of Dr French. The last of the papers began to turn black with the heat. Both men, now empty-handed, stared in fascination as all details of the murders went up in smoke.

'French was a widower apparently. No one picked up on this, which is a pity. We might have investigated him sooner. He worked under Westcott; you know. We missed this, too. It was all there had we had enough men to look. He joined the Hermetic Order and then struck out on his own as his tastes evolved.'

'And the others?'

'We should be able to gain convictions for kidnapping and accessory to attempted murder for the co-conspirators,' answered Smith-Cumming.

Kell nodded and replied, as much to himself, 'Justice.'

There was nothing in this for Smith-Cumming, so he left the comment hanging. He studied Kell for a moment, a half-smile on his lips.

'Are you staying to see Kit?'

The Medium Murders

He watched as Kell turned his back and began to walk away, laughing. Smith-Cumming's grin broadened, and he went over to a park seat near the warmth of the fire. In the distance, he saw a familiar figure strolling towards him. A sadness fell on him. What they had done was wrong. Worse than being a lie, it was a denial to the victims. Kit would see it this way. He would be angry. He had the luxury of being right. Smith-Cumming had no such luxury. He had his duty. This would be his guide, as it always was.

'Hello, Kit. Good to see you,' said Smith-Cumming rising from the bench.

A few weeks after…

Henry Cavendish stood up in the ballroom of Cavendish Hall. It had been transformed into a dining room for the fifty guests at the wedding of Esther Cavendish to Dr Richard Bright. As Henry looked around the room at his guests. Mary studied him. She marvelled, once more, at how much he'd changed over the last year.

He seemed taller. He'd certainly filled out. And he had Jane Edmunds by his side. Beside Jane Edmunds was Henry's mother, Aunt Emily. This was astonishing enough and augured well in the evolution of their aunt from harridan to matriarch.

'I never thought I would be giving a father of the bride speech at the age of nineteen,' started Henry. This brought laughter but Esther also felt a lump in her throat. She turned to Richard Bright and smiled. Kit had never seen any man look happier. With good reason. He was delighted for his two friends. At long last they were married. The laughter, meanwhile, subsided and Henry continued.

'I immediately wish to acknowledge my unworthiness. Two finer men than I should have been here today. If I may, I would like our first toast to be to their memory. Arthur and John Cavendish.'

Henry raised his glass and the assembled guests rose and toasted the memory of Esther's father and grandfather. Kit squeezed Mary's hand as he saw the tears appear in her eyes.

Henry continued to speak.

'But today is a happy occasion, to be followed by yet another celebration in February…'

Mary looked at Kit and her eyes narrowed. Only three months. It seemed a lifetime. How much had happened in the last year. What would the rest of their lives be like if this was just the first few months? She couldn't wait.

And then there was the matter of Kit's family. She would meet them at last. Some questions would finally be answered.

The Medium Murders

A few weeks later again....

'It's bigger than I thought,' said Mary. Kit detected a slight trace of nerves. They were disembarking from Kit's Rolls which had just driven up the long driveway of Cleves, Kit's ancestral home. It was, to all intents and purposes, a palace, although Kit referred to it as the country home.

The house was certainly much larger than Cavendish Hall. It was built in an English Baroque style and set in an estate of over two thousand acres. The house was square with towers at each corner.

'Are you going to lock me in a tower?' asked Mary hopefully.

'I will lock him and his father in the tower,' came the voice of Aunt Agatha behind them. 'Come on, get a weave on. Sooner this is over the better.'

To back this up, her umbrella appeared. This was enough to force Kit and Mary to move forward to avoid being prodded by their impatient aunt. The large doors at the front opened and out stepped Wedge, the elderly family butler.

'Master Kit, how good to see you, sir,' said Wedge. 'Lady Frost, Lady Mary.'

Wedge bowed to the new arrivals and Kit shook his hand.

'Hallo, old fellow, how have you been keeping?'

Jack Murray

'Oh, you know, sir, I'm not getting any younger.'

Mary liked him on first sight. He'd known Kit all his life. And liked Kit, this much was evident. There was just a hint of fear in the respectful greeting to Aunt Agatha which made Mary smile. The nerves were with her full bore now. She smiled at Wedge and looked ahead into the great hallway.

Kit took Mary's hand and walked with her forward into Cleves. The hallway seemed to be the size of Cavendish Hall. Enormous portraits by Lawrence and Raeburn adorned the walls, although she could not see one of Kit.

Then a young man appeared from one of the doors and walked towards them.

'Hello, Kit,' said the young man unenthusiastically.

'Hello, Edmund,' replied Kit with a smile, taking his half-brother into a hug. Mary detected that the greeting was a little forced as if Kit was willing himself to like his brother.

She looked at him. He was as tall as Kit and very good looking. There was something of the old Henry in him: an unresolved tension between the natural arrogance of privilege and the insecurity of youth. He looked at Mary in a way that made her blood run cold. She read what he was thinking, and she didn't like it one bit.

She smiled and put out her hand, 'Hello, Edmund, I've been so looking forward to meeting you.'

The Medium Murders

It felt like she was shaking hands with a lettuce.

While all this was going on, Mary was aware of another door opening and someone coming towards her. She turned away from Edmund and met the eyes of Kit's father.

Lancelot Aston was as tall as his two sons. Unlike his brother Alastair, he had a full head of silver hair which was brushed neatly back off his forehead. He wore a pencil thin moustache and a wide smile. His gait was unhurried, graceful, and panther-like. The dark suit was perfectly cut; he made no effort to acknowledge Kit. As far as this man was concerned, Mary was the only person in the hall.

When he finally reached Mary, he took her extended hand in both of his. His hands were warm and soft.

'My, my Kit. Bravo, my boy.'

Each word was spoken slowly and felt like a cat purring. His blue eyes were fixed on Mary's while he spoke. He took her arm and turned to lead her into the room from which he'd come.

'This is a pleasure, poppet.'

Mary turned to look at Kit. Her eyes narrowed. There was an amused frown on her face. And Kit knew exactly what she was thinking. Then she mouthed one word to him.

Poppet?

Jack Murray

THE END

If you enjoyed The Medium Murders, please leave a review. It really makes a difference:

The Medium Murders

Research Notes

This is a work of fiction. However, it references real-life individuals. Gore Vidal, in his introduction to Lincoln, writes that placing history in fiction or fiction in history has been unfashionable since Tolstoy and that the result can be accused of being neither. He defends the practice, pointing out that writers from Aeschylus to Shakespeare to Tolstoy have done so with not inconsiderable success and merit.

I have mentioned a number of key real-life individuals and events in this novel. My intention, in the following section, is to explain a little more about their connection to this period and this story.

For further reading on this period and the specific topics within this work of fiction I would recommend the following: Brian McDonald – Alice and the Forty Elephants. Conan Doyle and the Mysterious World of Light – Matt Wingett. Churchill, Walking with Destiny – Andrew Roberts. MI6: The History of the Secret Intelligence Service – Keith Jeffrey

Winston Churchill (1874 – 1965)

As incredible as it may seem, Winston Churchill was inducted or initiated into the Ancient Order of Druids in August 1908. The ceremony occurred at Blenheim Palace, at the Temple of Diana, where a day later he proposed to Clementine Hozier. They married a matter of weeks after. There is no question that Churchill saw the ceremony as anything other than a social occasion. Churchill was a long-time Mason and, therefore, familiar with such curious and arcane rituals. The idea that he was blackmailed by anyone, least of all his own security services is, as previously stated, pure fiction.

Sir Conan Doyle (1859 – 1920)

Jack Murray

Arthur Conan Doyle's fascination with the paranormal began early in his medical career. He investigated séances when he was a young doctor in Southsea. His interests extended as far as telepathy and hypnosis. In 1887, the year of his first Sherlock Holmes novel, he became convinced that spirit communication was possible.

Throughout the period when his fame and the fame of his creation grew, Conan Doyle investigated poltergeists, automatic writing and spirit photography. He confirmed his belief in this 'new revelation' in 1916 as the Great War was at its height. Supporters were many, including Harry Houdini, for a while, but so where his opponents, one of whom included Father Bernard Vaughan.

Sir Mansfield Smith Cumming (1853 – 1923)

Cumming helped found the British Secret Service in 1909, then known as Special Intelligence Bureau. Over the next few years, he became known as "C". Like Kit Aston, he lost part of his leg following a motoring accident before the war.

After the end of the war the Intelligence Service was forced into drastic cuts as a consequence of economic realities. This applied to both MI6 and MI5. This was certainly something the War Office considered in the aftermath of the war. That it did not happen is a tribute to the strong and effective lobbying by Smith-Cumming. The idea that MI6 in some way blackmailed the War Secretary on this matter is, of course, fiction.

Major-General Sir Vernon George Waldegrave Kell (1873 – 1942)

Kell was a British Army general who founded and became first Director of the British Security Service, otherwise known as MI5. He was known as K. The Home Section of the Secret Service Bureau had the responsibility of investigating espionage, sabotage and subversion within and without Britain. The section headed by Cumming became responsible for secret operations outside Britain.

The relationship between Kell and Smith-Cumming was marked by a degree of suspicion that one would look to oust the other and take over a unified service. However, they forged a highly effective partnership during the war.

The Medium Murders

The Hermetic Order of The Golden Dawn
This was a secret society devoted to the study of the occult, metaphysics, and paranormal activities during the late 19th and early 20th centuries. It was active in Britain but ultimately spread as far afield as Europe and the US. It is one of the largest single influences on 20th-century Western occultism. It was founded by Samuel Liddell Mathers, William Wynn Westcott and William Woodman.

Many celebrities of the time belonged to the Golden Dawn, such as the actress Florence Farr, the Irish revolutionary Maud Gonne, the muse of fellow member Irish poet William Butler Yeats, and Aleister Crowley.

The order had three orders within: the first order contained all the members or adepts. It was open to men and women and they confined their activities to the study of esoteric philosophy. The second order concerned itself with magic including astral travel and alchemy. The third order was closed to all except the founders Mathers and Westcott who claimed to be in contact with the "Secret Chiefs".

The order splintered, as the story explains, around 1900 for a variety of reasons although the actions of Samuel Mathers in driving through the membership of the controversial Aleister Crowley was a critical point.

Father Bernard Vaughan (1847 -1922)
Vaughan was a Jesuit priest from a well-to-do background. His brother Herbert was Archbishop of Westminster. Vaughan was a trenchant critic of spiritualism and Conan Doyle in particular. During the war he flew over to France to provide ministry to the troops engaged in the conflict.

Charles 'Wag" McDonald (1885 – 1943)
McDonald was a leader of a south London criminal gang known as the 'Elephant Boys' who were based in the Elephant and Castle area of London. He was assisted by his brother Wal and they formed an effective partnership with Billy Kimber (who features in

the TV series 'Peaky Blinders'). McDonald led an interesting life. He fought in the Boer War before to returning to England to take over the leadership of the Elephant Boys. He then volunteered for active service during the Great War. When he came back from France, he took over leadership of the gang once more before escaping to the US in 1921. He worked in Hollywood for several years, getting to know many of the stars. His life and the life of gangs in the area have been captured in a number of books by his descendant, Brian McDonald.

Alice Diamond (1896 – 1952)

Alice Diamond was an English career criminal, linked to organised shoplifting. Her career in crime began in 1912. By 1915 she was the leader of a gang known as the 'Forty Elephants' due to their association with the Elephant Boys led by Charles 'Wag' McDonald. Her chief lieutenant was Maggie Hill.

They were an odd couple. Diamond was tall and had a dominating personality. Hill was much smaller, intense and violent. They lived the high life when they could, accepting the cost of this would be occasional spells in jail.

She was imprisoned on a number of occasions. In fact, one of these periods of incarceration took place at the same time in which this book has been set. Some artistic license has ensured Alice Diamond's inclusion in the book. Alice Diamond never married but was in a relationship with Wag McDonald's brother, Bert.

William 'Billy' Hill (1911 – 1984)

Hill was an English criminal, linked to smuggling, protection, robbery, black market activity during World War II, and violence. He was one of the leaders of organised crime in London from the 1930's through to the 1960's. He was also implicated in defrauding London's high society of millions at key gambling locations in London. He is reputed to have supplied real guns to the filmmakers involved in the production of Mickey Spillane's 'The Girl Hunters' in 1963.

The Medium Murders

Jack Murray

About the Author

Jack Murray lives just outside London with his family. Born in Ireland he has spent most of his adult life in the England. His first novel, 'The Affair of the Christmas Card Killer' has been a global success. Four further Kit Aston novels have followed: 'The Chess Board Murders', 'The French Diplomat Affair' and 'The Phantom' and 'The Frisco Falcon'. 'The Medium Murders' is the fifth in the Kit Aston series.

Jack has also written a spin-off series featuring Aunt Agatha as a young woman. There are two in the series.

Another new series will begin in June 2021 featuring the grandson of Chief Inspector Jellicoe. It is set in the late fifties / early sixties.

In 2022, a new series will commence set in the period leading up to and during World War II. The series will include some of the minor characters from the Kit Aston series.

The Medium Murders

Acknowledgements

It is not possible to write a book on your own. There are contributions from so many people either directly or indirectly over many years. Listing them all would be an impossible task.

Special mention therefore should be made to my wife and family who have been patient and put up with my occasional grumpiness when working on this project.

My brother Edward, and John Convery helped in proofing and made supportive comments that helped me tremendously. I have been very lucky to receive badly needed editing from Kathy Lance who has helped tighten up some of the grammatical issues that, frankly, plagued my earlier books. She has been a Godsend!

My late father and mother both loved books. They encouraged a love of reading in me. In particular, they liked detective books, so I must tip my hat to the two greatest writers of this genre, Sir Arthur and Dame Agatha.

Following writing, comes the business of marketing. My thanks to Mark Hodgson and Sophia Kyriacou for their advice on this important area. Additionally, a shout out to the wonderful folk on 20Booksto50k.

Finally, my thanks to the teachers who taught and nurtured a love of writing.

Printed in Great Britain
by Amazon